THE BLACK MONK
& OTHER STORIES

ANTON CHEKHOV

THE BLACK MONK & OTHER STORIES

ALAN SUTTON
1985

Alan Sutton Publishing Limited
30 Brunswick Road
Gloucester

British Library Cataloguing in Publication Data

Chekhov, A.P.
  The black monk and other stories.
  I. Title
  891.73'3[F]   PG3456.A13

  ISBN 0-86299-230-3

Cover picture: detail from Peasants *by
Z. Serbryakova.
Photograph, Novosti Press Agency*

Typesetting and origination by
Alan Sutton Publishing Limited.
Photoset Bembo 9/10
Printed in Great Britain
by The Guernsey Press Company Limited
Guernsey, Channel Islands.

CONTENTS

BIOGRAPHICAL NOTE

Anton Pavlovich Chekhov was a Russian of remarkable talent. He was a medical doctor, with a great respect for science, and a writer with a mystical awareness, a fine appreciation of the dual nature of humanity and of the world, and a realisation of the horror and of the beauty of earthly existence. He conveyed his observations always with clear-sighted truthfulness, often with humour, and sometimes with poignant lyricism in the many stories and the few plays which he wrote during his short life. He was an individual who allied himself with no religion, nor with any political party; yet he lead a strictly ethical life, and was actively concerned with the social conditions he found around him.

His grandfather was born a serf, but had been resourceful enough to make sufficient money to buy his family's freedom. Chekhov's father, on the other hand, was more religious and artistic than practical, and made little success of providing for his wife and six children in the general store where the family lived in Taganrog, a small harbour town on the Sea of Azov in Southern Russia. Anton, born on 17 January 1860, was the third son, and he and his two elder brothers were, from an early age, called upon to work for long hours in the shop and chant for long hours in the church. The physical conditions of those early years were wretched, and it is not surprising that Anton and one of his brothers developed consumption in their twenties. Although home comforts were in short supply, education was not, and Anton attended the local state school until he was nineteen. During that time he had his first experience of the theatre, when touring companies visited Taganrog. The boys had to obtain permission from school for every performance they wished to attend, so the light-hearted Chekhov would often go in disguise, heavily made-up to avoid recognition by monitoring teachers. Before he left school, his father was forced to flee to Moscow for financial reasons; his two elder brothers were already there, and his mother and younger sister and brothers soon followed, leaving Anton to sell off their effects and provide for himself by giving private lessons while he finished his schooling.

At nineteen, however, Chekhov left Taganrog and went to Moscow, entering the medical faculty of the University and living in slum conditions with his family. One year later he started writing, to make money. He wrote short stories, often humorous, for journals and magazines in Moscow and St Petersberg. In 1880 he sold nine of them; by 1885 he was producing more than a hundred pieces of work a year. His first collection in book form was published in 1884, after he had completed his medical training. Two years later he was asked to write regularly for *Novoye Vremia*, the most influential Russian daily, and he received an important letter of encouragement from the novelist Grigorovich, finally convincing him of his talent as a writer, and making him take his writing more seriously than in the past. He continued with short stories, but also experimented in the field of drama, producing five one act sketches which he called 'vaudevilles', and two full-length plays: *Ivanov* and *The Wood Demon* (later to be re-written as *Uncle Vanya*).

Socially and financially Chekhov was now well-established and able to move with his mother, sister Maria, and younger brother into the house in Sadovaia-Kudrinskaia, where he lived until 1892, and which is now the Chekhov Museum. He had achieved a position among the cultural élite of Moscow. One of his life-long friendships which dated from those days was with the Romantic painter, Levitan, and another was with Suvorin, the editor of *Novoye Vremia*. He also had a close relationship with his sister, but, although he had friendships with women – he was both handsome and charming – he committed himself to none, feeling that in order to do justice to his talents, he must maintain emotional independence.

It was during those years that his consumption made itself unpleasantly evident. His elder brother, Nicholas, was worse affected, and died in 1889. This loss was one of the motivating forces which made Chekhov decide to visit the grim island of Sakhalin. He had started to prepare a thesis on the history of medicine, but then realised that he would prefer to study a topic more immediate and relevant. So, in spite of poor health, he made the terrific journey across Russia (before the railway was opened) to Sakhalin Island, just North of Japan, to study and make a detailed report on the Russian convict colony out there. Chekhov was profoundly moved by the human degradation he witnessed – an example of the horror of the world. He wrote factually and directly about his findings in *The Island of Sakhalin*, and fictionally and indirectly in various short stories, *Murder in Exile*, *Groussev*, *The Babas* and others. Drained by the shock of his experiences, he longed for culture, beauty and comfort when he returned home, finding these on his first visit to Europe in 1891.

He travelled in Europe on several occasions during the next ten years, but never came to England. He was in Paris at the time of the Dreyfus Affair, and admired and supported Emile Zola's defence of the Jew. On one occasion, he bought books in Nice for the public library in Taganrog.

Although Chekhov enjoyed his visits abroad, he prefered to work at home. For the benefit of his health, and to ensure the privacy which he needed in order to work, he left Moscow in 1892 and bought an estate outside the city at Melikhovo. He loved his new home and garden and found peace in the natural surroundings. He was now in his thirties, aware that he was not immortal, and frustrated by the apparent worthlessness of his life. He had been affected briefly by Tolstoy's grand philosophy, but realised that, for him, truth was not to be found in the thoughts of others, that there was no overall pattern, reason or order in the world. He admitted his feeling of ignorance: 'We shall not try to play the quack but will admit frankly that we cannot understand anything in this world.' Only imbeciles and quacks understand and know everything,' he wrote to a friend. For Chekhov, as for the mystic, reality was to be found in the moment, in isolation. He thought that the only purpose of literature was to portray the truth as the writer perceived it: 'Man will only grow better when he has seen himself as he is'. But he longed to do something noble and significant with his life: 'To save his soul, the Muslim digs a well. It would be a good thing if each of us left behind him a school, a well or something else, so that one's life should not pass and be lost in eternity without leaving a trace of its passage on this earth', he wrote in his diary.

During the next six years Chekhov fulfilled this desire to benefit the common good. He maintained a demanding medical practice and funded and established three schools in the area, as well as supplying various libraries. He was awarded a 'hereditary nobility' by Nicholas II for his 'exemplary zeal and exertions directed towards the education of the people.' It was during these years that Chekhov wrote *The Muzhiks*, an important story about peasant life, *The Black Monk*, and *Ward 6*, which attacked some aspects of Tolstoy's philosophy. He also wrote *The Seagull*, which was produced in St Petersberg in 1896, and a disastrous failure.

When he was thirty-seven, Chekhov's health had deteriorated to such an extent that he was recommended to move south. So in 1898 he had a new house and a new garden to create, this time on the outskirts of Yalta, on the Crimea. Once again he became involved in welfare work, his major achievement being the establishment of the Chekhov Sanitorium, for which he personally requested subscriptions from affluent Russians. During those last years of his life, he became friends with the young novelists Bunin, Kuprin and Gorki. It was in support of the latter, whom he saw as a destroyer of evil, that Chekhov resigned from the Moscow Academy of Belles Lettres. Another important connection was that with the newly-formed Moscow Arts Theatre, under the direction of Nemirovich-Danchenko and Stanislavski. The company successfully performed *The Seagull* in 1898, followed soon after by *Uncle Vanya* (1899). Chekhov met and fell in love with one of the leading actresses, Olga Knipper, and it was for her that he wrote *The Three Sisters* (1901). His final play, *The Cherry Orchard*, was first produced by the company a few months before his death in January, 1904.

Stanislavski, in his autobiography, gives a few personal glimpses of Chekhov. Of his genius he says: 'Chekhov, like no one else, was able to create inward and outward artistic truth. This is why he was able to say the truth about men.' He recalls that Chekhov had very little to say about the manner of the production of his plays, but that he was 'very proud of his medical calling, much more than of his talents as a writer.' He remembers Chekhov's humour: 'it was impossible not to laugh in Chekhov's presence', and he relates the practical joke Chekhov played on the theatre company, when he invited them all to supper at a friend's house while he went off and quietly married Olga Knipper, thus avoiding all ceremony and the hated embarrassment of being a centre of attention.

In 1901 Chekhov married. He and Olga lived apart much of the time, as she continued with her career and he was unable to spend long in Moscow, but she went with him on his last visit to Europe, and was with him when he died on a night early in July 1904, at the Black Forest sanitorium of Badenweiler. His body was later interred in the cemetery of the New Maiden Convent in Moscow.

SHEILA MICHELL

THE BLACK MONK

THE BLACK MONK

I

Andréï Vasilyevitch Kovrin, *Magister,* had worn himself out, and unsettled his nerves. He made no effort to undergo regular treatment; but only incidentally, over a bottle of wine, spoke to his friend the doctor; and his friend the doctor advised him to spend all the spring and summer in the country. And in the nick of time came a long letter from Tánya Pesótsky, asking him to come and stay with her father at Borisovka. He decided to go.

But first (it was in April) he travelled to his own estate, to his native Kovrinka, and spent three weeks in solitude; and only when the fine weather came drove across the country to his former guardian and second parent, Pesótsky, the celebrated Russian horticulturist. From Kovrinka to Borisovka, the home of the Pesótskys, was a distance of some seventy versts, and in the easy, springed calêche the drive along the roads, soft in springtime, promised real enjoyment.

The house at Borisovka was large, faced with a colonnade, and adorned with figures of lions with the plaster falling off. At the door stood a servant in livery. The old park, gloomy and severe, laid out in English fashion, stretched for nearly a verst from the house down to the river, and ended there in a steep clay bank covered with pines whose bare roots resembled shaggy paws. Below sparkled a deserted stream; overhead the snipe circled about with melancholy cries – all, in short, seemed to invite a visitor to sit down and write a ballad. But the gardens and orchards, which together with the seed-plots occupied some eighty acres, inspired very different feelings. Even in the worst of weather they were bright and joy-inspiring. Such wonderful roses, lilies, camelias, such tulips, such a host of flowering plants of every possible kind

3

and colour, from staring white to sooty black, – such a wealth of blossoms Kovrin had never seen before. The spring was only beginning, and the greatest rareties were hidden under glass; but already enough bloomed in the alleys and beds to make up an empire of delicate shades. And most charming of all was it in the early hours of morning, when dewdrops glistened on every petal and leaf.

In childhood the decorative part of the garden, called contemptuously by Pesótsky, 'the rubbish,' had produced on Kovrin a fabulous impression. What miracles of art, what studied monstrosities, what mockeries of nature! Espaliers of fruit trees, a pear tree shaped like a pyramidal popular, globular oaks and lindens, apple-tree houses, arches, monograms, candelabra – even the date 1862 in plum trees, to commemorate the year in which Pesótsky first engaged in the art of gardening. There were stately, symmetrical trees, with trunks erect as those of palms, which after examination proved to be gooseberry or currant trees. But what most of all enlivened the garden and gave it its joyous tone was the constant movement of Pesótsky's gardeners. From early morning to late at night, by the trees, by the bushes, in the alleys, and on the beds swarmed men as busy as ants, with barrows, spades, and watering-pots.

Kovrin arrived at Borisovka at nine o'clock. He found Tánya and her father in great alarm. The clear starlight night foretold frost, and the head gardener, Ivan Karlitch, had gone to town, so that there was no one who could be relied upon. At supper they spoke only of the impending frost; and it was decided that Tánya should not go to bed at all, but should inspect the gardens at one o'clock and see if all were in order, while Yegor Semiónovitch should rise at three o'clock, or even earlier.

Kovrin sat with Tánya all the evening, and after midnight accompanied her to the garden. The air already smelt strongly of burning. In the great orchard, called 'the commercial,' which every year brought Yegor Semiónovitch thousands of roubles profit, there already crept along the ground the thick, black, sour smoke which was to clothe the young leaves and save the plants. The trees were marshalled like chessmen in straight rows – like ranks of soldiers; and this pedantic regularity, together with the uniformity of height, made the garden seem monotonous and even tiresome. Kovrin and Tánya walked up and down the alleys, and watched the fires of dung, straw, and litter; but seldom met the workmen, who wandered in the smoke like shadows. Only the cherry and plum trees and a few apple trees were in blossom, but the whole garden was shrouded in smoke, and it was only when they reached the seed-plots that Kovrin was able to breathe.

'I remember when I was a child sneezing from the smoke,' he said, shrugging his shoulders, 'but to this day I cannot understand how smoke saves plants from the frost.'

'Smoke is a good substitute when there are no clouds,' answered Tánya.

'But what do you want the clouds for?'

'In dull and cloudy weather we have no morning frosts.'

'Is that so?' said Kovrin.

He laughed and took Tánya by the hand. Her broad, very serious, chilled face; her thick, black eye-brows; the stiff collar on her jacket which prevented her from moving her head freely; her dress tucked up out of the dew; and her whole figure, erect and slight, pleased him.

'Heavens! how she has grown!' he said to himself. 'When I was here last time, five years ago, you were quite a child. You were thin, long-legged, and untidy, and wore a short dress, and I used to tease you. What a change in five years!'

'Yes, five years!' sighed Tánya. 'A lot of things have happened since then. Tell me, Andréï, honestly,' she said, looking merrily into his face, 'do you feel that you have got out of touch with us? But why do I ask? You are a man, you live your own interesting life, you . . . Some estrangement is natural. But whether that is so or not, Andrusha, I want you now to look on us as your own. We have a right to that.'

'I do, already, Tánya.'

'Your word of honour?'

'My word of honour.'

'You were surprised that we had so many of your photographs. But surely you know how my father adores you, worships you. You are a scholar, and not an ordinary man; you have built up a brilliant career, and he is firmly convinced that you turned out a success because he educated you. I do not interfere with his delusion. Let him believe it!'

Already dawn. The sky paled, and the foliage and clouds of smoke began to show themselves more clearly. The nightingale sang, and from the fields came the cry of quails. 'It is time for bed!' said Tánya. 'It is cold too.' She took Kovrin by the hand. 'Thanks, Andrusha, for coming. We are cursed with most uninteresting acquaintances, and not many even of them. With us it is always garden, garden, garden, and nothing else. Trunks, timbers,' she laughed, 'pippins, rennets, budding, pruning, grafting. . . . All our life goes into the garden, we never even dream of anything but apples and pears. Of course this is all very good and useful, but sometimes I cannot help wishing for change. I remember when you used to come and pay us visits, and when you came home for the holidays, how the whole house grew fresher and brighter, as if someone had taken the covers off the furniture. I was then a very little girl, but I understood. . . .'

Tánya spoke for a time, and spoke with feeling. Then suddenly it came into Kovrin's head that during the summer he might become attached to this little, weak, talkative being, that he might get carried away, fall in love – in their position what was more probable and natural? The thought pleased him, amused him, and as he bent down to the kind, troubled face, he hummed to himself Pushkin's couplet:

'Oniégin, I will not conceal
That I love Tatyana madly.'

By the time they reached the house Yegor Semiónovitch had risen. Kovrin felt no desire to sleep; he entered into conversation with the old man, and returned with him to the garden. Yegor Semiónovitch was tall, broad-shouldered, and fat. He suffered from shortness of breath, yet walked so quickly that it was difficult to keep up with him. His expression was always troubled and hurried, and he seemed to be thinking that if he were a single second late everything would be destroyed.

'There, brother, is a mystery for you!' he began, stopping to recover breath. 'On the surface of the ground, as you see, there is frost, but raise the thermometer a couple of yards on your stick, and it is quite warm. . . . Why is that?'

'I confess I don't know,' said Kovrin, laughing.

'No! . . . You can't know everything. . . . The biggest brain cannot comprehend everything. You are still engaged with your philosophy?'

'Yes, . . . I am studying psychology, and philosophy generally.'

'And it doesn't bore you?'

'On the contrary, I couldn't live without it.'

'Well, God grant . . .' began Yegor Semiónovitch, smoothing his big whiskers thoughtfully. 'Well, God grant . . . I am very glad for your sake, brother, very glad. . . .'

Suddenly he began to listen, and making a terrible face, ran off the path and soon vanished among the trees in a cloud of smoke.

'Who tethered this horse to the tree?' rang out a despairing voice. 'Which of you thieves and murderers dared to tether this horse to the apple tree? My God, my God! Ruined, ruined, spoiled, destroyed! The garden is ruined, the garden is destroyed! My God!'

When he returned to Kovrin his face bore an expression of injury and impotence.

'What on earth can you do with these accursed people?' he asked in a whining voice, wringing his hands. 'Stepka brought a manure cart here last night and tethered the horse to an apple tree . . . tied the reins, the idiot, so tight, that the bark is rubbed off in three places. What can you do with men like this? I speak to him and he blinks his eyes and looks stupid. He ought to be hanged!'

When at last he calmed down, he embraced Kovrin and kissed him on the cheek.

'Well, God grant . . . God grant! . . .' he stammered. 'I am very, very glad that you have come. I cannot say how glad. Thanks!'

Then, with the same anxious face, and walking with the same quick step, he went round the whole garden, showing his former ward the orangery, the hothouses, the sheds, and two beehives which he described as the miracle of the century.

As they walked about, the sun rose, lighting up the garden. It grew hot. When he thought of the long, bright day before him, Kovrin remembered that it was but the beginning of May, and that he had before him a whole summer of long, bright, and happy days; and suddenly through him pulsed the joyous, youthful feeling which he had felt when as a child he played in this same garden. And in turn, he embraced the old man and kissed him tenderly. Touched by remembrances, the pair went into the house and drank tea out of the old china cups, with cream and rich biscuits; and these trifles again reminded Kovrin of his childhood and youth. The splendid present and the awakening memories of the past mingled, and a feeling of intense happiness filled his heart.

He waited until Tánya awoke, and having drunk coffee with her, walked through the garden, and then went to his room and began to work. He read attentively, making notes; and only lifted his eyes from his books when he felt that he must look out of the window or at the fresh roses, still wet with dew, which stood in vases on his table. It seemed to him that every little vein in his body trembled and pulsated with joy.

II

But in the country Kovrin continued to live the same nervous and untranquil life as he had lived in town. He read much, wrote much, studied Italian; and when he went for walks, thought all the time of returning to work. He slept so little that he astonished the household; if by chance he slept in the daytime for half an hour, he could not sleep all the following night. Yet after these sleepless nights he felt active and gay.

He talked much, drank wine, and smoked expensive cigars. Often, nearly every day, young girls from the neighbouring country-houses drove over to Borisovka, played the piano with Tánya, and sang. Sometimes the visitor was a young man, also a neighbour, who played the violin well. Kovrin listened eagerly to their music and singing, but was exhausted by it, so exhausted sometimes that his eyes closed involuntarily, and his head drooped on his shoulders.

One evening after tea he sat upon the balcony, reading. In the drawing-room Tánya – a soprano, one of her friends – a contralto, and the young violinist studied the well-known serenade of Braga. Kovrin listened to the words, but though they were Russian, could not understand their meaning. At last, laying down his book and listening attentively, he understood. A girl with a disordered imagination heard by night in a garden some mysterious sounds, sounds so beautiful and strange that she was forced to recognise their harmony and holiness, which to us mortals are incomprehensible, and therefore flew back to heaven. Kovrin's eyelids drooped. He rose, and in exhaustion walked up and down the drawing-room, and then up and down the hall. When the music ceased, he took Tánya by the hand and went out with her to the balcony.

'All day – since early morning,' he began, 'my head has been taken up with a strange legend. I cannot remember whether I read it, or where I heard it, but the legend is very remarkable and not very coherent. I may begin by saying that it is not very clear. A thousand years ago a monk, robed in black, wandered in the wilderness – somewhere in Syria or Arabia. . . . Some miles away the fishermen saw another black monk moving slowly over the surface of the lake. The second monk was a mirage. Now put out of your mind all the laws of optics, which legend, of course, does not recognise, and listen. From the first mirage was produced another mirage, from the second a third, so that the image of the Black Monk is eternally reflected from one stratum of the atmosphere to another. At one time it was seen in Africa, then in Spain, then in India, then in the Far North. At last it issued from the limits of the earth's atmosphere, but never came across conditions which would cause it to disappear. Maybe it is seen today in Mars or in the constellation of the Southern Cross. Now the whole point, the very essence of the legend, lies in the prediction that exactly a thousand years after the monk went into the wilderness, the mirage will again be cast into the atmosphere of the earth and show itself to the world of men. This term of a thousand years, it appears, is now expiring. . . . According to the legend we must expect the Black Monk today or tomorrow.'

'It is a strange story,' said Tánya, whom the legend did not please.

'But the most astonishing thing,' laughed Kovrin, 'is that I cannot remember how this legend came into my head. Did I read it? Did I hear it? Or can it be that I dreamed of the Black Monk? I cannot remember. But the legend interests me. All day long I thought of nothing else.'

Releasing Tánya, who returned to her visitors, he went out of the house, and walked lost in thought beside the flower-beds. Already the sun was setting. The freshly watered flowers exhaled a damp, irritating smell. In the house the music had again begun, and from the distance the violin produced the effect of a human voice. Straining his memory in an attempt to recall where he had heard the legend, Kovrin walked slowly across the park, and then, not noticing where he went, to the river-bank.

By the path which ran down among the uncovered roots to the water's edge Kovrin descended, frightening the snipe, and disturbing two ducks. On the dark pine trees glowed the rays of the setting sun, but on the surface of the river darkness had already fallen. Kovrin crossed the stream. Before him now lay a broad field covered with young rye. Neither human dwelling nor human soul was visible in the distance; and it seemed that the path must lead to the unexplored, enigmatical region in the west where the sun had already set – where still, vast and majestic, flamed the afterglow.

'How open it is – how peaceful and free!' thought Kovrin, walking along the path. 'It seems as if all the world is looking at me from a hiding-place and waiting for me to comprehend it.'

A wave passed over the rye, and the light evening breeze blew softly on his uncovered head. Yet a minute more and the breeze blew again, this time more strongly, the rye rustled, and from behind came the dull murmur of the pines. Kovrin stopped in amazement. On the horizon, like a cyclone or waterspout, a great, black pillar rose up from earth to heaven. Its outlines were undefined; but from the first it might be seen that it was not standing still, but moving with inconceivable speed towards Kovrin; and the nearer it came the smaller and smaller it grew. Involuntarily Kovrin rushed aside and made a path for it. A monk in black clothing, with grey hair and black eyebrows, crossing his hands upon his chest, was borne past. His bare feet were above the ground. Having swept some twenty yards past Kovrin, he looked at him, nodded his head, and smiled kindly and at the same time slyly. His face was pale and thin. When he had passed by Kovrin he again began to grow, flew across the river, struck inaudibly against the clay bank and pine trees, and, passing through them, vanished like smoke.

'You see,' stammered Kovrin, 'after all, the legend was true!'

Making no attempt to explain this strange phenomenon; satisfied with the fact that he had so closely and so plainly seen not only the black clothing but even the face and eyes of the monk; agitated agreeably, he returned home.

In the park and in the garden visitors were walking quietly; in the house the music continued. So he alone had seen the Black Monk. He felt a strong desire to tell what he had seen to Tánya and Yegor Semiónovitch, but feared that they would regard it as a hallucination, and decided to keep his counsel. He laughed loudly, sang, danced a mazurka, and felt in the best of spirits; and the guests and Tánya noticed upon his face a peculiar expression of ecstasy and inspiration, and found him very interesting.

III

When supper was over and the visitors had gone, he went to his own room, and lay on the sofa. He wished to think of the monk. But in a few minutes Tánya entered.

'There, Andrusha, you can read father's articles . . .' she said. 'They are splendid articles. He writes very well.'

'Magnificent!' said Yegor Semiónovitch, coming in after her, with a forced smile. 'Don't listen to her, please! . . . Or read them only if you want to go to sleep – they are a splendid soporific.'

'In my opinion they are magnificent,' said Tánya, deeply convinced. 'Read them, Andrusha, and persuade father to write more often. He could write a whole treatise on gardening.'

Yegor Semiónovitch laughed, blushed, and stammered out the conventional phrases used by abashed authors. At last he gave in.

'If you must read them, read first these papers of Gauché's, and the Russian articles,' he stammered, picking out the papers with trembling hands. 'Otherwise you won't understand them. Before you read my replies you must know what I am replying to. But it won't interest you . . . stupid. And it's time for bed.'

Tánya went out. Yegor Semiónovitch sat on the end of the sofa and sighed loudly.

'Akh, brother mine . . .' he began after a long silence. 'So you see, my dear *Magister*, I write articles, and exhibit at shows, and get medals sometimes. . . . Pesótsky, they say, has apples as big as your head. . . . Pesótsky has made a fortune out of his gardens. . . . In one word:

"Rich and glorious is Kotchubéi."'

'But I should like to ask you what is going to be the end of all this? The gardens – there is no question of that – are splendid, they are models. . . . Not gardens at all, in short, but a whole institution of high political importance, and a step towards a new era in Russian agriculture and Russian industry. . . . But for what purpose? What ultimate object?'

'That question is easily answered.'

'I do not mean in that sense. What I want to know is what will happen with the garden when I die? As things are, it would not last without me a single month. The secret does not lie in the fact that the garden is big and the workers many, but in the fact that I love the work – you understand? I love it, perhaps, more than I love myself. Just look at me! I work from morning to night. I do everything with my own hands. All grafting, all pruning, all planting – everything is done by me. When I am helped I feel jealous, and get irritated to the point of rudeness. The whole secret is in love, in a sharp master's eye, in a master's hands, and in the feeling when I drive over to a friend and sit down for half an hour, that I have left my heart behind me and am not myself – all the time I am in dread that something has happened to the garden. Now suppose I die tomorrow, who will replace all this? Who will do the work? The head gardeners? The workmen? Why the whole burden of my present worries is that my greatest enemy is not the hare or the beetle or the frost, but the hands of the stranger.'

'But Tánya?' said Kovrin, laughing. 'Surely she is not more dangerous than a hare? . . . She loves and understands the work.'

'Yes, Tánya loves it and understands it. If after my death the garden should fall to her as mistress, then I could wish for nothing better. But suppose – which God forbid – she should marry!' Yegor Semiónovitch whispered and looked at Kovrin with frightened eyes. 'That's the whole crux. She might marry, there would be children, and there would be no time to attend to the garden. That is bad enough. But what I fear most of all is that she may marry some spendthrift who is always in want of money, who will lease the garden to tradesmen, and the whole thing will go to the devil in the first year. In a business like this a woman is the scourge of God.'

Yegor Semiónovitch sighed and was silent for a few minutes.

'Perhaps you may call it egoism. But I do not want Tánya to marry. I am afraid! You've seen that fop who comes along with a fiddle and makes a noise. I know Tánya would never marry him, yet I cannot bear the sight of him. . . . In short, brother, I am a character . . . and I know it.'

Yegor Semiónovitch rose and walked excitedly up and down the room. It was plain that he had something very serious to say, but could not bring himself to the point.

'I love you too sincerely not to talk to you frankly,' he said, thrusting his hands into his pockets. 'In all delicate questions I say what I think, and dislike mystification. I tell you plainly, therefore, that you are the only man whom I should not be afraid of Tánya marrying. You are a clever man, you have a heart, and you would not see my life's work ruined. And what is more, I love you as my own son . . . and am proud of you. So if you and Tánya were to end . . . in a sort of romance . . . I should be very glad and very happy. I tell you this straight to your face, without shame, as becomes an honest man.'

Kovrin smiled. Yegor Semiónovitch opened the door, and was leaving the room, but stopped suddenly on the threshold.

'And if you and Tánya had a son, I could make a horticulturist out of him,' he added. 'But that is an idle fancy. Good night!'

Left alone, Kovrin settled himself comfortably, and took up his host's articles. The first was entitled 'Intermediate Culture,' the second 'A Few Words in Reply to the Remarks of Mr. Z. about the Treatment of the Soil of a New Garden,' the third 'More about Grafting.' The others were similar in scope. But all breathed restlessness and sickly irritation. Even a paper with the peaceful title of 'Russian Apple Trees' exhaled irritability. Yegor Semiónovitch began with the words 'Audi alteram partem,' and ended it with 'Sapienti sat'; and between these learned quotations flowed a whole torrent of acid words directed against 'the learned ignorance of our patent horticulturists who observe nature from their academic chairs,' and against M. Gauché, 'whose fame is founded on the admiration of the profane and *dilletanti*.' And finally Kovrin came across an uncalled-for and quite insincere expression of regret that it is no longer legal to flog peasants who are caught stealing fruit and injuring trees.

'His is good work, wholesome and fascinating,' thought Kovrin, 'yet in these pamphlets we have nothing but bad temper and war to the knife. I suppose it is the same everywhere; in all careers men of ideas are nervous, and victims of this kind of exalted sensitiveness. I suppose it must be so.'

He thought of Tánya, so delighted with her father's articles, and then of Yegor Semiónovitch. Tánya, small, pale, and slight, with her collar-bone showing, with her widely-opened, her dark and clever eyes, which it seemed were always searching for something. And Yegor Semiónovitch with his little, hurried steps. He thought again of Tánya, fond of talking, fond of argument, and always accompanying even the most insignificant phrases with mimicry and gesticulation. Nervous — she must be nervous in the highest degree.

Again Kovrin began to read, but he understood nothing, and threw down his books. The agreeable emotion with which he had danced the mazurka and listened to the music still held possession of him, and aroused a multitude of thoughts. It flashed upon him that if this strange, unnatural monk had been seen by him alone, he must be ill, ill to the point of suffering from hallucinations. The thought frightened him, but not for long.

He sat on the sofa, and held his head in his hands, curbing the inexplicable joy which filled his whole being; and then walked up and down the room for a minute, and returned to his work. But the thoughts which he read in books no longer satisfied him. He longed for something vast, infinite, astonishing. Towards morning he undressed and went unwillingly to bed; he felt that he had better rest. When at last he heard Yegor Semiónovitch going to his work in the garden, he rang, and ordered the servant to bring him some wine. He drank several glasses; his consciousness became dim, and he slept.

IV

Yegor Semiónovitch and Tánya often quarrelled and said disagreeable things to one another. This morning they had both been irritated, and Tánya burst out crying and went to her room, coming down neither to dinner nor to tea. At first Yegor Semiónovitch marched about, solemn and dignified, as if wishing to give everyone to understand that for him justice and order were the supreme interests of life. But he was unable to keep this up for long; his spirits fell, and he wandered about the park and sighed, 'Akh, my God!' At dinner he ate nothing, and at last, tortured by his conscience, he knocked softly at the closed door, and called timidly:

'Tánya! Tánya!'

Through the door came a weak voice, tearful but determined:

'Leave me alone! . . . I implore you.'

The misery of father and daughter reacted on the whole household, even on the labourers in the garden. Kovrin, as usual, was immersed in his own interesting work, but at last even he felt tired and uncomfortable. He determined to interfere, and disperse the cloud before evening. He knocked at Tánya's door, and was admitted.

'Come, come! What a shame!' he began jokingly; and then looked with surprise at her tear-stained and afflicted face covered with red spots. 'Is it so serious, then? Well, well!'

'But if you knew how he tortured me!' she said, and a flood of tears gushed out of her big eyes. 'He tormented me!' she continued, wringing her hands. 'I never said a word to him. . . . I only said there was no need to keep unnecessary labourers, if . . . if we can get day workmen. . . . You know the men have done nothing for the whole week. I . . . I only said this, and he roared at me, and said a lot of things . . . most offensive . . . deeply insulting. And all for nothing.'

'Never mind!' said Kovrin, straightening her hair. 'You have had your scoldings and your cryings, and that is surely enough. You can't keep up this for ever . . . it is not right . . . all the more since you know he loves you infinitely.'

'He has ruined my whole life,' sobbed Tánya. 'I never hear anything but insults and affronts. He regards me as superfluous in his own house. Let him! He will have cause! I shall leave here tomorrow, and study for a position as tele-graphist. . . . Let him!'

'Come, come. Stop crying, Tánya. It does you no good. . . . You are both irritable and impulsive, and both in the wrong. Come, and I will make peace!'

Kovrin spoke gently and persuasively, but Tánya continued to cry, twitching her shoulders and wringing her hands as if she had been overtaken by a real misfortune. Kovrin felt all the sorrier owing to the smallness of the cause of her sorrow. What a trifle it took to make this little creature unhappy for a whole day, or, as she had expressed it, for a whole life! And as he consoled Tánya, it occurred to him that except this girl and her father there was not one in the world who loved him as a kinsman; and had it not been for them, he, left fatherless and motherless in early childhood, must have lived his whole life without feeling one sincere caress, or tasting ever that simple, unreasoning love which we feel only for those akin to us by blood. And he felt that his tired, strained nerves, like magnets, responded to the nerves of this crying, shuddering girl. He felt, too, that he could never love a healthy, rosy-cheeked woman; but pale, weak, unhappy Tánya appealed to him.

He felt pleasure in looking at her hair and her shoulders; and he pressed her hand, and wiped away her tears. . . . At last she ceased crying. But she still continued to complain of her father, and of her insufferable life at home, imploring Kovrin to try to realise her position. Then by degrees she began to smile, and to sigh that God had cursed her with such a wicked temper; and in the end laughed aloud, called herself a fool, and ran out of the room.

A little later Kovrin went into the garden. Yegor Semiónovitch and Tánya, as if nothing had happened, were walking side by side up the alley, eating rye-bread and salt. Both were very hungry.

V

Pleased with his success as peacemaker, Kovrin went into the park. As he sat on a bench and mused, he heard the rattle of a carriage and a woman's laugh – visitors evidently again. Shadows fell in the garden, the sound of a violin, the music of a woman's voice reached him almost inaudibly; and this reminded him of the Black Monk. Whither, to what country, to what planet, had that optical absurdity flown?

Hardly had he called to mind the legend and painted in imagination the black apparition in the rye-field when from behind the pine trees opposite to him, walked inaudibly – without the faintest rustling – a man of middle height. His grey head was uncovered, he was dressed in black, and barefooted like a beggar. On his pallid, corpse-like face stood out sharply a number of black spots. Nodding his head politely the stranger or beggar walked noiselessly to the bench and sat down, and Kovrin recognised the Black Monk. For a minute they looked at one another, Kovrin with astonishment, but the monk kindly and, as before, with a sly expression on his face.

'But you are a mirage,' said Kovrin. 'Why are you here, and why do you sit in one place? That is not in accordance with the legend.'

'It is all the same,' replied the monk softly, turning his face towards Kovrin. 'The legend, the mirage, I – all are products of your own excited imagination. I am a phantom.'

'That is to say you don't exist?' asked Kovrin.

'Think as you like,' replied the monk, smiling faintly. 'I exist in your imagination, and as your imagination is a part of Nature, I must exist also in Nature.'

'You have a clever, a distinguished face – it seems to me as if in reality you had lived more than a thousand years,' said Kovrin. 'I did not know that my imagination was capable of creating such a phenomenon. Why do you look at me with such rapture? Are you pleased with me?'

'Yes. For you are one of the few who can justly be named the elected of God. You serve eternal truth. Your thoughts, your intentions, your astonishing science, all your life bear the stamp of divinity, a heavenly impress; they are dedicated to the rational and the beautiful, and that is, to the Eternal.'

'You say, to eternal truth. Then can eternal truth be accessible and necessary to men if there is no eternal life?'

'There is eternal life,' said the monk.

'You believe in the immortality of men.'

'Of course. For you, men, there awaits a great and a beautiful future. And the more the world has of men like you the nearer will this future be brought. Without you, ministers to the highest principles, living freely and consciously, humanity would be nothing; developing in the natural order it must wait the end of its earthly history. But you, by some thousands of years, hasten it into the kingdom of eternal truth – and in this is your high service. You embody in yourself the blessing of God which rested upon the people.'

'And what is the object of eternal life?' asked Kovrin.

'The same as all life – enjoyment. True enjoyment is in knowledge, and eternal life presents innumerable, inexhaustible fountains of knowledge; it is in this sense it was said: "In My Father's house are many mansions. . . ."'

'You cannot conceive what a joy it is to me to listen to you,' said Kovrin, rubbing his hands with delight.

'I am glad.'

'Yet I know that when you leave me I shall be tormented by doubt as to your reality. You are a phantom, a hallucination. But that means that I am psychically diseased, that I am not in a normal state?'

'What if you are? That need not worry you. You are ill because you have overstrained your powers, because you have borne your health in sacrifice to one idea, and the time is near when you will sacrifice not merely it but your life also. What more could you desire? It is what all gifted and noble natures aspire to.'

'But if I am psychically diseased, how can I trust myself?'

'And how do you know that the men of genius whom all the world trusts have not also seen visions? Genius, they tell you now, is akin to insanity. Believe me, the healthy and the normal are but ordinary men – the herd. Fears as to a nervous age, over-exhaustion and degeneration can trouble seriously only those whose aims in life lie in the present – that is the herd.'

'The Romans had as their ideal: *mens sana in corpore sano.*'

'All that the Greeks and Romans said is not true. Exaltations, aspirations, excitements, ecstacies – all those things which distinguish poets, prophets, martyrs to ideas from ordinary men are incompatible with the animal life, that is, with physical health. I repeat, if you wish to be healthy and normal go with the herd.'

'How strange that you should repeat what I myself have so often thought!' said Kovrin. 'It seems as if you had watched me and listened to my secret thoughts. But do not talk about me. What do you imply by the words: eternal truth?'

The monk made no answer. Kovrin looked at him, but could not make out his face. His features clouded and melted away; his head and arms disappeared; his body faded into the bench and into the twilight, and vanished utterly.

'The hallucination has gone,' said Kovrin, laughing. 'It is a pity.'

He returned to the house lively and happy. What the Black Monk had said to him flattered, not his self-love, but his soul, his whole being. To be the elected, to minister to eternal truth, to stand in the ranks of those who hasten by thousands of years the making mankind worthy of the kingdom of Christ, to deliver humanity from thousands of years of struggle, sin, and suffering, to give to one idea everything, youth, strength, health, to die for the general welfare – what an exalted, what a glorious ideal! And when through his memory flowed his past life, a life pure and chaste and full of labour, when he remembered what he had learnt and what he had taught, he concluded that in the. words of the monk there was no exaggeration.

Through the park, to meet him, came Tánya. She was wearing a different dress from that in which he had last seen her.

'You here?' she cried. 'We were looking for you, looking . . . But what has happened?' she asked in surprise, looking into his glowing, enraptured face, and into his eyes, now full of tears. 'How strange you are, Andrusha!'

'I am satisfied, Tánya,' said Kovrin, laying his hand upon her shoulder. 'I am more than satisfied; I am happy! Tánya, dear Tánya, you are inexpressibly dear to me. Tánya, I am so glad!'

He kissed both her hands warmly, and continued:

'I have just lived through the brightest, most wonderful, most unearthly moments. . . . But I cannot tell you all, for you would call me mad, or refuse to believe me. . . . Let me speak of you! Tánya, I love you, and have long loved you. To have you near me, to meet you ten times a day, has become a necessity for me. I do not know how I shall live without you when I go home.'

'No!' laughed Tánya. 'You will forget us all in two days. We are little people, and you are a great man.'

'Let us talk seriously,' said he. 'I will take you with me, Tánya! Yes? You will come? You will be mine?'

Tánya cried 'What?' and tried to laugh again. But the laugh did not come, and, instead, red spots stood out on her cheeks. She breathed quickly, and walked on rapidly into the park.

'I did not think . . . I never thought of this . . . never thought,' she said, pressing her hands together as if in despair.

But Kovrin hastened after her, and, with the same glowing, enraptured face, continued to speak.

'I wish for a love which will take possession of me altogether, and this love only you, Tánya, can give me. I am happy! How happy!'

She was overcome, bent, withered up, and seemed suddenly to have aged ten years. But Kovrin found her beautiful, and loudly expressed his ecstacy:

'How lovely she is!'

VI

When he learned from Kovrin that not only had a romance resulted, but that a wedding was to follow, Yegor Semiónovitch walked from corner to corner, and tried to conceal his agitation. His hands shook, his neck seemed swollen and purple; he ordered the horses to be put into his racing droschky, and drove away. Tánya, seeing how he whipped the horses and how he pushed his cap down over his ears, understood his mood, locked herself into her room, and cried all day.

In the orangery the peaches and plums were already ripe. The packing and despatch to Moscow of such a delicate load required much attention, trouble, and bustle. Owing to the heat of the summer every tree had to be watered; the process was costly in time and working-power; and many caterpillars appeared, which the workmen, and even Yegor Semiónovitch and Tánya, crushed with their fingers, to the great disgust of Kovrin. The autumn orders for fruit and trees had to be attended to, and a vast correspondence carried on. And at the very busiest time, when it seemed no one had a free moment, work began in the fields and deprived the garden of half its workers. Yegor Semiónovitch, very sunburnt, very irritated, and very worried, galloped about, now to the garden, now to the fields; and all the time shouted that they were tearing him to bits, and that he would put a bullet through his brain.

On top of all came the bustle over Tánya's trousseau, to which the Pesótskys attributed infinite significance. With the eternal snipping of scissors, rattle of sewing-machines, smell of flat-irons, and the caprices of the nervous and touchy dressmaker, the whole house seemed to spin round. And, to make matters worse, visitors arrived every day, and these visitors had to be amused, fed, and lodged for the night. Yet work and worry passed unnoticed in a mist of joy. Tánya felt as if love and happiness had suddenly burst upon her, although ever since her fourteenth year she had been certain that Kovrin would marry nobody but herself. She was eternally in a state of astonishment, doubt, and disbelief in herself. At one moment she was seized by such great joy that she felt she must fly away to the clouds and pray to God; but a moment later she remembered that when August came she would have to leave the home of her childhood and forsake her father; and she was frightened by the thought – God knows whence it came – that she was trivial, insignificant, and unworthy of a great man like Kovrin. When such thoughts came she would run up to her room, lock herself in, and cry bitterly for hours. But when visitors were present, it broke in upon her that Kovrin was a singularly handsome man, that all the women loved him and envied her; and in these moments her heart was as full of rapture and pride as if she had conquered the whole world. When he dared to smile on any other woman she trembled with jealousy, went to her room, and again – tears. These new feelings possessed her altogether; she helped her father mechanically, noticing neither pears nor caterpillars, nor workmen, nor how swiftly time was passing by.

Yegor Semiónovitch was in much the same state of mind. He still worked from morning to night, flew about the gardens, and lost his temper; but all the while he was wrapped in a magic reverie. In his sturdy body contended two men, one the real Yegor Semiónovitch, who, when he listened to the gardener, Ivan Karlovitch's report of some mistake or disorder, went mad with excitement, and tore his hair; and the other the unreal Yegor Semiónovitch – a half-intoxicated old man, who broke off an important conversation in the middle of a word, seized the gardener by the shoulder, and stammered:

'You may say what you like, but blood is thicker than water. His mother was an astonishing, a most noble, a most brilliant woman. It was a pleasure to see her good, pure, open, angel face. She painted beautifully, wrote poetry, spoke five foreign languages, and sang. . . . Poor thing, Heaven rest her soul, she died of consumption!'

The unreal Yegor Semiónovitch sighed, and after a moment's silence continued:

'When he was a boy growing up to manhood in my house he had just such an angel face, open and good. His looks, his movements, his words were as gentle and graceful as his mother's. And his intellect! It is not for nothing he has the degree of *Magister*. But you just wait, Ivan Karlovitch; you'll see what he'll be in ten years' time. Why, he'll be out of sight!'

But here the real Yegor Semiónovitch remembered himself, seized his head and roared:

'Devils! Frost-bitten! Ruined, destroyed! The garden is ruined; the garden is destroyed!'

Kovrin worked with all his former ardour, and hardly noticed the bustle about him. Love only poured oil on the flames. After every meeting with Tánya, he returned to his rooms in rapture and happiness, and set to work with his books and manuscripts with the same passion with which he had kissed her and sworn his love. What the Black Monk had told him of his election by God, of eternal truth, and of the glorious future of humanity, gave to all his work a peculiar, unusual significance. Once or twice every week, either in the park or in the house, he met the monk, and talked with him for hours; but this did not frighten, but on the contrary delighted him, for he was now assured that such apparitions visit only the elect and exceptional who dedicate themselves to the ministry of ideas.

Assumption passed unobserved. Then came the wedding, celebrated by the determined wish of Yegor Semiónovitch with what was called éclat, that is, with meaningless festivities which lasted for two days. Three thousand roubles were consumed in food and drink; but what with the vile music, the noisy toasts, the fussing servants, the clamour, and the closeness of the atmosphere, no one appreciated the expensive wines or the astonishing hors d'oeuvres specially ordered from Moscow.

VII

One of the long winter nights. Kovrin lay in bed, reading a French novel. Poor Tánya, whose head every evening ached as the result of the unaccustomed life in town, had long been sleeping, muttering incoherent phrases in her dreams.

The clock struck three. Kovrin put out the candle and lay down, lay for a long time with closed eyes unable to sleep owing to the heat of the room and Tánya's continued muttering. At half-past four he again lighted the candle. The Black Monk was sitting in a chair beside his bed.

'Good night!' said the monk, and then, after a moment's silence, asked, 'What are you thinking of now?'

'Of glory,' answered Kovrin. 'In a French novel which I have just been reading, the hero is a young man who does foolish things, and dies from a passion for glory. To me this passion is inconceivable.'

'Because you are too clever. You look indifferently on fame as a toy which cannot interest you.'

'That is true.'

'Celebrity has no attraction for you. What flattery, joy, or instruction can a man draw from the knowledge that his name will be graven on a monument, when time will efface the inscription sooner or later? Yes, happily there are too many of you for brief human memory to remember all your names.'

'Of course,' said Kovrin. 'And why remember them? . . . But let us talk of something else. Of happiness, for instance. What is this happiness?'

When the clock struck five he was sitting on the bed with his feet trailing on the carpet and his head turned to the monk, and saying:

'In ancient times a man became frightened at his happiness, so great it was, and to placate the gods laid before them in sacrifice his beloved ring. You have heard? Now I, like Polycrates, am a little frightened at my own happiness. From morning to night I experience only joy – joy absorbs me and stifles all other feelings. I do not know the meaning of grief, affliction, or weariness. I speak seriously, I am beginning to doubt.'

'Why?' asked the monk in an astonished tone. 'Then you think joy is a supernatural feeling? You think it is not the normal condition of things? No! The higher a man has climbed in mental and moral development the freer he is, the greater satisfaction he draws from life. Socrates, Diogenes, Marcus Aurelius knew joy and not sorrow. And the apostle said, "rejoice exceedingly." Rejoice and be happy!'

'And suddenly the gods will be angered,' said Kovrin jokingly. 'But it would hardly be to my taste if they were to steal my happiness and force me to shiver and starve.'

Tánya awoke, and looked at her husband with amazement and terror. He spoke, he turned to the chair, he gesticulated, and laughed; his eyes glittered and his laughter sounded strange.

'Andrusha, whom are you speaking to?' she asked, seizing the hand which he had stretched out to the monk. 'Andrusha, who is it?'

'Who?' answered Kovrin. 'Why, the monk! . . . He is sitting there.' He pointed to the Black Monk.

'There is no one there . . . no one, Andrusha; you are ill.'

Tánya embraced her husband, and, pressing against him as if to defend him against the apparition, covered his eyes with her hand.

'You are ill,' she sobbed, trembling all over. 'Forgive me, darling, but for a long time I have fancied you were unnerved in some way. . . . You are ill . . . psychically, Andrusha.'

The shudder communicated itself to him. He looked once more at the chair, now empty, and suddenly felt weakness in his arms and legs. He began to dress.

'It is nothing, Tánya, nothing . . .' he stammered, and still shuddered. 'But I am a little unwell. . . . It is time to recognise it.'

'I have noticed it for a long time, and father noticed it,' she said, trying to restrain her sobs. 'You have been speaking so funnily to yourself, and smiling so strangely, . . . and you do not sleep. O, my God, my God, save us!' she cried in terror. 'But do not be afraid, Andrusha, do not fear, . . . for God's sake do not be afraid. . . .'

She also dressed. . . . It was only as he looked at her that Kovrin understood the danger of his position, and realised the meaning of the Black Monk and of their conversations. It became plain to him that he was mad.

Both, themselves not knowing why, dressed and went into the hall; she first, he after her. There they found Yegor Semiónovitch in his dressing-gown. He was staying with them, and had been awakened by Tánya's sobs.

'Do not be afraid, Andrusha,' said Tánya, trembling as if in fever. 'Do not be afraid . . . father, this will pass off . . . it will pass off.'

Kovrin was so agitated that he could hardly speak. But he tried to treat the matter as a joke. He turned to his father-in-law and attempted to say:

'Congratulate me . . . it seems I have gone out of my mind.'
But his lips only moved, and he smiled bitterly.

At nine o'clock they put on his overcoat and a fur cloak,
wrapped him up in a shawl, and drove him to the doctor's. He
began a course of treatment.

VIII

Again summer. By the doctor's orders Kovrin returned to the
country. He had recovered his health, and no longer saw the
Black Monk. It only remained for him to recruit his physical
strength. He lived with his father-in-law, drank much milk,
worked only two hours a day, never touched wine, and gave
up smoking.

On the evening of the 19th June, before Elijah's day, a
vesper service was held in the house. When the priest took the
censor from the sexton, and the vast hall began to smell like a
church, Kovrin felt tired. He went into the garden. Taking no
notice of the gorgeous blossoms around him he walked up and
down, sat for a while on a bench, and then walked through the
park. He descended the sloping bank to the margin of the
river, and stood still, looking questioningly at the water. The
great pines, with their shaggy roots, which a year before had
seen him so young, so joyous, so active, no longer whispered,
but stood silent and motionless, as if not recognising him. . . .
And, indeed, with his short-clipped hair, his feeble walk, and
his changed face, so heavy and pale and changed since last
year, he would hardly have been recognised anywhere.

He crossed the stream. In the field, last year covered with
rye, lay rows of reaped oats. The sun had set, and on the
horizon flamed a broad, red afterglow, fortelling stormy
weather. All was quiet, and, gazing towards the point at
which a year before he had first seen the Black Monk, Kovrin
stood twenty minutes watching the crimson fade. When he
returned to the house, tired and unsatisfied, Yegor Semiónovitch and Tánya were sitting on the steps of the terrace,
drinking tea. They were talking together, and, seeing Kovrin,
stopped. But Kovrin knew by their faces that they had been
speaking of him.

'It is time for you to have your milk,' said Tánya to her husband.

'No, not yet,' he answered, sitting down on the lowest step. 'You drink it. I do not want it.'

Tánya timidly exchanged glances with her father, and said in a guilty voice:

'You know very well that the milk does you good.'

'Yes, any amount of good,' laughed Kovrin. 'I congratulate you, I have gained a pound in weight since last Friday.' He pressed his hands to his head and said in a pained voice: 'Why . . . why have you cured me? Bromide mixtures, idleness, warm baths, watching in trivial terror over every mouthful, every step . . . all this in the end will drive me to idiocy. I had gone out of my mind . . . I had the mania of greatness. . . . But for all that I was bright, active, and even happy . . . was interesting and original. Now I have become rational and solid, just like the rest of the world. I am a mediocrity, and it is tiresome for me to live. . . . Oh, how cruelly . . . how cruelly you have treated me! I had hallucinations . . . but what harm did that cause to anyone? I ask you what harm?'

'God only knows what you mean!' sighed Yegor Semiónovitch. 'It is stupid even to listen to you.'

'Then you need not listen.'

The presence of others, especially of Yegor Semiónovitch, now irritated Kovrin; he answered his father-in-law drily, coldly, even rudely, and could not look on him without contempt and hatred. And Yegor Semiónovitch felt confused, and coughed guiltily, although he could not see how he was in the wrong. Unable to understand the cause of such a sudden reversal of their former hearty relations, Tánya leaned against her father, and looked with alarm into his eyes. It was becoming plain to her that their relations every day grew worse and worse, that her father had aged greatly, and that her husband had become irritable, capricious, excitable, and uninteresting. She no longer laughed and sang, she ate nothing, and whole nights never slept, but lived under the weight of some impending terror, torturing herself so much that she lay insensible from dinner-time till evening. When the service was being held, it had seemed to her that her father was crying; and now as she sat on the terrace she made an effort not to think of it.

'How happy were Buddha and Mahomet and Shakespeare that their kind-hearted kinsmen and doctors did not cure them of ecstacy and inspiration!' said Kovrin. 'If Mahomet had taken potassium bromide for his nerves, worked only two hours a day, and drunk milk, that astonishing man could have left as little behind him as his dog. Doctors and kindhearted relatives only do their best to make humanity stupid, and the time will come when mediocrity will be considered genius, and humanity will perish. If you only had some idea,' concluded Kovrin peevishly, 'if you only had some idea how grateful I am!'

He felt strong irritation, and to prevent himself saying too much, rose and went into the house. It was a windless night, and into the window was borne the smell of tobacco plants and jalap. Through the windows of the great dark hall, on the floor and on the piano, fell the moonrays. Kovrin recalled the raptures of the summer before, when the air, as now, was full of the smell of jalap and the moonrays poured through the window. . . . To awaken the mood of last year he went to his room, lighted a strong cigar, and ordered the servant to bring him wine. But now the cigar was bitter and distasteful, and the wine had lost its flavour of the year before. How much it means to get out of practice! From a single cigar, and two sips of wine, his head went round, and he was obliged to take bromide of potassium.

Before going to bed Tánya said to him:

'Listen. Father worships you, but you are annoyed with him about something, and that is killing him. Look at his face; he is growing old, not by days but by hours! I implore you, Andrusha, for the love of Christ, for the sake of your own dead father, for the sake of my peace of mind – be kind to him again!'

'I cannot, and I do not want to.'

'But why?' Tánya trembled all over. 'Explain to me why!'

'Because I do not like him; that is all,' answered Kovrin carelessly, shrugging his shoulders. 'But better not talk of that; he is your father.'

'I cannot, cannot understand,' said Tánya. She pressed her hands to her forehead and fixed her eyes on one point.

'Something terrible, something incomprehensible is going on in this house. You, Andrusha, have changed; you are no longer yourself. . . . You – a clever, an exceptional man – get irritated over trifles. . . . You are annoyed by such little things that at any other time you yourself would have refused to believe it. No . . . do not be angry, do not be angry,' she continued, kissing his hands, and frightened by her own words. 'You are clever, good, and noble. You will be just to father. He is so good.'

'He is not good, but merely good-humoured. These vaudeville uncles – of your father's type – with well-fed, easygoing faces, are characters in their way, and once used to amuse me, whether in novels, in comedies, or in life. But they are now hateful to me. They are egoists to the marrow of their bones. . . . Most disgusting of all is their satiety, and this stomachic, purely bovine – or swinish – optimism.'

Tánya sat on the bed, and laid her head on a pillow.

'This is torture!' she said; and from her voice it was plain that she was utterly weary and found it hard to speak. 'Since last winter not a moment of rest. . . . It is terrible, my God! I suffer . . .'

'Yes, of course! I am Herod, and you and your papa the massacred infants. Of course!'

His face seemed to Tánya ugly and disagreeable. The expression of hatred and contempt did not suit it. She even observed that something was lacking in his face; ever since his hair had been cut off, it seemed changed. She felt an almost irresistible desire to say something insulting, but restrained herself in time, and overcome with terror, went out of the bedroom.

IX

Kovrin received an independent chair. His inaugural address was fixed for the 2nd of December, and a notice to that effect was posted in the corridors of the University. But when the day came a telegram was received by the University authorities that he could not fulfil the engagement, owing to illness.

Blood came from his throat. He spat it up, and twice in one month it flowed in streams. He felt terribly weak, and fell into a somnolent condition. But this illness did not frighten him, for he knew that his dead mother had lived with the same complaint more than ten years. His doctors, too, declared that there was no danger, and advised him merely not to worry, to lead a regular life, and to talk less.

In January the lecture was postponed for the same reason, and in February it was too late to begin the course. It was postponed till the following year.

He no longer lived with Tánya, but with another woman, older than himself, who looked after him as if he were a child. His temper was calm and obedient; he submitted willingly, and when Varvara Nikolaievna – that was her name – made arrangements for taking him to the Crimea, he consented to go, although he felt that from the change no good would come.

They reached Sevastopol late one evening, and stopped there to rest, intending to drive to Yalta on the following day. Both were tired by the journey. Varvara Nikolaievna drank tea, and went to bed. But Kovrin remained up. An hour before leaving home for the railway station he had received a letter from Tánya, which he had not read; and the thought of this letter caused him unpleasant agitation. In the depths of his heart he knew that his marriage with Tánya had been a mistake. He was glad that he was finally parted from her; but the remembrance of this woman, who towards the last had seemed to turn into a walking, living mummy, in which all had died except the great, clever eyes, awakened in him only pity and vexation against himself. The writing on the envelope reminded him that two years before he had been guilty of cruelty and injustice, and that he had avenged on people in no way guilty his spiritual vacuity, his solitude, his disenchantment with life. . . . He remembered how he had once torn into fragments his dissertation and all the articles written by him since the time of his illness, and thrown them out of the window, how the fragments flew in the wind and rested on the trees and flowers; in every page he had seen strange and baseless pretensions, frivolous irritation, and a mania for greatness. And all this had produced upon him an impression that he had written a description of his own faults. Yet when the last copybook had been torn up and thrown out of the window, he felt bitterness and vexation, and went to his wife and spoke to her cruelly. Heavens, how he had ruined her life! He remembered how once, wishing to cause her pain, he had told her that her father had played in their romance an unusual rôle, and had even asked him to marry her; and Yegor Semiónovitch, happening to overhear him, had rushed into the room, so dumb with consternation that he could not utter a word, but only stamped his feet on one spot and bellowed strangely as if his tongue had been cut out. And Tánya, looking at her father, cried out in a heartrending voice, and fell insensible on the floor. It was hideous.

The memory of all this returned to him at the sight of the well-known handwriting. He went out on to the balcony. It was warm and calm, and a salt smell came to him from the sea. The moonlight, and the lights around, were imaged on the surface of the wonderful bay – a surface of a hue impossible to name. It was a tender and soft combination of dark blue and green; in parts the water resembled copperas, and in parts, instead of water, liquid moonlight filled the bay. And all these combined in a harmony of hues which exhaled tranquillity and exaltation.

In the lower storey of the inn, underneath the balcony, the windows were evidently open, for women's voices and laughter could plainly be heard. There must be an entertainment.

Kovrin made an effort over himself, unsealed the letter, and, returning to his room, began to read:

'My father has just died. For this I am indebted to you, for it was you who killed him. Our garden is being ruined; it is managed by strangers; what my poor father so dreaded is taking place. For this also I am indebted to you. I hate you with all my soul, and wish that you may perish soon! Oh, how I suffer! My heart burns with an intolerable pain! . . . May you be accursed! I took you for an exceptional man, for a genius; I loved you, and you proved a madman. . . .'

Kovrin could read no more; he tore up the letter and threw the pieces away . . . He was overtaken by restlessness – almost by terror. . . . On the other side of the screen, slept Varvara

Nikolaievna; he could hear her breathing. From the storey beneath came the women's voices and laughter, but he felt that in the whole hotel there was not one living soul except himself. The fact that wretched, overwhelmed Tánya had cursed him in her letter, and wished him ill, caused him pain; and he looked fearfully at the door as if fearing to see again that unknown power which in two years had brought about so much ruin in his own life and in the lives of all who were dearest to him.

By experience he knew that when the nerves give way the best refuge lies in work. He used to sit at the table and concentrate his mind upon some definite thought. He took from his red portfolio a copybook containing the conspectus of a small work of compilation which he intended to carry out during his stay in the Crimea, if he became tired of inactivity. . . . He sat at the table, and worked on this conspectus, and it seemed to him that he was regaining his former peaceful, resigned, impersonal mood. His conspectus led him to speculation on the vanity of the world. He thought of the great price which life demands for the most trivial and ordinary benefits which it gives to men. To reach a chair of philosophy under forty years of age; to be an ordinary professor; to expound commonplace thoughts – and those thoughts the thoughts of others – in feeble, tiresome, heavy language; in one word, to attain the position of a learned mediocrity, he had studied fifteen years, worked day and night, passed through a severe psychological disease, survived an unsuccessful marriage – been guilty of many follies and injustices which it was torture to remember. Kovrin now clearly realised that he was a mediocrity, and he was willingly reconciled to it, for he knew that every man must be satisfied with what he is.

The conspectus calmed him, but the torn letter lay upon the floor and hindered the concentration of his thoughts. He rose, picked up the fragments, and threw them out of the window. But a light wind blew from the sea, and the papers fluttered back on to the window sill. Again he was overtaken by restlessness akin to terror, and it seemed to him that in the whole hotel except himself there was not one living soul. . . . He went on to the balcony. The bay, as if alive, stared up at him from its multitude of light and dark-blue eyes, its eyes of turquoise and fire, and beckoned him. It was warm and stifling; how delightful, he thought, to bathe!

Suddenly beneath the balcony a violin was played, and two women's voices sang. All this was known to him. The song which they sang told of a young girl, diseased in imagination, who heard by night in a garden mysterious sounds, and found in them a harmony and a holiness incomprehensible to us mortals. . . . Kovrin held his breath, his heart ceased to beat, and the magical, ecstatic rapture which he had long forgotten trembled in his heart again.

A high, black pillar, like a cyclone or waterspout, appeared on the opposite coast. It swept with incredible swiftness across the bay towards the hotel; it became smaller and smaller, and Kovrin stepped aside to make room for it. . . . The monk, with uncovered grey head, with black eyebrows, barefooted, folding his arms upon his chest, swept past him, and stopped in the middle of the room.

'Why did you not believe me?' he asked in a tone of reproach, looking caressingly at Kovrin. 'If you had believed me when I said you were a genius, these last two years would not have been passed so sadly and so barrenly.'

Kovrin again believed that he was the elected of God and a genius; he vividly remembered all his former conversation with the Black Monk, and wished to reply. But the blood flowed from his throat on to his chest, and he, not knowing what to do, moved his hands about his chest till his cuffs were red with the blood. He wished to call Varvara Nikolaievna, who slept behind the screen, and making an effort to do so, cried:

'Tánya!'

He fell on the floor, and raising his hands, again cried: 'Tánya!'

He cried to Tánya, cried to the great garden with the miraculous flowers, cried to the park, to the pines with their shaggy roots, to the rye-field, cried to his marvellous science, to his youth, his daring, his joy, cried to the life which had been so beautiful. He saw on the floor before him a great pool of blood, and from weakness could not utter a single word. But an inexpressible, infinite joy filled his whole being.

Beneath the balcony the serenade was being played, and the Black Monk whispered to him that he was a genius, and died only because his feeble, mortal body had lost its balance, and could no longer serve as the covering of genius.

When Varvara Nikolaievna awoke, and came from behind her screen, Kovrin was dead. But on his face was frozen an immovable smile of happiness.

ON THE WAY

ON THE WAY

In the room which the innkeeper, the Cossack Semión Tchistoplui, called 'The Traveller,' – meaning thereby, 'reserved exclusively for travellers,' – at a big, unpainted table, sat a tall and broad-shouldered man of about forty years of age. With his elbows on the table and his head resting on his hands, he slept. A fragment of a tallow candle, stuck in a pomade jar, illumined his fair hair, his thick, broad nose, his sunburnt cheeks, and the beetling brows that hung over his closed eyes. . . . Taken one by one, all his features – his nose, his cheeks, his eyebrows – were as rude and heavy as the furniture in 'The Traveller'; taken together they produced an effect of singular harmony and beauty. Such, indeed, is often the character of the Russian face; the bigger, the sharper the individual features, the softer and more benevolent the whole. The sleeper was dressed as one of good class, in a threadbare jacket bound with new wide braid, a plush waistcoat, and loose black trousers, vanishing in big boots.

On a bench which stretched the whole way round the room slept a girl some eight years of age. She lay upon a foxskin overcoat, and wore a brown dress and long black stockings. Her face was pale, her hair fair, her shoulders narrow, her body slight and frail; but her nose ended in just such an ugly lump as the man's. She slept soundly, and did not seem to feel that the crescent comb which had fallen from her hair was cutting into her cheek.

'The Traveller' had a holiday air. The atmosphere smelt of newly-washed floors; there were no rags on the line which stretched diagonally across the room; and in the ikon corner, casting a red reflection upon the image of St. George the Victory-Bringer, burned a lamp. With a severe and cautious gradation from the divine to the earthy, there stretched from each side of the image a row of gaudily-painted pictures. In the dim light thrown from the lamp and candle-end these pictures seemed to form a continuous belt covered with black patches; but when the tiled stove, wishing to sing in accord with the weather, drew in the blast with a howl, and the logs, as if angered, burst into ruddy flames and roared with rage, rosy patches quivered along the walls; and above the head of the sleeping man might be seen first the faces of seraphim, then the Shah Nasr Edin, and finally a greasy, sunburnt boy, with staring eyes, whispering something into the ear of a girl with a singularly blunt and indifferent face.

The storm howled outside. Something wild and angry, but deeply miserable, whirled round the inn with the fury of a beast, and strove to burst its way in. It banged against the doors, it beat on the windows and roof, it tore the walls, it threatened, it implored, it quieted down, and then with the joyous howl of triumphant treachery it rushed up the stove pipe; but here the logs burst into flame, and the fire, like a chained hound, rose up in rage to meet its enemy. There was a sobbing, a hissing, and an angry roar. In all this might be distinguished both irritated weariness and unsatisfied hate, and the angered impotence of one accustomed to victory.

Enchanted by the wild, inhuman music, 'The Traveller' seemed numbed into immobility for ever. But the door creaked on its hinges, and into the inn came the potboy in a new calico shirt. He walked with a limp, twitched his sleepy eyes, snuffed the candle with his fingers, and went out. The bells of the village church of Rogatchi, three hundred yards away, began to strike twelve. It was midnight. The storm played with the sounds as with snowflakes, it chased them to infinite distances, it cut some short and stretched some into long undulating notes; and it smothered others altogether in the universal tumult. But suddenly a chime resounded so loudly through the room that it might have been rung under the window. The girl on the foxskin overcoat started and raised her head. For a moment she gazed vacantly at the black window, then turned her eyes upon Nasr Edin, on whose face the firelight gleamed, and finally looked at the sleeping man.

'Papa!' she cried.

But her father did not move. The girl peevishly twitched her eyebrows, and lay down again with her legs bent under her. A loud yawn sounded outside the door. Again the hinges squeaked, and indistinct voices were heard. Someone entered, shook the snow from his coat, and stamped his feet heavily.

'Who is it?' drawled a female voice.

'Mademoiselle Ilováisky,' answered a bass.

Again the door creaked. The storm tore into the cabin and howled. Someone, no doubt the limping boy, went to the door of 'The Traveller,' coughed respectfully, and raised the latch.

'Come in, please,' said the female voice. 'It is all quite clean, honey!'

The door flew open. On the threshold appeared a bearded muzhik, dressed in a coachman's caftan, covered with snow from head to foot. He stooped under the weight of a heavy portmanteau. Behind him entered a little female figure, not half his height, faceless and handless, rolled into a shapeless bundle, and covered also with snow. Both coachman and bundle smelt of damp. The candle-flame trembled.

'What nonsense!' cried the bundle angrily. 'Of course we can go on! It is only twelve versts more, chiefly wood. There is no fear of our losing the way.'

'Lose our way or not, it's all the same . . . the horses won't go an inch farther,' answered the coachman. 'Lord bless you, miss. . . . As if I had done it on purpose!'

'Heaven knows where you've landed me! . . . Hush! there's someone asleep. You may go!'

The coachman shook the caked snow from his shoulders, set down the portmanteau, snuffled, and went out. And the little girl, watching, saw two tiny hands creeping out of the middle of the bundle, stretching upward, and undoing the network of shawls, handkerchiefs, and scarfs. First on the floor fell a heavy shawl, then a hood, and after it a white knitted muffler. Having freed its head, the bundle removed its cloak, and shrivelled suddenly into half its former size. Now it appeared in a long, grey ulster, with immense buttons and yawning pockets. From one pocket it drew a paper parcel. From the other came a bunch of keys, which the bundle put down so incautiously that the sleeping man started and opened his eyes. For a moment he looked around him vacantly, as if not realising where he was, then shook his head, walked to the corner of the room, and sat down. The bundle took off its ulster, again reduced itself by half, drew off its shoes, and also sat down.

It no longer resembled a bundle. It was a woman, a tiny, fragile brunette of some twenty years of age, thin as a serpent, with a long pale face, and curly hair. Her nose was long and sharp, her chin long and sharp, her eyelashes long; and thanks to a general sharpness the expression of her face was stinging. Dressed in a tight-fitting black gown, with lace on the neck and sleeves, with sharp elbows and long, rosy fingers, she called to mind portraits of English ladies of the middle of the century. The serious, self-centred expression of her face served only to increase the resemblance.

The brunette looked around the room, glanced sidelong at the man and girl, and, shrugging her shoulders, went over and sat at the window. The dark windows trembled in the damp west wind. Outside great flakes of snow, flashing white, darted against the glass, clung to it for a second, and were whirled away by the storm. The wild music grew louder.

There was a long silence. At last the little girl rose suddenly, and, angrily ringing out every word, exclaimed:

'Lord! Lord! How unhappy I am! The most miserable being in the world!'

The man rose, and with a guilty air, ill-suited to his gigantic stature and long beard, went to the bench.

'You're not sleeping, dearie? What do you want?' He spoke in the voice of a man who is excusing himself.

'I don't want anything! My shoulder hurts! You are a wicked man, father, and God will punish you; Wait! You'll see how he'll punish you!'

'I know it's painful, darling . . . but what can I do?' He spoke in the tone employed by husbands when they make excuses to their angry wives. 'If your shoulder hurts it is the long journey that is guilty. Tomorrow it will be over, then we shall rest, and the pain will stop. . . .'

'Tomorrow! Tomorrow! . . . Every day you say tomorrow! We shall go on for another twenty days!'

'Listen, friend, I give you my word of honour that this is the last day. I never tell you untruths. If the storm delayed us, that is not my fault.'

'I can bear it no longer! I cannot! I cannot!'

Sasha pulled in her leg sharply, and filled the room with a disagreeable whining cry. Her father waved his arm, and looked absent-mindedly at the brunette. The brunette shrugged her shoulders, and walked irresolutely towards Sasha.

'Tell me, dear,' she said, 'why are you crying? It is very nasty to have a sore shoulder . . . but what can be done?'

'The fact is, mademoiselle,' said the man apologetically, 'we have had no sleep for two nights, and drove here in a villainous cart. No wonder she is ill and unhappy. A drunken driver . . . the luggage stolen . . . all the time in a snowstorm . . . but what's the good of crying? . . . I, too, am tired out with sleeping in a sitting position, so tired that I feel almost drunk. Listen, Sasha . . . even as they are things are bad enough . . . yet you must cry!'

He turned his head away, waved his arm, and sat down.

'Of course, you mustn't cry!' said the brunette. 'Only babies cry. If you are ill, dearie, you must undress and go to sleep. . . . Come, let me undress you!'

With the girl undressed and comforted, silence again took possession of the room. The brunette sat at the window, and looked questioningly at the wall, the ikon, and the stove. Apparently things around seemed very strange to her, the room, the girl with her fat nose and boy's short nightgown, and the girl's father. That strange man sat in the corner, looking vacantly about him like a drunken man, and rubbing his face with his hands. He kept silence, blinked his eyes; and judging from his guilty figure no one would expect that he would be the first to break the silence. Yet it was he who began. He smoothed his trousers, coughed, laughed, and said:

'A comedy, I swear to God! . . . I look around, and can't believe my eyes. Why did destiny bring us to this accursed inn? What did she mean to express by it? But life sometimes makes such a *salto mortale*, that you look and can't believe your eyes. Are you going far, miss?'

'Not very far,' answered the brunette. 'I was going from home, about twenty versts away, to a farm of ours where my father and brother are staying. I am Mademoiselle Ilováisky, and the farm is Ilováisk. It is twelve versts from here. What disagreeable weather!'

'It could hardly be worse.'

The lame pot-boy entered the room, and stuck a fresh candle end in the pomade jar.

'Get the samovar!' said the man.

'Nobody drinks tea at this hour,' grinned the boy. 'It is a sin before Mass.'

'Don't you mind . . . it is not you that'll burn in hell, but we. . . .'

While they drank their tea the conversation continued. Mdlle. Ilováisky learned that the stranger's name was Grigóri Petróvitch Likharyóff, that he was a brother of Likharyóff, the Marshal of the Nobility in the neighbouring district, that he had himself once been a landed proprietor, but had gone through everything. And in turn Likharyóff learned that his companion was Márya Mikháilovna Ilováisky, that her father had a large estate, and that all the management fell upon her shoulders, as both father and brother were improvident, looked at life through their fingers, and thought of little but greyhounds. . . .

'My father and brother are quite alone on the farm,' said Mdlle. Ilováisky, moving her fingers (she had a habit in conversation of moving her fingers before her stinging face, and after every phrase, licking her lips with a pointed tongue); 'they are the most helpless creatures on the face of the earth, and can't lift a finger to help themselves. My father is muddle-headed, and my brother every evening tired off his feet. Imagine! . . . who is to get them food after the Fast? Mother is dead, and our servants cannot lay a cloth without my supervision. They will be without proper food, while I spend all night here. It is very funny!'

Mdlle. Ilováisky shrugged her shoulders, sipped her tea, and said:

'There are certain holidays which have a peculiar smell. Easter, Trinity, and Christmas each has its own smell. Even atheists love these holidays. My brother, for instance, says there is no God, but at Easter he is the first to run off to the morning service.'

Likharyóff lifted his eyes, turned them on his companion and laughed.

'They say that there is no God,' continued Mdlle. Ilováisky, also laughing, 'but why then, be so good as to tell me, do all celebrated writers, scholars, and clever men generally, believe at the close of their lives?'

'The man who in youth has not learnt to believe does not believe in old age, be he a thousand times a writer.'

Judged by his cough, Likharyóff had a bass voice, but now either from fear of speaking too loud, or from a needless bashfulness, he spoke in a tenor. After a moment's silence, he sighed and continued:

'This is how I understand it. Faith is a quality of the soul. It is the same as talent . . . it is congenital. As far as I can judge from my own case, from those whom I have met in life, from all that I see around me, this congenital faith is inherent in all Russians to an astonishing degree. . . . May I have another cup? . . . Russian life presents itself as a continuous series of faiths and infatuations, but unbelief or negation it has not – if I may so express it – even smelt. That a Russian does not believe in God is merely a way of saying that he believes in something else.'

Likharyóff took from Mdlle. Ilováisky another cup of tea, gulped down half of it an once, and continued:

'Let me tell you about myself. In my soul Nature planted exceptional capacity for belief. Half my life have I lived an atheist and a Nihilist, yet never was there a single moment when I did not believe. Natural gifts display themselves generally in early childhood, and my capacity for faith showed itself at a time when I could walk upright underneath the table. My mother used to make us children eat a lot, and when she gave us our meals, she had a habit of saying, "Eat, children; there's nothing on earth like soup!" I believed this; I ate soup ten times a day, swallowed it like a shark to the point of vomiting and disgust. My nurse used to tell me fairy tales, and I believed in ghosts, in fairies, in wood-demons, in every kind of monster. I remember well! I used to steal corrosive sublimate from father's room, sprinkle it on gingerbread, and leave it in the attic, so that the ghosts might eat it and die. But when I learned to read and to understand what I read, my beliefs got beyond description. I even ran away to America, I joined a gang of robbers, I tried to enter a monastery, I hired boys to torture me for Christ's sake. When I ran away to

America I did not go alone, but took with me just such another fool, and I was glad when we froze nearly to death, and when I was flogged. When I ran away to join the robbers, I returned every time with a broken skin. Most untranquil childhood! But when I was sent to school, and learned that the earth goes round the sun, and that white light so far from being white is composed of seven primary colours, my head went round entirely. At home everything seemed hideous, my mother, in the name of Elijah, denying lightning conductors, my father indifferent to the truths I preached. My new enlightenment inspired me! Like a madman I rushed about the house; I preached my truths to the stable boys, I was driven to despair by ignorance, I flamed with hatred against all who saw in white light only white. . . . But this is nonsense. . . . Serious, so to speak, manly infatuations began with me only at college. . . . Have you completed a university course?'

'At Novotcherkask – in the Don Institute.'

'But that is not a university course. You can hardly know what this science is. All sciences, whatever they may be, have only one and the same passport, without which they are meaningless – an aspiration to truth! Every one of them – even your wretched pharmacology – has its end, not in profit, not in convenience and advantage to life, but in truth. It is astonishing! When you begin the study of any science you are captivated from the first. I tell you, there is nothing more seductive and gracious, nothing so seizes and overwhelms the human soul, as the beginning of a science. In the first five or six lectures you are exalted by the very brightest hopes – you seem already the master of eternal truth. . . . Well, I gave myself to science passionately, as to a woman loved. I was its slave, and, except it, would recognise no other sun. Day and night, night and day, without unbending my back, I studied. I learnt off formulas by heart; I ruined myself on books; I wept when I saw with my own eyes others exploiting science for personal aims. . . . But I got over my infatuation soon. The fact is, every science has a beginning, but it has no end – it is like a recurring decimal. Zoology discovered thirty-five thousand species of insects; chemistry counts sixty elementary substances. If, as time goes by, you add to these figures ten ciphers, you will be just as far from the end as now, for all contemporary scientific research consists in the multiplication of figures. . . . This I began to understand when I myself discovered the thirty-five-thousand-and-first species, and gained no satisfaction. But I had no disillusion to outlive, for a new faith immediately appeared. I thrust myself into Nihilism with its proclamations, its hideous deeds, its tricks of all sorts. I went down to the people; I served as factory-hand; I greased the axles of railway carriages; I turned myself into a bargee. It was while thus wandering all over the face of Russia that I first saw Russian life. I became an impassioned admirer of that life. I loved the Russian people to distraction; I loved and trusted in its God, in its language, in its creations. . . . And so on eternally. . . . In my time I have been a Slavophile, and bored Aksakoff with my letters; and an Ukrainophile, and an archaeologist, and a collector of specimens of popular creative art. . . . I have been carried away by ideas, by men, by events, by places. . . . I have been carried away unceasingly. . . . Five years ago I embodied the negation of property; my latest faith was non-resistance to evil.'

Sasha sighed gustily and moved. Likharyóff rose and went over to her.

'Will you have some tea, darling?' he asked tenderly.

'Drink it yourself!' answered Sasha.

'You have lived a varied life,' said Márya Mikháilovna. 'You have something to remember.'

'Yes, yes; it is all very genial when you sit at the tea-table and gossip with a good companion; but you do not ask me what has all this gaiety cost me. With what have I paid for the diversity of my life? You must remember, in the first place, that I did not believe like a German Doctor of Philosophy. I did not live as a hermit, but my every faith bent me as a bow, and tore my body to pieces. Judge for yourself! Once I was as rich as my brother: now I am a beggar. Into this whirlpool of infatuation I cast my own estate, the property of my wife, the money of many others. I am forty-two today, with old age staring me in the face, and I am homeless as a dog that has lost his master by night. In my whole life I have never known repose. My soul was in constant torment; I suffered even from my hopes. . . . I have worn myself out with heavy unregulated work; I have suffered deprivation; five times I have been in prison. I have wandered through Archangel and Tobolsk . . . the very memory sickens me. I lived, but in the vortex never felt the process of life. Will you believe it, I never noticed how my wife loved me – when my children were born. What more can I tell you? To all who loved me I brought misfortune. . . . My mother has mourned for me now fifteen years, and my own brothers, who through me have been made to blush, who have been made to bend their backs, whose hearts have been sickened, whose money has been wasted, have grown at last to hate me like poison.'

Likharyóff rose and again sat down.

'If I were only unhappy I should be thankful to God,' he continued, looking at Mdlle. Ilováisky. 'But my personal unhappiness fades away when I remember how often in my infatuations I was ridiculous, far from the truth, unjust, cruel, dangerous! How often with my whole soul have I hated ánd despised those whom I ought to have loved, and loved those whom I ought to have hated! Today, I believe; I fall down on my face and worship; tomorrow, like a coward, I flee from the gods and friends of yesterday, and silently swallow some scoundrel! God alone knows how many times I have wept with shame for my infatuations! Never in my life have I consciously lied or committed a wrong, yet my conscience is unclean! I cannot even boast that my hands are unstained with blood, for before my own eyes my wife faded to death – worn out by my improvidence. My own wife! . . . Listen; there are now in fashion two opposing opinions of woman. One class measures her skull to prove that she is lower than man, to determine her defects, to justify their own animality. The other would employ all their strength in lifting woman to their own level – that is to say, force her to learn by heart thirty-five thousand species of insects, to talk and write the same nonsense as they themselves talk and write.'

Likharyhóff's face darkened.

'But I tell you that woman always was and always will be the slave of man!' he said in a bass voice, thumping his fist upon the table. 'She is wax – tender, plastic wax – from which man can mould what he will. Lord in heaven! Yet out of some trumpery infatuation for manhood she cuts her hair, forsakes her family, dies in a foreign land. . . . Of all the ideas to which she sacrifices herself not one is feminine! . . . Devoted, unthinking slave! Skulls I have never measured; but this I say from bitter, grievous experience: The proudest, the most independent women – once I had succeeded in communicating to them my inspiration, came after me, unreasoning, asking no questions, obeying my every wish. Of a nun I made a Nihilist, who, as I afterwards learned, killed a gendarme. My wife never forsook me in all my wanderings, and like a weathercock changed her faith as I changed my infatuations.'

With excitement Likharyóff jumped up, and walked up and down the room.

'Noble, exalted slavery!' he exclaimed, gesticulating. 'In this, in this alone, is hidden the true significance of woman's life. . . . Out of all the vile nonsense which accumulated in my head during my relations with women, one thing, as water from a filter, has come out pure, and that is neither ideas, nor philosophy, nor clever phrases, but this extraordinary submissiveness to fate, this uncommon benevolence, this all-merciful kindness.'

Lakharyóff clenched his fists, concentrated his eyes upon a single point, and, as if tasting every word, filtered through his clenched teeth:

'This magnanimous endurance, faith to the grave, the poetry of the heart. It is in this . . . yes, it is in this that the meaning of life is found, in this unmurmuring martyrdom, in the tears that soften stone, in the infinite all-forgiving love, which sweeps into the chaos of life in lightness and warmth. . . .'

Márya Mikháilovna rose slowly, took a step towards Likharyóff, and set her eyes piercingly upon his face. By the tears which sparkled on his eyelashes, by the trembling, passionate voice, by the flushed cheeks, she saw at a glance that women were not the accidental theme of his conversation. No, they were the object of his new infatuation, or, as he had put it, of his new belief. For the first time in her life she saw before her a man in the ecstacy of a burning, prophetic faith. Gesticulating – rolling his eyes, he seemed insane and ecstatical; but in the fire of his eyes, in the torrent of his words, in all the movements of his gigantic body, she saw only such beauty, that, herself not knowing what she did, she stood silently before him as if rooted to the ground, and looked with rapture into his face.

'Take my mother, for example!' he said, with an imploring look, stretching out his arms to her. 'I poisoned her life, I disgraced in her eyes the race of Likharyóff, I brought her only such evil as is brought by the bitterest foe, and . . . what? My brothers give her odd kopecks for wafers and collections, and she, violating her religious feeling, hoards up those kopecks, and sends them secretly to me! Such deeds as this educate and ennoble the soul more than all your theories, subtle phrases, thirty-five thousand species! . . . But I might give you a thousand instances! Take your own case! Outside storm and darkness, yet through storm and darkness and cold, you drive, fearless, to your father and brother, that their holidays may be warmed by your caresses, although they, it may well be, have forgotten your existence. But wait! The day will come when you will learn to love a man, and you will go after him to the North Pole. . . . You would go!'

'Yes . . . if I loved him.'

'You see!' rejoiced Likharyóff, stamping his feet. 'Oh, God, how happy I am to have met you here! . . . Such has always been my good fortune . . . everywhere I meet with kind acquaintances. Not a day passes that I do not meet some man for whom I would give my soul! In this world there are many more good people than evil! Already you and I have spoken frankly and out of the heart, as if we had known one another a thousand years. It is possible for a man to live his own life, to keep silent for ten years, to be reticent with his own wife and friends, and then some day suddenly he meets a cadet in a railway carriage, and reveals to him his whole soul. . . . You . . . I have the honour to see you for the first time, but I have confessed myself as I never did before. Why?'

Likharyóff rubbed his hands and smiled gaily. Then he walked up and down the room and talked again of women. The church bell chimed for the morning service.

'Heavens!' wept Sasha. 'He won't let me sleep with his talk!'

'Akh, yes!' stammered Likharyóff. 'Forgive me, darling. Sleep, sleep. . . . In addition to her, I have two boys,' he whispered. 'They live with their uncle, but she cannot bear to be a day without her father. . . . Suffers, grumbles, but sticks to me as a fly to honey. . . . But I have been talking nonsense, mademoiselle, and have prevented you also from sleeping. Shall I make your bed?'

Without waiting for an answer, he shook out the wet cloak, and stretched it on the bench with the fur on top, picked up the scattered mufflers and shawls, and rolled the ulster into a pillow – all this silently, with an expression of servile adoration, as though he were dealing not with women's rags, but with fragments of holy vessels. His whole figure seemed to express guilt and confusion, as if in the presence of such a tiny being he were ashamed of his height and strength. . . .

When Mdlle. Ilováisky had lain down he extinguished the candle, and sat on a stool near the stove. . . .

'Yes,' he whispered, smoking a thick cigarette, and puffing the smoke into the stove. 'Nature has set in every Russian an enquiring mind, a tendency to speculation, and extraordinary capacity for belief: but all these are broken into dust again our improvidence, indolence, and fantastic triviality. . . .'

Márya Mikháilovna looked in astonishment into the darkness, but she could see only the red spot on the ikon, and the quivering glare from the stove on Likharyóff's face. The darkness, the clang of the church bells, the roar of the storm, the limping boy, peevish Sasha and unhappy Likharyóff – all these mingled, fused in one great impression, and the whole of God's world seemed to her fantastic, full of mystery and magical forces. The words of Likharyóff resounded in her ears, and human life seemed to her a lovely, poetical fairy-tale, to which there was no end.

The great impression grew and grew, until it absorbed all consciousness and was transformed into a sweet sleep. Mdlle. Ilováisky slept. But in sleep she continued to see the lamp, and the thick nose with the red light dancing upon it. She was awakened by a cry.

'Papa, dear,' tenderly implored a child's voice. 'Let us go back to uncle's! There is a Christmas tree. Stepa and Kolya are there!'

'What can I do, darling?' reasoned a soft, male bass. 'Try and understand me. . . .'

And to the child's crying was added the man's. The cry of this double misery breaking through the howl of the storm, touched upon the ears of the girl with such soft, human music, that she could not withstand the emotion, and wept also. And she listened as the great black shadow walked across the room, lifted up the fallen shawl and wrapped it round her feet.

Awakened again by a strange roar, she sprang up and looked around her. Through the windows, covered half-way up in snow, gleamed the blue dawn. The room itself was full of a grey twilight, through which she could see the stove, the sleeping girl, and Nasr Edin. The lamp and stove had both gone out. Through the wide-opened door of the room could be seen the public hall of the inn with its tables and benches. A man with a blunt, gipsy face and staring eyes stood in the middle of the room in a pool of melted snow, and held up a stick with a red star on the top. Around him was a throng of boys immovable as statues, and covered with snow. The light of the star, piercing though its red paper covering, flushed their wet faces. The crowd roared in discord, and out of their roar Mdlle. Ilováisky understood only one quatrain:–

> 'Hey, boy, bold and fearless,
> Take a knife sharp and shiny,
> Come, kill and kill the Jew,
> The sorrowing son . . .'

At the counter stood Likharyóff, looking with emotion at the singers, and tramping his feet in time. Seeing Márya Mikháilovna he smiled broadly, and entered the room. She also smiled.

'Congratulations!' he said. 'I see you have slept well.'

Mdlle. Ilováisky looked at him silently, and continued to smile.

After last night's conversation he seemed to her no longer tall and broad-shouldered, but a little man. A big steamer seems small to those who have crossed the ocean.

'It is time for me to go,' she said. 'I must get ready. Tell me, where are you going to?'

'I? First to Klinushka station, thence to Siergievo, and from Siergievo a drive of forty versts to the coalmines of a certain General Shashkovsky. My brothers have got me a place as manager . . . I will dig coal.'

'Allow me . . . I know these mines. Shashkovsky is my uncle. But . . . why are you going there?' asked Márya Mikháilovna in surprise.

'As manager. I am to manage the mines.'

'I don't understand.' She shrugged her shoulders. 'You say you are going to these mines. Do you know what that means? Do you know that it is all bare steppe, that there is not a soul near . . . that the tedium is such that you could not live there a single day? The coal is bad, nobody buys it, and my uncle is a maniac, a despot, a bankrupt. . . . He will not even pay your salary.'

'It is the same,' said Likharyóff indifferently. 'Even for the mines, thanks!'

Mdlle. Ilováisky again shrugged her shoulders, and walked up and down the room in agitation.

'I cannot understand, I cannot understand,' she said, moving her fingers before her face. 'This is inconceivable . . . it is madness. Surely you must realise that this . . . it is worse than exile. It is a grave for a living man. Akh, heavens!' she said passionately, approaching Likharyóff and moving her fingers before his smiling face. Her upper lip trembled, and her stinging face grew pale. 'Imagine it . . . a bare steppe . . . and solitude. Not a soul to say a word to . . . and you . . . infatuated with women! Mines and women!'

Mdlle. Ilováisky seemed ashamed of her warmth, and, turning away from Likharyóff, went over to the window.

'No . . . no . . . you cannot go there!' she said, rubbing her finger down the window-pane.

Not only through her head, but through her whole body ran a feeling that here behind her stood an unhappy, forsaken, perishing man. But he, as if unconscious of his misery, as if he had not wept the night before, looked at her and smiled good-humouredly. It would have been better if he had continued to cry. For a few minutes in agitation she walked up and down the room, and then stopped in the corner and began to think. Likharyóff said something, but she did not hear him. Turning her back to him, she took a credit note from her purse, smoothed it in her hand, and then, looking at him, blushed and thrust it into her pocket.

Outside the inn resounded the coachman's voice. Silently, with a severe, concentrated expression. Mdlle. Ilováisky began to put on her wraps. Likharyóff rolled her up in them, and chattered gaily. But every word caused her intolerable pain. It is not pleasant to listen to the jests of the wretched or dying.

When the transformation of a living woman into a formless bundle was complete, Mdlle. Ilováisky looked for the last time around 'The Traveller,' stood silent a moment, and then went out slowly. Likharyóff escorted her.

Outside, God alone knows why, the storm still raged. Great clouds of big, soft snowflakes restlessly whirled over the ground, finding no abiding place. Horses, sledges, trees, the bull tethered to the post – all were white, and seemed made of down.

'Well, God bless you!' stammered Likharyóff, as he helped Márya Mikháilovna into the sledge. 'Don't think ill of me!'

Mdlle. Ilováisky said nothing. When the sledge started and began to circle round a great snowdrift, she looked at Likharyóff as if she wished to say something. Likharyóff ran up to the sledge, but she said not a word, and only gazed at him through her long eyelashes to which the snowflakes already clung.

Whether it be that his sensitive mind read this glance aright, or whether, as it may have been, that his imagination led him astray, it suddenly struck him that but a little more and this girl would have forgiven him his age, his failures, his misfortunes, and followed him, neither questioning nor reasoning, to the ends of the earth. For a long time he stood as if rooted to the spot, and gazed at the track left by the sledge-runners. The snowflakes settled swiftly on his hair, his beard, his shoulders. But soon the traces of the sledge-runners vanished, and he, covered with snow, began to resemble a white boulder, his eyes all the time continuing to search for something through the clouds of snow.

A FAMILY COUNCIL

A FAMILY COUNCIL

To prevent the skeleton in the Uskoff family cupboard escaping into the street, the most rigorous measures were taken. One half of the servants was packed off to the theatre and circus, and the other half sat imprisoned in the kitchen. Orders were given to admit no one. The wife of the culprit's uncle, her sister, and the governess, although initiated into the mystery, pretended that they knew nothing whatever about it; they sat silently in the dining-room, and dared not show their faces in the drawing-room or hall.

Sasha Uskoff, aged twenty-five, the cause of all this upheaval, arrived some time ago; and on the advice of kind-hearted Ivan Markovitch, his maternal uncle, sat demurely in the corridor outside the study door, and prepared himself for sincere, open-hearted confession.

On the other side of the door the family council was being held. The discussion ran on a ticklish and very disagreeable subject. The facts of the matter were as follows. Sasha Uskoff had discounted at a bankers a forged bill of exchange, the term of which expired three days before; and now his two paternal uncles, and Ivan Markovitch, an uncle on his mother's side, were discussing the solemn problem: should the money be paid and the family honour saved, or should they wash their hands of the whole matter, and leave the law to take its course?

To people unconcerned and uninterested such questions seem very trivial, but for those with whom the solution lies they are extraordinarily complex. The three uncles had already had their say, yet the matter had not advanced a step.

'Heavens!' cried the Colonel, a paternal uncle, in a voice betraying both weariness and irritation. 'Heavens! who said that family honour was a prejudice? I never said anything of the kind. I only wanted to save you from looking at the matter from a false standpoint – to point out how easily you may make an irremediable mistake. Yet you don't seem to understand me! I suppose I am speaking Russian, not Chinese!'

'My dear fellow, we understand you perfectly,' interposed Ivan Markovitch soothingly.

'Then why do you say that I deny family honour? I repeat what I have said! Fam—ily hon—our false—ly under—stood is a pre—ju—dice! Falsely under—stood, mind you! That is my point of view. From any conviction whatever, to screen and leave unpunished a rascal, no matter who he is, is both contrary to law and unworthy of an honourable man. It is not the saving of the family honour, but civic cowardice. Take the Army, for example! The honour of the Army is dearer to a soldier than any other honour. But we do not screen our guilty members . . . we judge them! Do you imagine that the honour of the Army suffers thereby? On the contrary!'

The other paternal uncle, an official of the Crown Council, a rheumatic, taciturn, and not very intelligent man, held his peace all the time, or spoke only of the fact that if the matter came into court the name of the Uskoffs would appear in the newspapers; in his opinion, therefore, to avoid publicity it would be better to hush up the matter while there was still time. But with the exception of this reference to the newspapers, he gave no reason for his opinion.

But kind-hearted Ivan Markovitch, the maternal uncle, spoke fluently and softly with a tremula in his voice. He began with the argument that youth has its claims and its peculiar temptations. Which of us was not once young, and which of us did not sometimes go a step too far? Even leaving aside ordinary mortals, did not history teach that the greatest minds in youth were not always able to avoid infatuations and mistakes. Take for instance the biographies of great writers. What one of them did not gamble and drink, and draw upon himself the condemnation of all right-minded men? While on the one hand we remembered that Sasha's errors had overstepped the boundary into crime, on the other we must take into account that Sasha hardly received any education; he was expelled from the gymnasium when in the fifth form; he lost his parents in early childhood, and thus at the most susceptible age was deprived of control and all beneficent influences. He was a nervous boy, easily excited, without any naturally strong moral convictions, and he had been spoiled by happiness. Even if he were guilty, still he deserved the sympathy and concern of all sympathetic souls. Punished, of course, he must be; but then, had he not already been punished by his conscience, and the tortures which he must now be feeling as he awaited the decision of his relatives. The comparison with the Army which the Colonel had made was very flattering, and did great honour to his generous mind; the appeal to social feelings showed the nobility of his heart. But it must not be forgotten that the member of society in every individual was closely bound up with the Christian.

'And how should we violate our social duty,' asked Ivan Markovitch, 'if instead of punishing a guilty boy we stretch out to him the hand of mercy?'

Then Ivan Markovitch reverted to the question of the family honour. He himself had not the honour to belong to the distinguished family of Uskoff, but he knew very well that that illustrious race dated its origin from the thirteenth century, and that he could not forget for a moment that his beloved, unforgotten sister was the wife of a scion of the race. In one word – the Uskoff family was dear to him for many reasons, and he could not for a moment entertain the thought that for a paltry fifteen hundred roubles a shadow should be cast for ever upon the ancestral tree. And if all the arguments already adduced were insufficiently convincing then he, in conclusion, asked his brothers-in-law to explain the problem: What is a crime? A crime was an immoral action, having its impulse in an evil will. So most people thought. But could we affirm that the human will was free to decide? To this important question science coulgive no conclusive answer. Metaphysicians maintained various divergent theories. For instance, the new school of Lombroso refused to recognise free-will, and held that every crime was the product of purely anatomical peculiarities in the individual.

'Ivan Markovitch!' interrupted the Colonel imploringly. 'Do, for Heaven's sake, talk sense. We are speaking seriously about a serious matter . . . and you, about Lombroso! You are a clever man, but think for a moment – how can all this rattle-box rhetoric help us to decide the question?'

Sasha Uskoff sat outside the door and listened. He felt neither fear nor shame nor tedium – only weariness and spiritual vacuity. He felt that it did not matter a kopeck whether he was forgiven or not; he had come here to await his sentence and to offer a frank explanation, only because he was begged to do so by kindly Ivan Markovitch. He was not afraid of the future. It was all the same to him, here in the corridor, in prison, or in Siberia.

'Siberia is only Siberia – the devil take it!'

Life has wearied Sasha, and has become insufferably tedious. He is inextricably in debt, he has not a kopeck in his pocket, his relatives have become odious to him; with his friends and with women he must part sooner or later, for they are already beginning to look at him contemptuously as a parasite. The future is dark.

Sasha, in fact, is indifferent, and only one thing affects him. That is, that through the door he can hear himself being spoken of as a scoundrel and a criminal. All the time he is itching to jump up, burst into the room, and, in answer to the detestable metallic voice of the Colonel, to cry:

'You are a liar!'

A criminal – it is a horrid word. It is applied as a rule to murderers, thieves, robbers, and people incorrigibly wicked and morally hopeless. But Sasha is far from this. . . . True, he is up to his neck in debts, and never attempts to pay them. But then indebtedness is not a crime, and there are very few men who are not in debt. The Colonel and Ivan Markovitch are both in debt.

'What on earth am I guilty of?' asked Sasha.

He had obtained money by presenting a forged bill. But this was done by every young man he knew. Khandrikoff and Von Burst, for instance, whenever they wanted money, discounted bills with forged acceptances of their parents and friends, and when their own money came in met them. Sasha did exactly the same thing, and only failed to meet his bill owing to Khandrikoff's failure to lend the money which he had promised. It was not he, but circumstance which was at fault. . . .

It was true that imitating another man's signature was considered wrong, but that did not make it a crime but merely an ugly formality, a manoeuvre constantly adopted which injured nobody; and Sasha when he forged the Colonel's name had no intention of causing loss to anyone.

'It is absurd to pretend that I have been guilty of a crime,' thought Sasha. 'I have not the character of men who commit crimes. On the contrary, I am easy-going and sensitive . . . when I have money I help the poor. . . .'

While Sasha reasoned thus, the discussion continued on the other side of the door.

'But, gentlemen, this is only the beginning!' cried the Colonel. 'Suppose, for the sake of argument, that we let him off and pay the money! He will go on still in the same way and continue to lead his unprincipled life. He will indulge in dissipation, run into debt, go to our tailors and order clothes in our names. What guarantee have we that this scandal will be the last? As far as I am concerned, I tell you frankly that I do not believe in his reformation for one moment.'

The official of the Crown Council muttered something in reply. Then Ivan Markovitch began to speak softly and fluently. The Colonel impatiently shifted his chair, and smothered Ivan Markovitch's argument with his destable, metallic voice. As last the door opened, and out of the study came Ivan Markovitch with red spots on his meagre, clean-shaven face.

'Come!' he said, taking Sasha by the arm. 'Come in and make an open-hearted confession. Without pride, like a good boy . . . humbly and from the heart.'

Sasha went into the study. The official of the Crown Council continued to sit, but the Colonel, hands in pockets, and with one knee resting on his chair, stood before the table. The room was full of smoke and stiflingly hot. Sasha did not look at either the Colonel or his brother, but suddenly feeling ashamed and hurt, glanced anxiously at Ivan Markovitch and muttered:

'I will pay . . . I will give . . .'

'May I ask you on what you relied when you obtained the money on this bill?' rang out the metallic voice.

'I . . . Khandrikoff promised to lend me the money in time.'

Sasha said nothing more. He went out of the study and again sat on the chair outside the door. He would have gone away at once had he not been stifled with hatred and with a desire to tear the Colonel to pieces or at least to insult him to his face. But at this moment in the dim twilight around the dining-room door appeared a woman's figure. It was the Colonel's wife. She beckoned Sasha, and, wringing her hands, said with tears in her voice:

'*Alexandre*, I know that you do not love me, but . . . listen for a moment! My poor boy, how can this have happened? It is awful, awful! For Heaven's sake beg their forgiveness . . . justify yourself, implore them!'

Sasha looked at her twitching shoulders, and at the big tears which flowed down her cheeks; he heard behind him the dull, nervous voices of his exhausted uncles, and shrugged his shoulders. He had never expected that his aristocratic relatives would raise such a storm over a paltry fifteen hundred roubles. And he could understand neither the tears nor the trembling voices.

An hour later he heard indications that the Colonel was gaining the day. The other uncles were being won over to his determination to leave the matter to the law.

'It is decided!' said the Colonel stiffly. '*Basta!*'.

But having decided thus, the three uncles, even the inexorable Colonel, perceptibly lost heart.

'Heavens!' sighed Ivan Markovitch. 'My poor sister!'

And he began in a soft voice to announce his conviction that his sister, Sasha's mother, was invisibly present in the room. He felt in his heart that this unhappy, sainted woman was weeping, anguishing, interceding for her boy. For the sake of her repose in the other world it would have been better to spare Sasha.

Sasha heard someone whimpering. It was Ivan Markovitch. He wept and muttered something inaudible through the door. The Colonel rose and walked from corner to corner. The discussion began anew. . . .

The clock in the drawing-room struck two. The council was over at last. The Colonel, to avoid meeting a man who had caused him so much shame, left the room through the antechamber. Ivan Markovitch came into the corridor. He was plainly agitated, but rubbed his hands cheerfully. His tear-stained eyes glanced happily around him, and his mouth was twisted into a smile.

'It is all right, my boy!' he said to Sasha. 'Heaven be praised! You may go home, child, and sleep quietly. We have decided to pay the money, but only on the condition that you repent sincerely, and agree to come with me to the country tomorrow, and set to work.'

A minute afterwards, Ivan Markovitch and Sasha, having put on their overcoats and hats, went downstairs together. Uncle Ivan muttered something edifying. But Sasha didn't listen; he felt only that something heavy and painful had fallen from his shoulders. He was forgiven – he was free! Joy like a breeze burst into his breast and wrapped his heart with refreshing coolness. He wished to breathe, to move, to live. And looking at the street lamps and at the black sky he remembered that today at 'The Bear', Von Burst would celebrate his name-day. A new joy seized his soul.

'I will go!' he decided.

But suddenly he remembered that he had not a kopeck, and that his friends already despised him for his penuriousness. He must get money at all cost.

'Uncle, lend me a hundred roubles!' he said to Ivan Markovitch.

Ivan Markovitch looked at him in amazement, and staggered back against a lamp-post.'

'Lend me a hundred roubles!' cried Sasha, impatiently shifting from foot to foot, and beginning to lose his temper. 'Uncle, I beg of you . . . lend me a hundred roubles!'

His face trembled with excitement, and he nearly rushed at his uncle.

'You won't give them?' he cried, seeing that his uncle was too dumfounded to understand. 'Listen, if you refuse to lend them, I'll inform on myself tomorrow. I'll refuse to let you pay the money. I'll forge another tomorrow!'

Thunderstruck, terror-striken, Ivan Markovitch muttered something incoherent, took from his pocket a hundred-rouble note, and handed it silently to Sasha. And Sasha took it and hurriedly walked away.

And sitting in a droschky, Sasha grew cool again, and felt

his heart expand with renewed joy. The claims of youth of which kind-hearted uncle Ivan had spoken at the council-table had inspired and taken possession of him again. He painted in imagination the coming feast, and in his mind, among visions of bottles, women, and boon companions, twinkled a little thought:

'Now I begin to see that I was in the wrong.'

AT HOME

AT HOME

'They sent over from Grigorievitch's for some book, but I said that you were not at home. The postman has brought the newspapers and two letters. And, Yevgénïi Petróvitch, I really must ask you to do something in regard to Serózha. I caught him smoking the day before yesterday, and again today. When I began to scold him, in his usual way he put his hands over his ears, and shouted so as to drown my voice.'

Yevgénïi Petróvitch Buikovsky, Procuror of the District Court, who had only just returned from the Session House and was taking off his gloves in his study, looked for a moment at the complaining governess and laughed:

'Serózha smoking!' He shrugged his shoulders. 'I can imagine that whipper-snapper with a cigarette! How old is he?'

'Seven. Of course you may not take it seriously, but at his age smoking is a bad and injurious habit, and bad habits should be rooted out in their beginning.'

'Very true. But where does he get the tobacco?'

'On your table.'

'On my table! Ask him to come here.'

When the governess left the room, Buikovsky sat in his armchair in front of his desk, shut his eyes, and began to think. He pictured in imagination his Serózha with a gigantic cigarette a yard long, surrounded by clouds of tobacco smoke. The caricature made him laugh in spite of himself; but at the same time the serious, worried face of his governess reminded him of a time, now long passed by, a half-forgotten time, when smoking in the schoolroom or nursery inspired in teachers and parents a strange and not quite comprehensible horror. No other word but horror would describe it. The culprits were mercilessly flogged, expelled from school, their lives marred, and this, although not one of the schoolmasters or parents could say what precisely constitutes the danger and guilt of smoking. Even very intelligent men did not hesitate to fight a vice which they did not understand. Yevgénïi Petróvitch remembered the director of his own school, a benevolent and highly educated old man, who was struck with such terror when he caught a boy with a cigarette that he became pale, immediately convoked an extraordinary council of masters, and condemned the offender to expulsion. Such indeed appears to be the law of life; the more intangible the evil the more fiercely and mercilessly is it combated.

The Procuror remembered two or three cases of expulsion, and recalling the subsequent lives of the victims, he could not but conclude that such punishment was often a much greater evil than the vice itself. . . . But the animal organism is gifted with capacity to adapt itself rapidly, to accustom itself to changes, to different atmospheres, otherwise every man would feel that his rational actions were based upon an irrational foundation, and that there was little reasoned truth and conviction even in such responsibilities – responsibilities terrible in their results – as those of the schoolmaster, and lawyer, the writer. . . .

And such thoughts, light and inconsequential, which enter only a tired and resting brain, wandered about in Yevgénïi Petróvitch's head; they spring no one knows where or why, vanish soon, and, it would seem, wander only on the outskirts of the brain without penetrating far. For men who are obliged for whole hours, even for whole days, to think official thoughts all in the same direction, such free, domestic speculations are an agreeable comfort.

It was nine o'clock. Overhead from the second storey came the footfalls of someone walking from corner to corner; and still higher, on the third storey, someone was playing scales. The footsteps of the man who, judging by his walk, was thinking tensely or suffering from toothache, and the monotonous scales in the evening stillness, combined to create a drowsy atmosphere favourable to idle thoughts. From the nursery came the voices of Serózha and his governess.

'Papa has come?' cried the boy. 'Papa has co-o-me! Papa! papa!'

'*Votre père vous appelle, allez vite,*' cried the governess, piping like a frightened bird. . . . Do you hear?'

'What shall I say to him?' thought Yevgénii Petróvitch.

And before he had decided what to say, in came his son Serózha, a boy of seven years old. He was one of those little boys whose sex can be distinguished only by their clothes – weakly, pale-faced, delicate. . . . Everything about him seemed tender and soft; his movements, his curly hair, his looks, his velvet jacket.

'Good evening, papa,' he began in a soft voice, climbing on his father's knee, and kissing his neck. 'You wanted me?'

'Wait a minute, wait a minute, Sergéï Yevgénitch,' answered the Procuror, pushing him off. 'Before I allow you to kiss me I want to talk to you, and to talk seriously. . . . I am very angry with you, and do not love you any more . . . understand that, brother; I do not love you, and you are not my son. . . . No!'

Serózha looked earnestly at his father, turned his eyes on to the chair, and shrugged his shoulders.

'What have I done?' he asked in doubt, twitching his eyes. 'I have not been in your study all day and touched nothing.'

'Natálya Semiónovna has just been complaining to me that she caught you smoking. . . . Is it true? Do you smoke?'

'Yes, I smoked once, father. . . . It is true.'

'There, you see, you tell lies also,' said the Procuror, frowning, and trying at the same time to smother a smile. 'Natálya Semiónovna saw you smoking twice. That is to say, you are found out in three acts of misconduct – you smoke, you take another person's tobacco, and you lie. Three faults!'

'Akh, yes,' remembered Serózha, with smiling eyes. 'It is true. I smoked twice – today and once before.'

'That is to say you smoked not once but twice. I am very, very displeased with you! You used to be a good boy, but now I see you are spoiled and have become naughty.'

Yevgénii Petróvitch straightened Serózha's collar, and thought: 'What else shall I say to him?'

'It is very bad,' he continued. 'I did not expect this from you. In the first place you have no right to go to another person's table and take tobacco which does not belong to you.

A man has a right to enjoy only his own property, and if he takes another's then . . . he is a wicked man.' (This is not the way to go about it, thought the Procuror.) 'For instance, Natálya Semiónovna has a boxful of dresses. That is her box, and we have not, that is neither you nor I have, any right to touch it, as it is not ours. . . . Isn't that plain? You have your horses and pictures . . . I do not take them. Perhaps I have often felt that I wanted to take them . . . but they are yours, not mine!'

'Please, father, take them if you like,' said Serózha, raising his eyebrows. 'Always take anything of mine, father. This yellow dog which is on your table is mine, but I don't mind. . . .'

'You don't understand me,' said Buikovsky. 'The dog you gave me, it is now mine, and I can do with it what I like; but the tobacco I did not give to you. The tobacco is mine.' (How can I make him understand? thought the Procuror. Not in this way). 'If I feel that I want to smoke someone else's tobacco I first of all ask for permission. . . .'

And idly joining phrase to phrase, and imitating the language of children, Buikovsky began to explain what is meant by property. Serózha looked at his chest, and listened attentively (he loved to talk to his father in the evenings), then set his elbows on the table edge and began to concentrate his short-sighted eyes upon the papers and inkstand. His glance wandered around the table, and paused on a bottle of gum-arabic.

'Papa, what is gum made of?' he asked, suddenly lifting the bottle to his eyes.

Buikovsky took the bottle, put it back on the table, and continued:

'In the second place, you smoke. . . . That is very bad! If I smoke, then . . . it does not follow that everyone may. I smoke, and know . . . that it is not clever, and I scold myself, and do not love myself on account of it. . . .' (I am a nice teacher, thought the Procuror.) 'Tobacco seriously injures the health, and people who smoke die sooner than they ought to. It is particularly injurious to little boys like you. You have a weak chest, you have not yet got strong, and in weak people tobacco smoke produces consumption and other complaints. Uncle Ignatius died of consumption. If he had not smoked perhaps he would have been alive today.'

Serózha looked thoughtfully at the lamp, touched the shade with his fingers, and sighed.

'Uncle Ignatius played splendidly on the fiddle!' he said. 'His fiddle is now at Grigorievitch's.'

Serózha again set his elbows on the table and lost himself in thought. On his pale face was the expression of one who is listening intently or following the course of his own thoughts; sorrow and something like fright showed themselves in his big, staring eyes. Probably he was thinking of death, which had so lately carried away his mother and Uncle Ignatius. Death is a thing which carries away mothers and uncles and leaves on the earth only children and fiddles. Dead people live in the sky somewhere, near the stars, and thence look down upon the earth. How do they bear the separation?

'What shall I say to him?' asked the Procuror. 'He is not listening. Apparently he thinks there is nothing serious either in his faults or in my arguments. How can I explain it to him?'

The Procuror rose and walked up and down the room.

'In my time these questions were decided very simply,' he thought. 'Every boy caught smoking was flogged. The cowards and babies, therefore, gave up smoking, but the brave and cunning bore their floggings, carried the tobacco in their boots and smoked in the stable. When they were caught in the stable and again flogged, they smoked on the river-bank . . . and so on until they were grown up. My own mother in order to keep me from smoking used to give me money and sweets. Nowadays all these methods are regarded as petty or immoral. Taking logic as his standpoint, the modern teacher tries to inspire in the child good principles not out of fear, not out of wish for distinction or reward, but consciously.'

While he walked and talked, Serózha climbed on the chair next the table and began to draw. To prevent the destruction of business papers and the splashing of ink, his father had provided a packet of paper, cut especially for him, and a blue pencil.

'Today the cook was chopping cabbage and cut her finger,' he said, meantime sketching a house and twitching his eyebrows. 'She cried so loud that we were all frightened and ran into the kitchen. Such a stupid! Natálya Semiónovna ordered her to bathe her finger in cold water, but she sucked it. . . . How could she put her dirty finger in her mouth! Papa, that is bad manners!'

He further told how during dinner-time an organ-grinder came into the yard with a little girl who sang and danced to his music.

'He has his own current of thoughts,' thought the Procuror. 'In his head he has a world of his own, and he knows better than anyone else what is serious and what is not. To gain his attention and conscience it is no use imitating his language . . . what is wanted is to understand and reason also in his manner. He would understand me perfectly if I really disliked tobacco, if I were angry, or cried. . . . For that reason mothers are irreplaceable in bringing up children, for they alone can feel and cry and laugh like children. . . . With logic and morals nothing can be done. What shall I say to him?'

And Yevgénii Petróvitch found it strange and absurd that he, an experienced jurist, half his life struggling with all kinds of interruptions, prejudices, and punishments, was absolutely at a loss for something to say to his son.

'Listen, give me your word of honour that you will not smoke!' he said.

'Word of honour!' drawled Serózha, pressing hard on his pencil and bending down to the sketch. 'Word of honour!'

'But has he any idea what "word of honour" means?' Buikovsky asked himself. 'No, I am a bad teacher! If a schoolmaster or any of our lawyers were to see me now, he would call me a rag, and suspect me of super-subtelty. . . . But in school and in court all these stupid problems are decided much more simply than at home when you are dealing with those whom you love. Love is exacting and complicates the business. If this boy were not my son, but a pupil or a prisoner at the bar, I should not be such a coward and scatterbrains. . . .'

Yevgénii Petróvitch sat at the table and took up one of Serózha's sketches. It depicted a house with a crooked roof, and smoke which, like lightning, zigzagged from the chimney

to the edge of the paper; beside the house stood a soldier with
dots for eyes, and a bayonet shaped like the figure four.

'A man cannot be taller than a house,' said the Procuror.
'Look! the roof of your house only goes up to the soldier's
shoulder.'

Serózha climbed on his father's knee, and wriggled for a
long time before he felt comfortable.

'No, papa,' he said, looking at the drawing. 'If you drew the
soldier smaller you wouldn't be able to see his eyes.'

Was it necessary to argue? From daily observation the
Procuror had become convinced that children, like savages,
have their own artistic outlook, and their own requirements,
inaccessible to the understanding of adults. Under close
observation Serózha to an adult seemed abnormal. He found it
possible and reasonable to draw men taller than houses, and to
express with the pencil not only objects but also his own
sentiments. Thus, the sound of an orchestra he drew as a
round, smoky spot; whistling as a spiral thread. . . .
According to his ideas, sounds were closely allied with forms
and colour, and when painting letters he always coloured L
yellow, M red, A black, and so on.

Throwing away his sketch, Serózha again wriggled, settled
himself more comfortably, and occupied himself with his
father's beard. First he carefully smoothed it down, then
divided it in two, and arranged it to look like whiskers.

'Now you are like Iván Stepánovitch,' he muttered; 'but
wait, in a minute you will be like . . . like the porter. Papa,
why do porters stand in doorways? Is it to keep out robbers?'

The Procuror felt on his face the child's breath, touched
with his cheek the child's hair. In his heart rose a sudden
feeling of warmth and softness, a softness that made it seem
that not only his hands but all his soul lay upon the velvet of
Serózha's coat. He looked into the great, dark eyes of his
child, and it seemed to him that out of their big pupils looked
at him his mother, and his wife, and all whom he had ever
loved.

'What is the good of thrashing him?' he asked. 'Punishment
is . . . and why turn myself into a schoolmaster? . . .
Formerly men were simple; they thought less, and solved
problems bravely. . . . Now, we think too much; logic has

eaten us up. . . . The more cultivated a man, the more he thinks, the more he surrenders himself to subtleties, the less firm is his will, the greater his timidity in the face of affairs. And, indeed, if you look into it, what a lot of courage and faith in one's self does it need to teach a child, to judge a criminal, to write a big book. . . .'

The clock struck ten.

'Now, child, time for bed,' said the Procuror. 'Say good night, and go.'

'No, papa,' frowned Serózha. 'I may stay a little longer. Talk to me about something. Tell me a story.'

'I will, only after the story you must go straight to bed.'

Yevgénii Petróvitch sometimes spent his free evenings telling Serózha stories. Like most men of affairs he could not repeat by heart a single verse or remember a single fairy tale; and every time was obliged to improvise. As a rule he began with the jingle, 'Once upon a time, and a very good time it was,' and followed this up with all kinds of innocent nonsense, at the beginning having not the slightest idea of what would be the middle and the end. Scenery, characters, situations all came at hazard, and fable and moral flowed out by themselves without regard to the teller's will. Serózha dearly loved these improvisations, and the Procuror noticed that the simpler and less pretentious the plots, the more they affected the child.

'Listen,' he began, raising his eyes to the ceiling. 'Once upon a time, and a very good time it was, there lived an old, a very, very old tsar, with a long grey beard, and . . . this kind of moustaches. Well! He lived in a glass palace which shone and sparkled in the sun like a big lump of clean ice. . . . The palace . . . brother mine . . . the palace stood in a great garden where, you know, grew oranges . . . pears, cherry trees . . . and blossomed tulips, roses, water lilies . . . and birds of different colours sang. . . . Yes. . . . On the trees hung glass bells which, when the breeze blew, sounded so musically that it was a joy to listen. Glass gives out a softer and more tender sound than metal. . . . Well? Where was I? In the garden were fountains. . . . You remember you saw a fountain in the country, at Aunt Sonia's. Just the same kind of fountains stood in the king's garden, only they were much bigger, and the jets of water rose as high as the tops of the tallest populars.'

Yevgénii Petróvitch thought for a moment and continued:

'The old tsar had an only son, the heir to his throne – a little boy about your size. He was a good boy. He was never peevish, went to bed early, never touched anything on the table . . . and in all ways was a model. But he had one fault – he smoked.'

Serózha listened intently, and without blinking looked straight in his father's eyes. The Procuror continued, and thought: 'What next?' He hesitated for a moment, and ended his story thus:

'From too much smoking, the tsarevitch got ill with consumption, and died . . . when he was twenty years old. His sick and feeble old father was left without any help. There was no one to govern the kingdom and defend the palace. His enemies came and killed the old man, and destroyed the palace, and now in the garden are neither cherry trees nor birds nor bells. . . . So it was, brother.'

The end of the plot seemed to Yevgénii Petróvitch naïve and ridiculous. But on Serózha the whole story produced a strong impression. Again his eyes took on an expression of sorrow and something like fright; he looked thoughtfully at the dark window, shuddered, and said in a weak voice:

'I will not smoke any more.'

'They will tell me that this parable acted by means of beauty and artistic form,' he speculated. 'That may be so, but that is no consolation. . . . That does not make it an honest method. . . . Why is it morals and truth cannot be presented in a raw form, but only with mixtures, always sugared and gilded like a pill. This is not normal. . . . It is falsification, deception . . . a trick.'

And he thought of those assessors who find it absolutely necessary to make a speech; of the public which understands history only through epics and historical novels; and of himself drawing a philosophy of life not from sermons and laws, but from fables, romances, poetry. . . .

'Medicine must be sweetened, truth made beautiful. . . . And this good fortune man has taken advantage of from the time of Adam. . . . And after all maybe it is natural thus, and cannot be otherwise . . . there are in nature many useful and expedient deceits and illusions. . . .'

He sat down to his work, but idle, domestic thoughts long wandered in his brain. From the third storey no longer came the sound of the scales. But the occupant of the second storey long continued to walk up and down. . . .

IN EXILE

IN EXILE

Old Semión, nicknamed Wiseacre, and a young Tartar, whom
nobody knew by name, sat by the bonfire at the side of the
river. The other three ferrymen lay in the hut. Semión, an old
man of sixty, gaunt and toothless, but broad-shouldered and
healthy in appearance, was drunk; he would have been asleep
long ago if it had not been for the flagon in his pocket, and his
fear that his companions in the hut might ask him for vodka.
The Tartar was ill and tired; and sat there, wrapped up in his
rags, holding forth on the glories of life in Simbirsk, and
boasting of the handsome and clever wife he had left behind
him. He was about twenty-five years old, but now in the light
of the camp fire his pale face, with its melancholy and sickly
expression, seemed the face of a lad.

'Yes, you can hardly call it paradise,' said Wiseacre. 'You
can take it all in at a glance – water, bare banks, and clay about
you, and nothing more. Holy Week is over, but there is still
ice floating down the river, and this very morning snow.'

'Misery, misery!' moaned the Tartar, looking round him in
terror.

Ten paces below them lay the river, dark and cold,
grumbling, it seemed, at itself, as it clove a path through the
steep clay banks, and bore itself swiftly to the sea. Up against
the bank lay one of the great barges which the ferrymen call
karbases. On the opposite side, far away, rising and falling, and
mingling with one another, crept little serpents of fire. It was
the burning of last year's grass. And behind the serpents of fire
darkness again. From the river came the noise of little ice floes
crashing against the barge. Darkness only, and cold!

The Tartar looked at the sky. There were as many stars
there as in his own country, just the same blackness above
him. But something was lacking. At home in Simbirsk
government there were no such stars and no such heaven.

'Misery, misery!' he repeated.

'You'll get used to it,' said Wiseacre, grinning. 'You're young and foolish now – your mother's milk is still wet on your lips, only youth and folly could make you imagine there's no one more miserable than you. But the time'll come when you'll say, "God grant every one such a life as this!" Look at me, for instance. In a week's time the water will have fallen, we'll launch the small boat, you'll be off to Siberia to amuse yourselves, and I'll remain here and row from one side to another. Twenty years now I've been ferrying. Day and night! Salmon and pike beneath the water and I above it! And God be thanked! I don't want for anything! God grant everyone such a life!'

The Tartar thrust some brushwood into the fire, lay closer to it, and said:

'My father is ill. When he dies my mother and wife are coming. They promised me.'

'What do you want with a mother and wife?' asked Wiseacre, 'put that out of your head, it's all nonsense, brother! It's the devil's doing to make you think such thoughts. Don't listen to him, accursed! If he begins about women, answer him back, "Don't want them." If he comes about freedom, answer him back, "Don't want it." You don't want anything. Neither father, nor mother, nor wife, nor freedom, nor house, nor home. You don't want anything, d——n them!'

Wiseacre took a drink from his flask and continued:

'I, brother, am no simple mujik, but a sexton's son, and when I lived in freedom in Kursk wore a frockcoat, yet now I have brought myself to such a point that I can sleep naked on the earth and eat grass. And God grant everyone such a life! I don't want anything, and I don't fear anyone, and I know there is no one richer and freer than I in the world. The first day I came here from Russia I persisted, "I don't want anything." The devil took me on also about wife, and home, and freedom, but I answered him back "I don't want anything." I tired him out, and now, as you see, I live well, and don't complain. If anyone bates an inch to the devil, or listens to him even once, he's lost – there's no salvation for him – he sinks in the bog to the crown of his head, and never gets out.

'Don't think it's only our brother, the stupid mujik, that gets lost. The well-born and educated lose themselves also. Fifteen years ago they sent a gentleman here from Russia. He wouldn't share something with his brothers, and did something dishonest with a will. Belonged, they said, to a prince's or a baron's family – maybe he was an official, who can tell? Well, anyway he came, and the first thing he did was to buy himself a house and land in Mukhortinsk. "I want," he says, "to live by my work, by the sweat of my brow, because," he says, "I am no longer a gentleman, but a convict." "Well," I said, "may God help him, he can do nothing better." He was a young man, fussy, and fond of talking; mowed his own grass, caught fish, and rode on horseback sixty versts a day. That was the cause of the misfortune. From the first year he used to ride to Guirino, to the post office. He would stand with me in the boat and sigh: "Akh, Semión, how long they are sending me money from home." "You don't want it, Vassili Sergeyitch," I answered, "what good is money to you? Give up the old ways, forget them as if they never were, as if you had dreamt them, and begin to live anew. Pay no attention," I said, "to the devil, he'll bring you nothing but ill. At present, you want only money, but in a little time you'll want something more. If you want to be happy, don't wish for anything at all. Yes. . . . Already," I used to say to him, "fortune has done you and me a bad turn – there's no good begging charity from her, and bowing down to her – you must despise and laugh at her. Then she'll begin to laugh herself." So I used to talk to him.

'Well, two years after he came, he drove down to the ferry in good spirits. He was rubbing his hands and laughing. "I am going to Guirino," he says, "to meet my wife. She has taken pity on me, and is coming. She is a good wife." He was out of breath from joy.

'The next day he came back with his wife. She was a young woman, a good-looking one, in a hat, with a little girl in her arms. And my Vassili Sergeyitch bustles about her, feasts his eyes on her, and praises her up to the skies, "Yes, brother Semión, even in Siberia people live." "Well," I thought, "he won't always think so." From that time out, every week, he rode to Guirino to inquire whether money had been sent to him from Russia. Money he wanted without end. "For my sake," he used to say, "she is burying her youth and beauty in Siberia, and sharing my miserable life. For this reason I must procure her every enjoyment." And to make things gayer for her, he makes acquaintance with officials and all kinds of people. All this company, of course, had to be fed and kept in drink, a piano must be got, and a shaggy dog for the sofa – in one word, extravagance, luxury. . . . She didn't live with him long. How could she? Mud, water, cold, neither vegetable nor fruit, bears and drunkards around her, and she a woman from Petersburg, petted and spoiled. . . . Of course, she got sick of it. . . . Yes, and a husband, too, no longer a man, but a convict. . . . Well, after three years, I remember, on Assumption Eve, I heard shouting from the opposite bank. When I rowed across I saw the lady all wrapped up, and with her a young man, one of the officials. A troïka! I rowed them across, they got into the troïka and drove off. Towards morning, Vassili Sergeyitch drives up in hot haste. "Did my wife go by," he asked, "with a man in spectacles?" "Yes," I said, "seek the wind in the field." He drove after them, and chased them for five days. When I ferried him back, he threw himself into the bottom of the boat, beat his head against the planks, and howled. I laughed and reminded him, "even in Siberia people live!" But that only made him worse.

'After this he tried to regain his freedom. His wife had gone back to Russia, and he thought only of seeing her, and getting her to return to him. Every day he galloped off to one place or another, one day to the post office, the next to town to see the authorities. He sent in petitions asking for pardon and permission to return to Russia – on telegrams alone, he used to say, he spent two hundred roubles. He sold his land and mortgaged his house to a Jew. He got grey-haired and bent, and his face turned yellow like a consumptive's. He could not speak without tears coming into his eyes. Eight years he spent sending in petitions. Then he came to life again; he had got a new consolation. The daughter, you see, was growing up. He doted on her. And to tell the truth, she wasn't bad-looking – pretty, black-browed, and high-spirited. Every Sunday he rode with her to the church at Guirino. They would stand side by side in the boat, she laughing, and he never lifting his eyes from her. "Yes," he said, "Semión, even in Siberia people live, and are happy. See what a daughter I've got! you might go a thousand versts and never see another like her." The daughter, as I said, was really good-looking. "But wait a little," I used to say to myself, "the girl is young, the blood flows in her veins, she wants to live; and what is life here?" Anyway, brother, she began to grieve. Pined and declined, dwindled away, got ill, and now can't stand on her legs. onsumption! There's your Siberian happiness! That's the way people live in Siberia! . . . And my Vassili Sergeyitch spends his time driving about to doctors and bringing them home. Once let him hear there's a doctor or a magic curer within two or three hundred versts, and after him he must go. . . . It's terrible to think of the amount of money he spends, he might as well drink it. . . . She'll die all the same, nothing'll save her, and then he'll be altogether lost. Whether he hangs himself from grief or runs off to Russia it's all the same. If he runs away they'll catch him, then we'll have a trial and penal servitude, and the rest of it. . . .'

'It was very well for him,' said the Tartar, shuddering with the cold.

'What was well?'

'Wife and daughter. . . . Whatever he suffers, whatever punishment he'll have, at any rate he saw them. . . . *You* say you don't want anything. But to have nothing is bad. His wife lived with him three years, God granted him that. To have nothing is bad, but three years is good. You don't understand.'

Trembling with cold, finding only with painful difficulty the proper Russian words, the Tartar began to beg that God might save him from dying in a strange land, and being buried in the cold earth. If his wife were to come to him, even for one day, even for one hour, for such happiness he would consent to undergo the most frightful tortures, and thank God for them. Better one day's happiness than nothing!

And he again told the story of how he had left at home a handsome and clever wife. Then, putting both his hands to his head, he began to cry, and to assure Semión that he was guilty of nothing, and was suffering unjustly. His two brothers and his uncle had stolen a peasant's horses, and beaten the old man half to death. But society had treated him unfairly, and sent the three brothers to Siberia, while the uncle, a rich man, remained at home.

'You'll get used to it!' said Semión.

The Tartar said nothing, and only turned his wet eyes on the fire; his face expressed doubt and alarm, as if he did not yet understand why he lay there in darkness and in cold among strangers, and not at Simbirsk. Wiseacre lay beside the fire, laughed silently at something, and hummed a tune.

'What happiness can she have with her father?' he began after a few minutes' silence. 'He loves her, and finds her a consolation, that's true. But you can't put your finger in his eyes; he's a cross old man, a stern old man. And with young girls you don't want sternness. What they want is caresses, and ha! ha! ha! and ho! ho! ho! – perfume and pomade. Yes. . . . Akh, business, business!' He sighed, lifting himself clumsily. 'Vodka all gone – means it's time to go to bed. Well, I'm off, brother.'

The Tartar added some more brushwood to the fire, lay down again, and began to think of his native village and of his wife; if his wife would only come for a week, for a day, let her go back if she liked! Better a few days, even a day, than nothing! But if his wife kept her promise and came, what would he feed her with? Where would she live?

'How can you live without anything to eat?' he asked aloud.

For working day and night at an oar they paid him only ten kopecks a day. True, passengers sometimes gave money for tea and vodka, but the others shared this among themselves, gave nothing to the Tartar, and only laughed at him. From poverty he was hungry, cold, and frightened. His whole body ached and trembled. If he went into the hut there would be nothing for him to cover himself with. Here, too, he had nothing to cover himself with, but he might keep up the fire.

In a week the waters would have fallen, and the ferrymen, with the exception of Semión, would no longer be wanted. The Tartar must begin his tramp from village to village asking for bread and work. His wife was only seventeen years old; she was pretty, modest, and spoiled. How could she tramp with uncovered face through the villages and ask for bread? It was too horrible to think of.

When next the Tartar looked up it was dawn. The barge, the willows, and the ripples stood out plainly. You might turn round and see the clayey slope, with its brown thatched hut at the bottom, and above it the huts of the village. In the village the cocks already crowed.

The clayey slope, the barge, the river, the strange wicked people, hunger, cold, sickness – in reality there was none of this at all. It was only a dream, thought the Tartar. He felt that he was sleeping, and heard himself snore. Of course, he was at home in Simbirsk, he had only to call his wife by name and she would call back, in the next room lay his old mother. . . . What terrible things are dreams! . . . Where do they come from? . . . The Tartar smiled and opened his eyes. What river was this? The Volga?

It began to snow.

'Ahoy!' came a voice from the other side, 'boatman!'

The Tartar shook himself, and went to awaken his companions. Dragging on their sheepskin coats on the way, swearing in voices hoarse from sleep, the ferrymen appeared on the bank. After sleep, the river, with its piercing breeze, evidently seemed to them a nightmare. They tumbled lazily into the boat. The Tartar and three ferrymen took up the long, wide-bladed oars which looked in the darkness like the claws of a crab. Semión threw himself on his stomach across the helm. On the opposite bank the shouting continued, and twice revolver shots were heard. The stranger evidently thought that the ferrymen were asleep or had gone into the village to the kabak.

'You'll get across in time,' said Wiseacre in the tone of a man who is convinced that in this world there is no need for hurry. 'It's all the same in the end; you'll gain nothing by making a noise.'

The heavy, awkward barge parted from the bank, cleaving a path through the willows, and only the slow movement of the willows backward showed that it was moving at all. The ferrymen slowly raised their oars in time. Wiseacre lay on his stomach across the helm, and, describing a bow in the air, swung slowly from one side to the other. In the dim light it seemed as if the men were sitting on some long-clawed antediluvian animal, floating with it into the cold desolate land that is sometimes seen in nightmares.

The willows soon were passed and the open water reached. On the other bank the creak and measured dipping of the oars were already audible, and cries of 'Quicker, quicker!' came back across the water. Ten minutes more and the barge struck heavily against the landing-stage.

'It keeps on falling, it keeps on falling,' grumbled Semión, rubbing the snow from his face. 'Where it all comes from God only knows!'

On the bank stood a frail old man of low stature in a short foxskin coat and white lambskin cap. He stood immovable at some distance from the horses; his face had a gloomy concentrated expression, as if he were trying to remember something, and were angry with his disobedient memory. When Semión approached him, and, smiling, took off his cap, he began:

'I am going in great haste to Anastasevka. My daughter is worse. In Anastasevka, I am told, a new doctor has been appointed.'

The ferrymen dragged the cart on to the barge, and started back. The man, whom Semión called Vassili Sergeyitch, stood all the time immovable, tightly compressing his thick fingers, and when the driver asked for permission to smoke in his presence, answered nothing, as if he had not heard. Semión, lying on his stomach across the helm, looked at him maliciously, and said:

'Even in Siberia people live! Even in Siberia!'

Wiseacre's face bore a triumphant expression, as if he had demonstrated something, and rejoiced that things had justified his prediction. The miserable, helpless expression of the man in the foxskin coat evidently only increased his delight.

'It's muddy travelling at this time, Vassili Sergeyitch,' he said, as they harnessed the horses on the river bank. 'You might have waited another week or two till it got drier. For the matter of that, you might just as well not go at all. . . . If there was any sense in going it would be another matter, but you yourself know that you might go on for ever and nothing would come of it. . . . Well?'

Vassili Sergeyitch silently handed the men some money, climbed into the cart, and drove off.

'After that doctor again,' said Semión, shuddering from the cold. 'Yes, look for a real doctor – chase the wind in the field, seize the devil by the tail, damn him. Akh, what characters these people are! Lord forgive me, a sinner!'

The Tartar walked up to Semión, and looked at him with hatred and repulsion. Then, trembling, and mixing Tartar words with his broken Russian, he said:

'He is a good man, a good man, and you are bad. You are bad. He is a good soul, a great one, but you are a beast. . . . He is living, but you are dead. . . . God made men that they might have joys and sorrows, but you ask for nothing. . . . You are a stone, – earth! A stone wants nothing, and you want nothing. . . . You are a stone, and God has no love for you. But him He loves!'

All laughed; the Tartar alone frowned disgustedly, shook his hand, and, pulling his rags more closely round him, walked back to the fire. Semión and the ferrymen returned to the hut.

'Cold!' said one ferryman in a hoarse voice, stretching himself on the straw with which the floor was covered.

'Yes, it's not warm,' said another. 'A galley-slave's life!'

All lay down. The door opened before the wind, and snowflakes whirled through the hut. But no one rose to shut it, all were too cold and lazy.

'I, for one, am all right,' said Semión. 'God grant everyone such a life.'

'You, it is known, were born a galley-slave – the devil himself wouldn't take you.'

From the yard came strange sounds like the whining of a dog.

'What's that? Who's there?'

'It's the Tartar crying.'

'Well . . . what a character!'

'He'll get used to it,' said Semión, and went off to sleep. Soon all the others followed his example. But the door remained unshut.

ROTHSCHILD'S FIDDLE

ROTHSCHILD'S FIDDLE

The town was small – no better than a village – and it was inhabited almost entirely by old people who died so seldom that it was positively painful. In the hospital, and even in the prison, coffins were required very seldom. In one word, business was bad. If Yacob Ivanof had been coffin-maker in the government town, he would probably have owned his own house, and called himself Yakob Matvieitch; but, as it was, he was known only by the name of Yakob, with the street nickname given for some obscure reason of 'Bronza'; and lived as poorly as a simple muzhik in a little, ancient cabin with only one room; and in this room lived he, Marfa, the stove, a double bed, the coffins, a joiner's bench, and all the domestic utensils.

Yet Yakob made admirable coffins, durable and good. For muzhiks and petty tradespeople he made them all of one size, taking himself as model; and this method never failed him, for though he was seventy years of age, there was not a taller or stouter man in the town, not even in the prison. For women and for men of good birth he made his coffins to measure, using for this purpose an iron yardwand. Orders for children's coffins he accepted very unwillingly, made them without measurement, as if in contempt, and every time when paid for his work exclaimed:

'Thanks. But I confess I don't care much for wasting time on trifles.'

In addition to coffin-making Yakob drew a small income from his skill with the fiddle. At weddings in the town there usually played a Jewish orchestra, the conductor of which was the tinsmith Moses Ilitch Shakhkes, who kept more than half the takings for himself. As Yakob played very well upon the fiddle, being particularly skilful with Russian songs, Shakhkes sometimes employed him in the orchestra, paying him fifty kopecks a day, exclusive of gifts from the guests. When Bronza sat in the orchestra he perspired and his face grew purple; it was always hot, the smell of garlic was suffocating; the fiddle whined, at his right ear snored the double-bass, at his left wept the flute, played by a lanky, red-haired Jew with a whole network of red and blue veins upon his face, who bore the same surname as the famous millionaire Rothschild. And even the merriest tunes this accursed Jew managed to play sadly. Without any tangible cause Yakob had become slowly penetrated with hatred and contempt for Jews, and especially for Rothschild; he began with irritation, then swore at him, and once even was about to hit him; but Rothschild flared up, and, looking at him furiously, said:

'If it were not that I respect you your talents, I should send you flying out of the window.'

Then he began to cry. So Bronza was employed in the orchestra very seldom, and only in cases of extreme need when one of the Jews was absent.

Yakob had never been in a good humour. He was always overwhelmed by the sense of the losses which he suffered. For instance, on Sundays and saints' days it was a sin to work, Monday was a tiresome day – and so on; so that in one way or another, there were about two hundred days in the year when he was compelled to sit with his hands idle. That was one loss! If anyone in the town got married without music, or if Shakhkes did not employ Yakob, that was another loss. The Inspector of Police was ill for two years, and Yakob waited with impatience for his death, yet in the end the Inspector transferred himself to the government town for the purpose of treatment, where he got worse and died. There was another loss, a loss at the very least of ten roubles, as the Inspector's coffin would have been an expensive one lined with brocade. Regrets for his losses generally overtook Yakob at night; he lay in bed with the fiddle beside him, and, with his head full of such speculations, would take the bow, the fiddle giving out through the darkness a melancholy sound which made Yakob feel better.

On the sixth of May last year Marfa was suddenly taken ill. She breathed heavily, drank much water and staggered. Yet next morning she lighted the stove, and even went for water.

Towards evening she lay down. All day Yakob had played on the fiddle, and when it grew dark he took the book in which every day he inscribed his losses, and from want of something better to do, began to add them up. The total amounted to more than a thousand roubles. The thought of such losses so horrified him that he threw the book on the floor and stamped his feet. Then he took up the book, snapped his fingers, and sighed heavily. His face was purple, and wet with perspiration. He reflected that if this thousand roubles had been lodged in the bank the interest per annum would have amounted to at least forty roubles. That meant that the forty roubles were also a loss. In one word, wherever you turn, everywhere you meet with loss, and profits none.

'Yakob,' cried Marfa unexpectedly, 'I am dying.'

He glanced at his wife. Her face was red from fever and unusually clear and joyful; and Bronza, who was accustomed to see her pale, timid, and unhappy-looking, felt confused. It seemed as if she were indeed dying, and were happy in the knowledge that she was leaving for ever the cabin, the coffins, and Yakob. And now she looked at the ceiling and twitched her lips, as if she had seen Death her deliverer, and were whispering with him.

Morning came; through the window might be seen the rising of the sun. Looking at his old wife, Yakob somehow remembered that all his life he had never treated her kindly, never caressed her, never pitied her, never thought of buying her a kerchief for her head, never carried away from the weddings a piece of tasty food, but only roared at her, abused her for his losses, and rushed at her with shut fists. True, he had never beaten her, but he had often frightened her out of her life and left her rooted to the ground with terror. Yes, and he had forbidden her to drink tea, as the losses without that were great enough; so she drank always hot water. And now, beginning to understand why she had such a strange, enraptured face, he felt uncomfortable.

When the sun had risen high he borrowed a cart from a neighbour, and brought Marfa to the hospital. There were not many patients there, and he had to wait only three hours. To his joy he was received not by the doctor but by the feldscher, Maxim Nikolaitch, an old man of whom it was said that, although he was drunken and quarrelsome, he knew more than the doctor.

'May your health be good!' said Yakob, leading the old woman into the dispensary. 'Forgive me, Maxim Nikolaitch, for troubling you with my empty affairs. But there, you can see for yourself my object is ill. The companion of my life, as they say, excuse the expression. . . .'

Contracting his grey brows and smoothing his whiskers, the feldscher began to examine the old woman, who sat on the tabouret, bent, skinny, sharp-nosed, and with open mouth so that she resembled a bird that is about to drink.

'So . . .' said the feldscher slowly, and then sighed. 'Influenza and may be a bit of a fever. There is typhus now in the town. . . . What can I do? She is a old woman, glory be to God. . . . How old?'

'Sixty-nine years, Maxim Nikolaitch.'

'An old woman. It's high time for her.'

'Of course! Your remark is very just,' said Yakob, smiling out of politeness. 'And I am sincerely grateful for your kindness; but allow me to make one remark; every insect is fond of life.'

The feldscher replied in a tone which implied that upon him alone depended her life or death. 'I will tell you what you'll do, friend; put on her head a cold compress, and give her these powders twice a day. And good-bye to you.'

By the expression of the feldscher's face, Yacob saw that it was a bad business, and that no powders would make it any better; it was quite plain to him that Marfa was beyond repair, and would assuredly die, if not today then tomorrow. He touched the feldscher on the arm, blinked his eyes, and said in a whisper:

'Yes, Maxim Nikolaitch, but you will let her blood.'

'I have no time, no time, friend. Take your old woman, and God be with you!'

'Do me this one kindness!' implored Yakob. 'You yourself know that if she merely had her stomach out of order, or some internal organ wrong, then powders and mixtures would cure; but she has caught cold. In cases of cold the first thing is to bleed the patient.'

But the feldscher had already called for the next patient, and into the dispensary came a peasant woman with a little boy.

'Be off!' he said to Yakob, with a frown.

'At least try the effect of leeches. I will pray God eternally for you.'

The feldscher lost his temper, and roared:

'Not another word.'

Yakob also lost his temper, and grew purple in the face; but he said nothing more and took Marfa under his arm and led her out of the room. As soon as he had got her into the cart, he looked angrily and contemptuously at the hospital and said:

'What an artist! He will let the blood of a rich man, but for a poor man grudges even a leech. Herod!'

When they arrived home, and entered the cabin, Marfa stood for a moment holding on to the stove. She was afraid that if she were to lie down Yakob would begin to complain about his losses, and abuse her for lying in bed and doing no work. And Yakob looked at her with tedium in his soul and remembered that tomorrow was John the Baptist, and the day after Nikolai the Miracle-worker, and then came Sunday, and after that Monday – another idle day. For four days no work could be done, and Marfa would be sure to die on one of these days. Her coffin must be made today. He took the iron yardwand, went up to the old woman and took her measure. After that she lay down, and Yakob crossed himself, and began to make a coffin.

When the work was finished, Bronza put on his spectacles and wrote in his book of losses:

'Marfa Ivanova's coffin – 2 roubles, 40 kopecks.'

And he sighed. All the time Marfa had lain silently with her eyes closed. Towards evening, when it was growing dark, she called her husband:

'Rememberest, Yakob?' she said, looking at him joyfully. 'Rememberest, fifty years ago God gave us a baby with yellow hair. Thou and I then sat every day by the river . . . under the willow . . . and sang songs.' And laughing bitterly she added: 'The child died.'

'That is all imagination,' said Yakob.

Later on came the priest, administered to Marfa the Sacrament and extreme unction. Marfa began to mutter something incomprehensible, and towards morning, died.

The old-women neighbours washed her, wrapped her in her winding sheet, and laid her out. To avoid having to pay the deacon's fee, Yakob himself read the psalms; and escaped a fee also at the graveyard, as the watchman there was his god-father. Four peasants carried the coffin free, out of respect for the deceased. After the coffin walked a procession of old women, beggars, and two cripples. The peasants on the road crossed themselves piously. And Yakob was very satisfied that everything passed off in honour, order, and cheapness, without offence to anyone. When saying good-bye for the last time to Marfa, he tapped the coffin with his fingers, and thought 'An excellent piece of work.'

But while he was returning from the graveyard he was overcome with extreme weariness. He felt unwell, he breathed feverishly and heavily, he could hardly stand on his feet. His brain was full of unaccustomed thoughts. He remembered again that he had never taken pity on Marfa and never caressed her. The fifty-two years during which they had lived in the same cabin stretched back to eternity, yet in the whole of that eternity he had never thought of her, never paid any attention to her, but treated her as if she were a cat or a dog. Yet every day she had lighted the stove, boiled and baked, fetched water, chopped wood, slept with him on the same bed; and when he returned drunk from weddings, she had taken his fiddle respectfully, and hung it on the wall, and put him to bed – all this silently with a timid, worried expression on her face. And now he felt that he could take pity on her, and would like to buy her a present, but it was too late. . . .

Towards Yakob smiling and bowing came Rothschild.

'I was looking for you, uncle,' he said. 'Moses Ilitch sends his compliments, and asks you to come across to him at once.'

Yakob felt inclined to cry.

'Begone!' i shouted, and continued his path.

'You can't mean that,' cried Rothschild in alarm, running after him. 'Moses Ilitch will take offence! He wants you at once.'

The way in which the Jew puffed and blinked, and the multitude of his red freckles awoke in Yakob disgust. He felt disgust, too, for his green frock-coat, with its black patches, and his whole fragile, delicate figure.

'What do you mean by coming after me, garlic?' he shouted. 'Keep off!'

The Jew also grew angry, and cried:

'If you don't take care to be a little politer I will send you flying over the fence.'

'Out of my sight!' roared Yakob, rushing on him with clenched fists. 'Out of my sight, abortion, or I will beat the soul out of your cursed body! I have no peace with Jews.'

Rothschild was frozen with terror; he squatted down and waved his arms above his head, as if warding off blows, and then jumped up and ran for his life. While running he hopped, and flourished his hands; and the twitching of his long, fleshless spine could plainly be seen. The boys in the street were delighted with the incident, and rushed after him, crying, 'Jew! Jew!' The dogs pursued him with loud barks. Someone laughed, then someone whistled, and the dogs barked louder and louder. Then, it must have been, a dog bit Rothschild, for there rang out a sickly, despairing cry.

Yakob walked past the common, and then along the outskirts of the town; and the street boys cried, 'Bronza! Bronza!' With a piping note snipe flew around him, and ducks quacked. The sun baked everything, and from the water came scintillations so bright that it was painful to look at. Yakob walked along the path by the side of the river, and watched a stout, red-cheeked lady come out of the bathing-place. Not far from the bathing-place sat a group of boys catching crabs with meat; and seeing him they cried maliciously, 'Bronza! Bronza!' And at this moment before him rose a thick old willow with an immense hollow in it, and on it a raven's nest. . . . And suddenly in Yakob's mind awoke the memory of the child with the yellow hair of whom Marfa had spoken. . . . Yes, it was the same willow, green, silent, sad. . . . How it had aged, poor thing!

He sat underneath it, and began to remember. On the other bank, where was now a flooded meadow, there then stood a great birch forest, and farther away, where the now bare hill glimmered on the horizon, was an old pine wood. Up and down the river went barges. But now everything was flat and smooth; on the opposite bank stood only a single birch, young and shapely, like a girl; and on the river were only ducks and geese where once had floated barges. It seemed that since those days even the geese had become smaller. Yakob closed his eyes, and in imagination saw flying towards him an immense flock of white geese.

He began to wonder how it was that in the last forty or fifty years of his life he had never been near the river, or if he had, had never noticed it. Yet it was a respectable river, and by no means contemptible; it would have been possible to fish in it, and the fish might have been sold to tradesmen, officials, and the attendant at the railway station buffet, and the money could have been lodged in the bank; he might have used it for rowing from country-house to country-house and playing on the fiddle, and everyone would have paid him money; he might even have tried to act as bargee – it would have been better than making coffins; he might have kept geese, killed them and sent them to Moscow in the winter-time – from the feathers alone he would have made as much as ten roubles a year. But he had yawned away his life, and done nothing. What losses! Akh, what losses! and if he had done all together – caught fish, played on the fiddle, acted as bargee, and kept geese – what a sum he would have amassed! But he had never even dreamed of this; life had passed without profits, without any satisfaction; everything had passed away unnoticed; before him nothing remained. But look backward – nothing but losses, such losses that to think of them it makes the blood run cold. And why cannot a man live without these losses? Why had the birch wood and the pine forest both been cut down? Why is the common pasture unused? Why do people do exactly what they ought not to do? Why did he all his life scream, roar, clench his fists, insult his wife? For what imaginable purpose did he frighten and insult the Jew? Why, indeed, do people prevent one another living in peace? All these are also losses! Terrible losses! If it were not for hatred and malice people would draw from one another incalculable profits.

Evening and night, twinkled in Yakob's brain the willow, the fish, the dead geese, Marfa with her profile like that of a bird about to drink, the pale, pitiable face of Rothschild, and an army of snouts thrusting themselves out of the darkness and muttering about losses. He shifted from side to side, and five times in the night rose from his bed and played on the fiddle.

In the morning he rose with an effort and went to the hospital. The same Maxim Nikolaitch ordered him to bind his head with a cold compress, and gave him powders; and by the expression of his face and by his tone Yakob saw that it was a bad business, and that no powders would make it any better. But upon his way home he reflected that from death at least there would be one profit; it would no longer be necessary to eat, to drink, to pay taxes, or to injure others; and as a man lies in his grave not one year, but hundreds and thousands of years, the profit was enormous. The life of man was, in short, a loss, and only his death a profit. Yet this consideration, though entirely just, was offensive and bitter; for why in this world is it so ordered that life, which is given to a man only once, passes by without profit?

He did not regret dying, but as soon as he arrived home and saw his fiddle, his heart fell, and he felt sorry. The fiddle could not be taken to the grave; it must remain an orphan, and the same thing would happen with it as had happened with the birchwood and the pineforest. Everything in this world decayed, and would decay! Yakob went to the door of the hut and sat upon the threshold stone, pressing his fiddle to his shoulder. Still thinking of life, full of decay and full of losses, he began to play, and as the tune poured out plaintively and touchingly, the tears flowed down his cheeks. And the harder he thought, the sadder was the song of the fiddle.

The latch creaked twice, and in the wicket door appeared Rothschild. The first half of the yard he crossed boldly, but seeing Yakob, he stopped short, shrivelled up, and apparently from fright began to make signs as if he wished to tell the time with his fingers.

'Come on, don't be afraid,' said Yakob kindly, beckoning him. 'Come!'

With a look of distrust and terror Rothschild drew near and stopped about two yards away.

'Don't beat me, Yakob, it is not my fault!' he said, with a bow. 'Moses Ilitch has sent me again. "Don't be afraid!" he said, "go to Yakob again and tell him that without him we cannot possibly get on." The wedding is on Wednesday.

Shapovaloff's daughter is marrying a wealthy man. . . . It will be a first-class wedding,' added the Jew, blinking one eye.

'I cannot go,' answered Yakob, breathing heavily. 'I am ill, brother.'

And again he took his bow, and the tears burst from his eyes and fell upon the fiddle. Rothschild listened attentively, standing by his side with arms folded upon his chest. The distrustful, terrified expression upon his face little by little changed into a look of suffering and grief, he rolled his eyes as if in an ecstacy of torment, and ejaculated 'Wachchch!' And the tears slowly rolled down his cheeks and made little black patches on his green frock-coat.

All day long Yakob lay in bed and worried. With evening came the priest, and, confessing him, asked whether he had any particular sin which he would like to confess; and Yakob exerted his fading memory, and remembering Marfa's unhappy face, and the Jew's despairing cry when he was bitten by the dog, said in a hardly audible voice:

'Give the fiddle to Rothschild.'

And now in the town everyone asks: Where did Rothschild get such an excellent fiddle? Did he buy it or steal it . . . or did he get it in pledge? Long ago he abandoned his flute, and now plays on the fiddle only. From beneath his bow issue the same mournful sounds as formerly came from the flute; but when he tries to repeat the tune that Yakob played when he sat on the threshold stone, the fiddle emits sounds so passionately sad and full of grief that the listeners weep; and he himself rolls his eyes and ejaculates 'Wachchch!' . . . But this new song so pleases everyone in the town that wealthy traders and officials never fail to engage Rothschild for their social gatherings, and even force him to play it as many as ten times.

A FATHER

A FATHER

'I don't deny it; I have had a drop too much. . . . Forgive me; the fact is I happened to pass by the public, and, all owing to the heat, I drank a couple of bottles. It's hot, brother!'

Old Musátoff took a rag from his pocket, and wiped the sweat from his clean-shaven, dissipated face.

'I have come to you, Bórenka, angel mine, just for a minute,' he continued, looking at his son, 'on very important business. Forgive me if I am in the way. Tell me, my soul . . . do you happen to have ten roubles to spare till Tuesday? You understand me . . . yesterday I ought to have paid for the rooms, but the money question . . . you understand. Not a kopeck!'

Young Musátoff went out silently, and behind the door began a whispered consultation with his housekeeper and the colleagues in the Civil Service with whom he shared the villa. In a minute he returned, and silently handed his father a ten-rouble note. The old gentleman took it carelessly, and without looking at it thrust it into his pocket, and said:

'*Merci!* And how is the world using you? We haven't met for ages.'

'Yes, it is a long time – since All Saints' Day.'

'Five times I did my best to get over to you, but never could get time. First one matter, then another . . . simply ruination! But, Boris, I may confess it, I am not telling the truth . . . I lie . . . I always lie. Don't believe me, Bórenka. I promised to let you have the ten roubles back on Tuesday; don't believe that either! Don't believe a single word I say! I have no business matters at all, simply idleness, drink, and shame to show myself in the street in this get-up. But you, Bórenka, will forgive me. Three times I sent the girl for money, and wrote you piteous letters. For the money, thanks! But don't believe the letters. . . . I lied. It hurts me to plunder you in this way,

101

angel mine; I know that you can hardly make both ends meet, and live – so to say – on locusts. But with impudence like mine you can do nothing. A rascal who only shows his face when he wants money! . . . Forgive me, Bórenka, I tell you the plain truth, because I cannot look with indifference upon your angel face. . . .'

A minute passed in silence. The old man sighed deeply, and began:

'Let us make the supposition, brother, that you were to treat me to a glass of beer.'

Without a word, Boris again went out and whispered outside the door. The beer was brought in. At the sight of the bottle Musátoff enlivened, and suddenly changed his tone.

'The other day I was at the races,' he began, making frightened faces. 'There were three of us, and together we put in the totalisator a three-rouble note on Shustri. And good luck to Shustri! With the risk of one rouble we each got back thirty-two. It is a noble sport. The old woman always pitches into me about the races, but I go. I love it!'

Boris, a young fair-haired man, with a sad, apathetic face, walked from corner to corner, and listened silently. When Musátoff interrupted his story in order to cough, he went up to him and said:

'The other day, papa, I bought myself a new pair of boots, but they turned out too small. I wish you would take them off my hands. I will let you have them cheap!'

'I shall be charmed!' said the old man, with a grimace. 'Only for the same price – without any reduction.'

'Very well. . . . We will regard that as a loan also.'

Boris stretched his arm under the bed, and pulled out the new boots. Old Musátoff removed his own awkward brown shoes – plainly someone else's – and tried the new boots on.

'Like a shot!' he exclaimed. 'Your hand on it. . . . I'll take them. On Tuesday, when I get my pension, I'll send the money. . . . But I may as well confess, I lie.' He resumed his former piteous tone. 'About the races I lied, and about the pension I lie. You are deceiving me, Bórenka. . . . I see very well through your magnanimous pretext. I can see through you! The boots are too small for you because your heart is too large! Akh, Borya, Borya, I understand it . . . and I feel it!'

'You have gone to your new rooms?' asked Boris, with the object of changing the subject.

'Yes, brother, into the new rooms. . . . Every month we shift. With a character like the old woman's we cannot stay anywhere.'

'I have been at the old rooms. But now I want to ask you to come to the country. In your state of health it will do you good to be in the fresh air.'

Musátoff waved his hand. 'The old woman wouldn't let me go, and myself I don't care to. A hundred times you have tried to drag me out of the pit. . . . I have tried to drag myself . . . but the devil an improvement! Give it up! In the pit I'll die as I have lived. At this moment I sit in front of you and look at your angel face . . . yet I am being dragged down into the pit. It's destiny, brother! You can't get flies from a dunghill to a rose bush. No. . . . Well, I'm off . . . it's getting dark.'

'If you wait a minute, we'll go together. I have business in town myself.'

Musátoff and his son put on their coats, and went out. By the time they had found a droschky it was quite dark, and the windows were lighted up.

'I know I'm ruining you, Bórenka,' stammered the father. 'My poor, poor children! What an affliction to be cursed with such a father! Bórenka, angel mine, I cannot lie when I see your face. Forgive me! . . . To what a pass, my God, has impudence brought me! This very minute I have taken your money, and shamed you with my drunken face; your brothers also I sponge on and put to shame. If you had seen me yesterday! I won't hide anything, Bórenka. Yesterday our neighbours – all the rascality, in short – came in to see the old woman. I drank with them, and actually abused you behind your back, and complained that you had neglected me. I tried, you understand, to get the drunken old women to pity me, and played the part of an unhappy father. That's my besetting sin; when I want to hide my faults, I heap them on the heads of my innocent children. . . . But I cannot lie to you, Bórenka, or hide things. I came to you in pride, but when I had felt your kindness and all-mercifulness, my tongue clove to the roof of my mouth, and all my conscience turned upside down.'

'Yes, father, but let us talk about something else.'

'Mother of God, what children I have!' continued the old man, paying no attention to his son. 'What a glory the Lord has sent me! Such children should be sent not to me, a good-for-nothing, but to a real man with a soul and a heart. I am not worthy of it!'

Musátoff took off his cap and crossed himself piously thrice.

'Glory be to Thee, O God!' he sighed, looking around as if seeking an ikon. 'Astonishing, priceless children! Three sons I have, and all of them the same! Sober, serious, diligent – and what intellects! Cabman, what intellects! Gregory alone has as much brains as ten ordinary men. French . . . and German . . . he speaks both . . . and you never get tired of listening. Children, children mine, I cannot believe that you are mine at all! I don't believe it! You, Bórenka, are a very martyr! I am ruining you . . . before long I shall have ruined you. You give me money without end, although you know very well that not a kopeck goes on necessaries. Only the other day I sent you a piteous letter about my illness. . . . But I lied; the money was wanted to buy rum. Yet you gave it to me sooner than offend your old father with a refusal. All this I know . . . and feel . . . Grisha also is a martyr. On Thursday, angel mine, I went to his office, drunk, dirty, ragged . . . smelling of vodka like a cellar. I went straight up to him and began in my usual vulgar slang, although he was with the other clerks, the head of the department – and petitioners all around! Disgraced him for his whole life! . . . Yet he never got the least confused, only a little pale; he smiled, and got up from his desk as if nothing were wrong – even introduced me to his colleagues. And he brought me the whole way home, without a word of reproach! I sponge on him even worse than on you!

'Then take your brother, Sasha! There's another martyr! Married to a colonel's daughter, moving in a circle of aristocrats, with a dot . . . and everything else. . . . He, at any rate, you would think would have nothing to do with me. Well, brother, what does he do? When he gets married the very first thing after the wedding he comes to me with his young wife, and pays me the first visit . . . to my lair, to the lair . . . I swear to God!'

The old man began to sob, but soon laughed again.

'At the very moment, as the fates would have it, when we were eating scraped radishes and kvas, and frying fish, with a stench in the room enough to stink out the devil. I was lying drunk as usual, and the old woman jumps up and greets them with a face the colour of beefsteak . . . in one word, a scandal. But Sasha bore it all.'

'Yes, our Sasha is a good man,' said Boris.

'Incomparable! You are all of you gold, both you and Grisha, and Sasha and Sonia. I torture, pester, disgrace, and sponge on you, yet in my whole life I have never heard a word of reproach, or seen a single sidelong look. If you had a decent father it would be different, but . . . You have never had anything from me but evil. I am a wicked, dissolute man. . . . Now, thank God, I have quieted down, and have no character left in me, but formerly, when you were little children, I had a character and no mistake. Whatever I said or did seemed to me gospel! I remember! I used to come back late from the club, drunk and irritated, and begin to abuse your poor mother about the household expenses. I would keep on at her all night, and imagine that she was in the wrong; in the morning you would get up and go to school, but all the time I would keep on showing her that I had a character. Heaven rest her soul, how I tortured the poor martyr! And when you came back from school and found me asleep you weren't allowed your dinner until I got up. And after dinner the same music! P'rhaps you remember. May God forbid that anyone else should be cursed with such a father! He sent you to me as a blessing. A blessing! Continue in this way, children, to the end. Honour thy father that thy days may be long in the land! For your goodness Heaven will reward you with long life! Cabman, stop!'

Musátoff alighted and ran into a beerhouse. After a delay of half an hour he returned, grunted tipsily, and took his seat.

'And where is Sonia now?' he asked. 'Still at the boarding-school?'

'No, she finished last May. She lives now with Sasha's aunt.'

'What?' exclaimed the old man. 'Left school? And a glorious girl, God bless her – went with her brothers. *Akh*, Bórenka, no mother, no one to console her! Tell me, Bórenka, does she know . . . does she know that I am alive? Eh?'

Boris did not answer. Five minutes passed in deep silence. The old man sobbed, wiped his face with a rag, and said:

'I love her, Bórenka! She was the only daughter, and in old age there is no consolation like a daughter. If I could only see her for a moment. Tell me, Bórenka, may I?'

'Of course, whenever you like.'

'And she won't object?'

'Of course not; she herself went to look for you.'

'I swear to God! There is a nest of angels! Cabman, eh? Arrange it, Bórenka, angel! Of course she is a young lady now, *délicatesse . . . consommé*, and all that sort of thing in the noble style. So I can't see her in this get-up. But all this, Bórenka, we can arrange. For three days I won't taste a drop – that'll bring my accursed drunken snout into shape. Then I will go to your place and put on a suit of your clothes, and get a shave and have my hair cut. Then you will drive over and take me with you? Is it agreed?'

'All right.'

'Cabman, stop!'

The old man jumped out of the carriage and ran into another beershop. Before they reached his lodgings he visited two more; and every time his son waited silently and patiently. When, having dismissed the cabman, they crossed the broad, muddy yard to the rooms of the 'old woman,' Musátoff looked confused and guilty, grunted timidly, and smacked his lips.

'Bórenka,' he began, in an imploring voice, 'if the old woman says anything of that kind to you – you understand – don't pay any attention to her. And be polite to her. She is very ignorant and impertinent, but not a bad sort at bottom. She has a good, warm heart.'

They crossed the yard and entered a dark hall. The door squeaked, the kitchen smelt, the samovar smoked, and shrill voices were heard. . . . While they passed through the kitchen Boris noticed only the black smoke, a rope with washing spread out, and the chimney of a samovar, through the chinks of which burst golden sparks.

'This is my cell,' said Musátoff, bowing his head, and showing his son into a little, low-ceilinged room, filled with atmosphere unbearable from proximity to the kitchen. At a table sat three women, helping one another to food. Seeing the guest, they looked at one another and stopped eating.

'Well, did you get it?' asked one, apparently 'the old woman,' roughly.

'Got it, got it,' stammered the old man. 'Now, Boris, do us the honour! Sit down! With us, brother – young man – everything is simple. . . . We live in a simple way.'

Musátoff fussed about without any visible reason. He was ashamed before his son, and at the same time apparently wished to bear himself before the women as a man of importance and a forsaken, unhappy father.

'Yes, brother mine – young man – we live simply, without show-off,' he stammered. 'We are plain folk, young man. . . . We are not like you . . . we do not trouble to throw dust in other people's eyes. No! . . . A drop of vodka, eh?'

One of the women, ashamed of drinking before a stranger, sighed and said:

'I must have another glass after these mushrooms. After mushrooms, whether you like it or not, you have to drink. . . . Ivan Gerasiuitch, ask him . . . perhaps he'll have a drink.'

'Drink, young man!' said Musátoff, without looking at his son. 'Wines and liqueurs we don't keep, brother, we live plainly.'

'I'm afraid our arrangements don't suit him,' sighed the old woman.

'Leave him alone, leave him alone, he'll drink all right.'

To avoid giving offence to his father, Boris took a glass, and drained it in silence. When the samovar was brought in he, silently and with a melancholy air – again to please his father – drank two cups of atrocious tea. And without a word he listened while the 'old woman' lamented the fact that in this world you will sometimes find cruel and godless children who forsake their parents in their old age.

'I know what you are thinking,' said the drunken old man, falling into his customary state of excitement. 'You are thinking that I have fallen in the world, that I have dirtied myself, that I am an object of pity! But in my mind this simple life is far more natural than yours, young man. I do not need

for anything . . . and I have no intention of humiliating myself
. . . I can stand a lot . . . but tolerance is at an end when a brat
of a boy looks at me with pity.'

When he had drank his tea, he cleaned a herring, and
squeezed onion on it with such vigour that tears of emotion
sprang into his eyes. He spoke again of the totalisator, of his
winnings, and of a hat of Panama straw for which he had paid
sixteen roubles the day before. He lied with the same appetite
with which he had drunk and devoured the herring. His son
sat silently for more than an hour, and then rose to take leave.

'I wouldn't think of detaining you,' said Musátoff stiffly. 'I
ask your pardon, young man, for not living in the way to
which you are accustomed.'

He bristled up, sniffed with dignity, and winked to the
women.

'Good-bye, young man!' he said, escorting his son into the
hall. '*Attendez!*'

But in the hall, where it was quite dark, he suddenly pressed
his face to his son's arm, and sobbed.

'If I could only see Sóniushka!' he whispered. 'Arrange it,
Bórenka, angel mine! I will have a shave, and put on one of
your suits . . . and make a severe face. I won't open my mouth
while she's present. I won't say a word. I swear to God!'

He glanced timidly at the door, from behind which came
the shrill voices of the women, smothered his sobs, and said in
a loud voice:

'Well, good-bye, young man! *Attendez!*'

TWO TRAGEDIES

TWO TRAGEDIES

At ten o'clock on a dark September evening six-year-old Andreï, the only son of Dr. Kiríloff, a Zemstvo physician, died from diphtheria. The doctor's wife had just thrown herself upon her knees at the bedside of her dead child, and was giving way to the first ecstacy of despair, when the hall-door bell rang loudly.

Owing to the danger of infection all the servants had been sent out of the house that morning; and Kiríloff, in his shirtsleeves, with unbuttoned waistcoat, with sweating face, and hands burned with carbolic acid, opened the door himself. The hall was dark, and the stranger who entered it was hardly visible. All that Kiríloff could distinguish was that he was of middle height, that he wore a white muffler, and had a big, extraordinarily pale face – a face so pale that at first it seemed to illumine the darkness of the hall.

'Is the doctor at home?' he asked quickly.

'I am the doctor,' answered Kiríloff, 'What do you want?'

'Ah, it is you. I am glad!' said the stranger. He stretched out through the darkness for the doctor's hand, found it, and pressed it tightly. I am very . . . very glad. We are acquaintances. My name is Abógin. . . . I had the pleasure of meeting you last summer at Gnutcheff's. I am very glad that you are in. . . . For the love of Christ do not refuse to come with me at once. . . . My wife is dangerously ill. . . . I have brought a trap.'

From Abógin's voice and movements it was plain that he was greatly agitated. Like a man frightened by a fire or by a mad dog, he could not contain his breath. He spoke rapidly in a trembling voice, and something inexpressibly sincere and childishly imploring sounded in his speech. But, like all men frightened and thunder-struck, he spoke in short abrupt phrases, and used many superfluous and inconsequential words.

111

'I was afraid I should not find you at home,' he continued. 'While I was driving here I was in a state of torture. . . . Dress and come at once, for the love of God. . . . It happened thus. Paptchinski – Alexander Semiónevitch – whom you know, had driven over. . . . We talked for awhile . . . then we had tea; suddenly my wife screamed, laid her hand upon her heart, and fell against the back of the chair. We put her on the bed. . . . I bathed her forehead with ammonia, and sprinkled her with water . . . she lies like a corpse. . . . It is aneurism. . . . Come. . . . Her father died from aneurism. . . .'

Kiríloff listened and said nothing. It seemed he had forgotten his own language. But when Abógin repeated what he had said about Paptchinski and about his wife's father, the doctor shook his head, and said apathetically, drawling every word:

'Excuse me, I cannot go. . . . Five minutes ago . . . my child died.'

'Is it possible?' cried Abógin, taking a step back. 'Good God, at what an unlucky time I have come! An amazingly unhappy day . . . amazing! What a coincidence . . . as if on purpose.'

Abógin put his hand upon the door-handle, and inclined his head as if in doubt. He was plainly undecided as to what to do; whether to go, or again to ask the doctor to come.

'Listen to me,' he said passionately, seizing Kiríloff by the arm; 'I thoroughly understand your position. God is my witness that I feel shame in trying to distract your attention at such a moment, but . . . what can I do? Judge yourself – whom can I apply to? Except you, there is no doctor in the neighbourhood. Come! For the love of God! It is not for myself I ask. . . . It is not I who am ill.'

A silence followed. Kiríloff turned his back to Abógin, for a moment stood still, and went slowly from the anteroom into the hall. Judging by his uncertain, mechanical gait, by the care with which he straightened the shade upon the unlit lamp, and looked into a thick book which lay upon the table – in this moment he had no intentions, no wishes, thought of nothing; and probably had even forgotten that in the anteroom a stranger was waiting. The twilight and silence of the hall

apparently intensified his stupor. Walking from the hall into
his study, he raised his right leg high, and sought with his
hands the doorpost. All his figure showed a strange
uncertainty, as if he were in another's house, or for the first
time in life were intoxicated, and were surrendering himself
questioningly to the new sensation. Along the wall of the
study and across the bookshelves ran a long zone of light.
Together with a heavy, close smell of carbolic and ether, this
light came from a slightly opened door which led from the
study into the bedroom. The doctor threw himself into an
armchair before the table. A minute he looked drowsily at the
illumined books, and then rose, and went into the bedroom.

In the bedroom reigned the silence of the grave. All, to the
smallest trifle, spoke eloquently of a struggle just lived
through, of exhaustion, and of final rest. A candle standing on
the stool among phials, boxes, and jars, and a large lamp upon
the dressing-table lighted the room. On the bed beside the
window lay a boy with open eyes and an expression of
surprise upon his face. He did not move, but his eyes, it
seemed, every second grew darker and darker, and vanished
into his skull. With her hands upon his body, and her face
hidden in the folds of the bedclothes, knelt the mother. Like
the child, she made no movement; life showed itself alone in
the bend of her back and in the position of her hands. She
pressed against the bed with all her being, with force and
eagerness, as if she feared to destroy the tranquil and
convenient pose which she had found for her weary body.
Counterpane, dressings, jars, pools on the floor, brushes and
spoons scattered here and there, the white bottle of lime-
water, the very air, heavy and stifling – all were dead and
seemed immersed in rest.

The doctor stopped near his wife, thrust his hands into his
trouser pockets, and turning his head, bent his gaze upon his
son. His face expressed indifference; only by the drops upon
his beard could it be seen that he had just been crying.

The repellent terror which we conceive when we speak of
death was absent from the room. The general stupefaction, the
mother's pose, the father's indifferent face, exhaled something
attractive and touching; exhaled that subtle, intangible beauty
of human sorrow which cannot be analysed or described, and

which music alone can express. Beauty breathed even in the grim tranquillity of the mourners. Kiríloff and his wife were silent; they did not weep, as if in addition to the weight of their sorrow they were conscious also of the poetry of their position. It seemed that they were thinking how in its time their youth had passed, how now with the child had passed even their right to have children at all. The doctor was forty-four years old, already grey, with the face of an old man; his faded and sickly wife, thirty-five. Andreï was not only their only son, but also their last.

In contrast with his wife, Kiríloff belonged to those natures which in time of spiritual pain feel a need for movement. After standing five minutes beside his wife, he, again lifting high his right leg, went from the bedroom into a little room half taken up by a long, broad sofa, and thence into the kitchen. After wandering about the stove and the cook's bed he bowed his head and went through a little door back to the anteroom.

Here again he saw the white muffler and the pale face.

'At last!' sighed Abógin, taking hold of the door-handle. 'Come, please!'

The doctor shuddered, looked at him, and remembered.

'Listen to me; have I not already told you I cannot come?' he said, waking up. 'How extraordinary!'

'Doctor, I am not made of stone. . . . I thoroughly understand your position. . . . I sympathise with you!' said Abógin, with an imploring voice, laying one hand upon his muffler. 'But I am not asking this for myself. . . . My wife is dying! If you had heard her cry, if you had seen her face, then you would understand my persistence! My God! and I thought that you had gone to get ready! Dr. Kiríloff, time is precious. Come, I implore you!'

'I cannot go,' said Kiríloff with a pause between each word. Then he returned to the hall.

Abógin went after him, and seized him by the arm.

'You are overcome by your sorrow – that I understand. But remember . . . I am not asking you to come and cure a toothache . . . not as an adviser . . . but to save a human life,' he continued, in the voice of a beggar. 'A human life should be supreme over every personal sorrow. . . . I beg of you manliness, an exploit! . . . In the name of humanity!'

'Humanity is a stick with two ends,' said Kiríloff with irritation. 'In the name of the same humanity I beg of you not to drag me away. How strange this seems! Here I am hardly standing on my legs, yet you worry me with your humanity! At the present moment I am good for nothing. . . . I will not go on any consideration! And for whom should I leave my wife? No. . . . No.'

Kiríloff waved his hands and staggered back.

'Do not . . . do not ask me,' he continued in a frightened voice. 'Excuse me. . . . By the Thirteenth Volume of the Code I am bound to go, and you have the right to drag me by the arm. . . . If you will have it, drag me . . . but I am useless. . . . Even for conversation I am not in a fit state. . . . Excuse me.'

'It is useless, doctor, for you to speak to me in that tone,' said Abógin, again taking Kiríloff's arm. 'The devil take your Thirteenth Volume! . . . To do violence to your will I have no right. If you will, come; if you don't, then God be with you; but it is not to your will that I appeal, but to your heart! . . . A young woman is at the point of death! This moment your own son has died, and who if not you should understand my terror?'

Abógin's voice trembled with agitation; in tremble and in tone was something more persuasive than in the words. He was certainly sincere; but it was remarkable that no matter how well chosen his phrases, they seemed to come from him stilted, soulless, inappropriately ornate, to such an extent that they seemed an insult to the atmosphere of the doctor's house and to his own dying wife. He felt this himself, and therefore, fearing to be misunderstood, he tried with all his force to make his voice sound soft and tender, so as to win if not with words at least by sincerity of tone. In general, phrases, however beautiful and profound, act only on those who are indifferent, and seldom satisfy the happy or unhappy; it is for this reason that the most touching expression of joy or sorrow is always silence; sweethearts understand one another best when they are silent; and a burning passionate eulogy spoken above a grave touches only the strangers present, and seems to widow and child inexpressive and cold.

Kiríloff stood still and said nothing. When Abógin used some more phrases about the high vocation of a physician, self-sacrifice, and so on, the doctor asked gloomily:

'Is it far?'

'Something between thirteen and fourteen versts. I have excellent horses. I give you my word of honour to bring you there and back in an hour. In a single hour!'

The last words acted on the doctor more powerfully than the references to humanity and the vocation of a doctor. He thought for a moment and said, with a sigh:

'All right. . . . I will go.'

With a rapid, steady gait he went into his study, and after a moment's delay returned with a long overcoat. Moving nervously beside him, shuffling his feet, and overjoyed, Abógin helped him into his coat. Together they left the house.

It was dark outside, but not so dark as in the anteroom. In the darkness was clearly defined the outline of the tall, stooping doctor, with his long, narrow beard and eagle nose. As for Abógin, in addition to his pale face the doctor could now distinguish a big head, and a little student's cap barely covering the crown. The white muffler gleamed only in front; behind, it was hidden under long hair.

'Believe me, I appreciate your generosity,' he muttered, seating the doctor in the calêche. 'We will get there in no time. Listen, Luka, old man, drive as hard as you can! Quick!'

The coachman drove rapidly. First they flew past a row of ugly buildings, with a great open yard; everywhere around it was dark, but from a window a bright light glimmered through the palisade, and three windows in the upper storey of the great block seemed paler than the air. After that they drove through intense darkness. There was a smell of mushroom dampness, and a lisping of trees; ravens awakened by the noise of the calêche stirred in the foliage, and raised a frightened, complaining cry, as if they knew that Kiríloff's son was dead, and that Abógin's wife was dying. They flashed past single trees, past a coppice; a pond, crossed with great black shadows, scintillated – and the calêche rolled across a level plain. The cry of the ravens was heard indistinctly far behind, and then ceased entirely.

For nearly the whole way Abógin and Kiríloff were silent. Only once, Abógin sighed and exclaimed:

'A frightful business! A man never so loves those who are near to him as when he is in danger of losing them.'

And when the calêche slowly crossed the river, Kiríloff started suddenly as if he were frightened by the plash of the water, and moved.

'Listen! Let me go for a moment,' he said wearily. 'I will come again. I must send a feldscher to my wife. She is alone!'

Abógin did not answer. The calêche, swaying and banging over the stones, crossed a sandy bank and rolled onward. Kiríloff, wrapped in weariness, looked around him. Behind, in the scanty starlight, gleamed the road; and the willows by the river bank vanished in the darkness. To the right stretched a plain, flat and interminable as heaven; and far in the distance, no doubt on some sodden marsh, gleamed will-of-the-wisps. On the left, running parallel to the road, stretched a hillock, shaggy with a small shrubbery, and over the hill hung immovably a great half-moon, rosy, half muffled in the mist and fringed with light clouds, which, it seemed, watched it on every side, that it might not escape.

On all sides Nature exhaled something hopeless and sickly; the earth, like a fallen woman sitting in her dark chamber and trying to forget the past, seemed tormented with remembrances of spring and summer, and waited in apathy in inevitable winter. Everywhere the world seemed a dark, unfathomable deep, an icy pit from which there was no escape either for Kiríloff or for Abógin or for the red half-moon. . . .

The nearer to its goal whirled the calêche, the more impatient seemed Abógin. He shifted, humped up, and looked over the coachman's shoulder. And when at last the carriage stopped before steps handsomely covered with striped drugget, he looked up at the lighted windows of the second storey, and panted audibly.

'If anything happens . . . I will never survive it,' he said, entering the hall with Kiríloff, and rubbing his hands in agitation. But after listening a moment, he added, 'There is no confusion . . . things must be going well.'

In the hall were neither voices nor footsteps, and the whole house, notwithstanding its brilliant lights, seemed asleep. Only now, for the first time, the doctor and Abógin, after their sojourn in darkness, could see one another plainly. Kiríloff was tall, round-shouldered, and ugly, and was carelessly dressed. His thick, almost negro, lips, his eagle nose, and his withered, indifferent glance, expressed something cutting, unkindly, and rude. His uncombed hair, his sunken temples, the premature grey in the long, narrow beard, through which appeared his chin, the pale grey of his skin, and his careless, angular manners, all reflected a career of need endured, of misfortune, of weariness with life and with men. Judging by his dry figure, no one would ever believe that this man had a wife, and that he had wept over his child.

Abógin was a contrast. He was a thick-set, solid blond, with a big head, with heavy but soft features; and he was dressed elegantly and fashionably. From his carriage, from his closely-buttoned frock-coat, from his mane of hair, and from his face, flowed something noble and leonine; he walked with his head erect and his chest expanded, he spoke in an agreeable baritone, and the way in which he took off his muffler and smoothed his hair breathed a delicate, femine elegance. Even his pallor, and the childish terror with which, while taking off his coat, he looked up the staircase, did not detract from his dignity, or diminish the satiety, health, and aplomb which his whole figure breathed.

'There is no one about . . . I can hear nothing,' he said, going upstairs. 'There is no confusion. . . . God is merciful!'

He led the doctor through the hall into a great drawing-room, with a black piano, and lustres in white covers. From this they went into a small, cosy, and well-furnished dining-room, full of a pleasant, rosy twilight.

'Wait a moment,' said Abógin, 'I shall be back immediately. I will look around and tell them you are here. . . .'

Kiríloff remained alone. The luxury of the room, the pleasant twilight, and even his presence in the unknown house of a stranger, which had the character of an adventure, apparently did not affect him. He lay back in the armchair and examined his hands, burnt with carbolic acid. Only faintly could he see the bright red lamp shade and a violoncello case. But looking at the other side of the room, where ticked a clock, he noticed a stuffed wolf, as solid and sated as Abógin himself.

Not a sound. . . . Then in a distant room someone loudly ejaculated 'Ah!'; a glass door, probably the door of a wardrobe, closed . . . and again all was silent. After waiting a moment Kiríloff ceased to examine his hands, and raised his eyes upon the door through which Abógin had gone.

On the threshold stood Abógin. But it was not the Abógin who had left the room. The expression of satiety, the delicate elegance had vanished; his face, his figure, his pose were contorted by a repulsive expression not quite of terror, not quite of physical pain. His nose, his lips, his moustaches, all his features twitched; it seemed they wished to tear themselves off his face; and his eyes were transfigured as if from torture.

Abógin walked heavily into the middle of the room, bent himself in two, groaned, and shook his fists.

'Deceived!' he shouted, with a strong hissing accentuation of the second syllable. 'Cheated! Gone! Got ill, and sent for a doctor, only to fly with that buffoon Paptchinski! My God!'

Abógin walked heavily up to the doctor, stretched up to his face his white, soft fists, and, shaking them, continued in a howl:

'Gone! Deceived! But why this extra lie? My God! My God! But why this filthy swindler's trick, this devilish reptile play? What have I ever done? Gone!'

The tears burst from his eyes. He turned on one foot and walked up and down the room. And now in his short coat, in the narrow, fashionable trousers, which made his legs seem too thin for his body, with his great head and mane, he still more closely resembled a lion. On the doctor's indifferent face appeared curiosity. He rose and looked at Abógin.

'Be so good as to tell me . . . where is the patient?'

'Patient! Patient!' cried Abógin, with a laugh, a sob, and a shaking of his fists. 'This is no sick woman, but a woman accursed! Meanness, baseness, lower than Satan himself could have conceived! Sent for a doctor, to fly with him – to fly with that buffoon, that clown, that Alphonse. Oh, God, better a thousand times that she had died! I cannot bear it. . . . I cannot bear it!'

The doctor drew himself up. His eyes blinked and filled with tears, his narrow beard moved to the right and to the left in accord with the movement of his jaws.

'Be so good as to inform me what is the meaning of this?' he asked, looking around him in curiosity. 'My child lies dead, my wife in despair is left alone in a great house. I myself can hardly stand on my feet, for three nights I have not slept, and what is this? I am brought here to play in some trivial comedy, to take the part of a property-man. . . . I don't understand it!'

Abógin opened one of his fists, flung upon the floor a crumpled paper, and trod on it as upon an insect which he wished to crush.

'And I never saw it! I never understood!' he said through his clenched teeth, shaking one of his fists beside his face, with an expression as if someone had trod upon a corn. 'I never noticed that he rode here every day, never noticed that today he came in a carriage! Why in a carriage? And I never noticed! Fool!'

'I don't understand . . . I really don't understand,' stammered Kiríloff. 'What is the meaning of this? This is practical joking at the expense of another . . . it is mocking at human suffering. It is impossible. . . . I have never heard of such a thing!'

With the dull astonishment depicted on his face of a man who is only beginning to understand that he has been badly insulted, the doctor shrugged his shoulders, and not knowing what to say, threw himself in exhaustion into the chair.

'Got tired of me, loved another! Well, God be with them! But why this deception, why this base, this traitorous trick?' cried Abógin in a whining voice. 'Why? For what? What have I done to her? Listen, doctor,' he said passionately, coming nearer to Kiríloff. 'You are the involuntary witness of my misfortune, and I will not conceal from you the truth. I swear to you that I loved that woman, that I loved her to adoration, that I was her slave. For her I gave up everything; I quarrelled with my parents, I threw up my career and my music, I forgave her what I could not have forgiven in my own mother or sister. . . . I have never said an unkind word to her. . . . I gave her no cause! But why this lie? I do not ask for love, but why this shameless deception? If a woman doesn't love, then let her say so openly, honestly, all the more since she knew my views on that subject. . . .'

With tears in his eyes, and with his body trembling all over, Abógin sincerely poured forth to the doctor his whole soul. He spoke passionately, with both hands pressed to his heart, he revealed family secrets without a moment's hesitation; and, it seemed, was even relieved when these secrets escaped him. Had he spoken thus for an hour, for two hours, and poured out his soul, he would certainly have felt better. Who knows whether the doctor might not have listened to him, sympathised with him as a friend, and, even without protest, become reconciled to his own unhappiness. . . . But it happened otherwise. While Abógin spoke, the insulted doctor changed. The indifference and surprise on his face gave way little by little to an expression of bitter offence, indignation, and wrath. His features became sharper, harder, and more disagreeable. And finally when Abógin held before his eyes the photograph of a young woman with a face handsome but dry and inexpressive as a nun's, and asked him could he, looking at this photograph, imagine that she was capable of telling a lie, the doctor suddenly leaped up, averted his eyes, and said, rudely ringing out every word:

'What do you mean by talking to me like this? I don't want to hear you! I will not listen!' He shouted and banged his fist upon the table. 'What have I to do with your stupid secrets, devil take them! You dare to communicate to me these base trifles! Do you not see that I have already been insulted enough? Am I a lackey who will bear insults without retaliation?'

Abógin staggered backwards, and looked at Kiríloff in amazement.

'Why did you bring me here?' continued the doctor, shaking his beard. . . . 'If you marry filth, then storm with your filth, and play your melodramas; but what affair is that of mine? What have I to do with your romances? Leave me alone! Display your well-born meanness, show off your humane ideas, (the doctor pointed to the violoncello case) play on your double basses and trombones, get as fat as a capon, but do not dare to mock the personality of another! If you cannot respect it, then rid it of your detestable attention!'

Abógin reddened. 'What does all this mean?' he asked.

'It means this: that it is base and infamous to play practical jokes on other men. I am a doctor; you regard doctors and all other working men who do not smell of scent and prostitution as your lackeys and your servants. But reflect, reflect – no one has given you the right to make a property man of a suffering human being!'

'You dare to speak this to me?' said Abógin; and his face again twitched, this time plainly from anger.

'Yes . . . and you, knowing of the misery in my home, have dared to drag me here to witness this insanity,' cried the doctor, again banging his fist upon the table. 'Who gave you the right to mock at human misfortune?'

'You are out of your mind,' said Abógin. 'You are not generous. I also am deeply unhappy, and . . .'

'Unhappy!' cried Kiríloff, with a contemptuous laugh. 'Do not touch that word; it ill becomes you. Oafs who have no money to meet their bills also call themselves unfortunate. Geese that are stuffed with too much fat are also unhappy. Insignificant curs!'

'You forget yourself, you forget yourself!' screamed Abógin. 'For words like those . . . people are horsewhipped. Do you hear me?'

He suddenly thrust his hand into his side pocket, took out a pocket-book, and taking two bank-notes, flung them on the table.

'There you have the money for your visit!' he said, dilating his nostrils. 'You are paid!'

'Do not dare to offer money to me,' cried Kiríloff, sweeping the notes on to the floor. 'For insults money is not the payment.'

The two men stood face to face, and in their anger flung insults at one another. It is certain that never in their lives had they uttered so many unjust, inhuman, and ridiculous words. In each was fully expressed the egoism of the unfortunate. And men who are unfortunate, egoistical, angry, unjust, and heartless are even less than stupid men capable of understanding one another. For misfortune does not unite, but severs; and those who should be bound by community of sorrow are much more unjust and heartless than the happy and contented.

'Be so good as to send me home!' cried the doctor at last.

Abógin rang sharply. Receiving no answer he rang again, and angrily flung the bell upon the floor; it fell heavily on the carpet and emitted a plaintive and ominous sound. . . . A footman appeared.

'Where have you been hiding yourself? May Satan take you!' roared Abógin, rushing at him with clenched fists. 'Where have

you been? Go, tell them at once to give this gentleman the
calêche, and get the carriage ready for me! . . . Stop!' he cried,
when the servant turned to go. 'Tomorrow let none of you
traitors remain in this house! The whole pack of you! I will get
others! Curs!'

Awaiting their carriages, Abógin and Kiríloff were silent.
The first had already regained his expression of satiety and his
delicate elegance. He walked up and down the room, shook
his head gracefully, and apparently thought something out.
His anger had not yet evaporated, but he tried to look as if he
did not notice his enemy. . . . The doctor stood, with one
hand on the edge of the table, and looked at Abógin with
deep, somewhat cynical and ugly contempt – with the eyes of
sorrow and misfortune when they see before them satiety and
elegance.

When, after a short delay, the doctor took his seat in the
calêche, his eyes retained their contemptuous look. It was
dark, much darker than an hour before. The red half-moon
had fallen below the hill, and the clouds that had guarded it lay
in black spots among the stars. A carriage with red lamps
rattled along the road, and overtook Kiríloff. It was Abógin,
driving away to protest . . . and make a fool of himself. . . .

And all the way home Kiríloff thought, not of his wife or of
dead Andreï, but of Abógin and of the people who lived in the
house which he had just left. His thoughts were unjust,
heartless, inhuman. He condemned Abógin and his wife, and
Paptchinski, and all that class of persons who live in a rosy
twilight and smell of perfumes; all the way he hated and
despised them to the point of torture; and his mind was full of
unshakeable convictions as to the worthlessness of such
people.

Time will pass; the sorrow of Kiríloff will pass away also,
but this conviction – unjust, unworthy of a human heart – will
never pass away, and will remain with the doctor to the day of
his death.

SLEEPYHEAD

SLEEPYHEAD

Night. Nursemaid Varka, aged thirteen, rocks the cradle where baby lies, and murmurs almost inaudibly:

> 'Bayu, bayushki, bayú!
> Nurse will sing a song to you! . . .'

In front of the ikon burns a green lamp; across the room from wall to wall stretches a cord on which hang baby-clothes and a great pair of black trousers. On the ceiling above the lamp shines a great green spot, and the baby-clothes and trousers cast long shadows on the stove, on the cradle, on Varka . . . When the lamp flickers, the spot and shadows move as if from a draught. It is stifling. There is a smell of soup and boots.

The child cries. It has long been hoarse and weak from crying, but still it cries, and who can say when it will be comforted? And Varka wants to sleep. Her eyelids droop, her head hangs, her neck pains her. . . . She can hardly move her eyelids or her lips, and it seems to her that her face is sapless and petrified, and that her head has shrivelled up to the size of a pinhead.

'*Bayu, bayushki, bayú!*' she murmurs, 'Nurse is making pap for you. . . .'

In the stove chirrups a cricket. In the next room behind that door snore Varka's master and the journeyman Athanasius. The cradle creaks plaintively, Varka murmurs – and the two sounds mingle soothingly in a lullaby sweet to the ears of those who lie in bed. But now the music is only irritating and oppressive, for it inclines to sleep, and sleep is impossible. If Varka, which God forbid, were to go to sleep, her master and mistress would beat her.

The lamp flickers. The green spot and the shadows move about, they pass into the half-open, motionless eyes of Varka,

127

and in her half-awakened brain blend in misty images. She
sees dark clouds chasing one another across the sky and crying
like the child. And then a wind blows; the clouds vanish; and
Varka sees a wide road covered with liquid mud; along the
road stretch waggons, men with satchels on their backs crawl
along, and shadows move backwards and forwards; on either
side through the chilly, thick mist are visible hills. And
suddenly the men with the satchels, and the shadows collapse
in the liquid mud. 'Why is this?' asks Varka. 'To sleep, to
sleep!' comes the answer. And they sleep soundly, sleep
sweetly; and on the telegraph wires perch crows, and cry like
the child, and try to awaken them.

'*Bayu, bayushki, bayú.* Nurse will sing a song to you,'
murmurs Varka; and now she sees herself in a dark and stifling
cabin.

On the floor lies her dead father, Yéfim Stépanoff. She
cannot see him, but she hears him rolling from side to side,
and groaning. In his own words he 'has had a rupture.' The
pain is so intense that he cannot utter a single word, and only
inhales air and emits through his lips a drumming sound.

'Bu, bu, bu, bu, bu. . . .'

Mother Pelageya has run to the manor-house to tell the
squire that Yéfim is dying. She has been gone a long time . . .
will she ever return? Varka lies on the stove, and listens to her
father's 'Bu, bu, bu, bu.' And then someone drives up to the
cabin door. It is the doctor, sent from the manor-house where
he is staying as a guest. The doctor comes into the hut; in the
darkness he is invisible, but Varka can hear him coughing and
hear the creaking of the door.

'Bring a light!' he says.

'Bu, bu, bu,' answers Yéfim.

Pelageya runs to the stove and searches for a jar of matches.
A minute passes in silence. The doctor dives into his pockets
and lights a match himself.

'Immediately, *batiushka,* immediately!' cries Pelageya,
running out of the cabin. In a minute she returns with a candle
end.

Yéfim's cheeks are flushed, his eyes sparkle, and his look is
piercing, as if he could see through the doctor and the cabin
wall.

'Well, what's the matter with you?' asks the doctor, bending over him. 'Ah! You have been like this long?'

'What's the matter? The time has come, your honour, to die. . . . I shall not live any longer. . . .'

'Nonsense. . . . We'll soon cure you!'

'As you will, your honour. Thank you humbly . . . only we understand. . . . If we must die, we must die. . . .'

Half an hour the doctor spends with Yéfim; then he rises and says:

'I can do nothing. . . . You must go to the hospital; there they will operate on you. You must go at once . . . without fail! It is late, and they will all be asleep at the hospital . . . but never mind, I will give you a note. . . . Do you hear?'

'*Batiushka,* how can he go to the hospital?' asks Pelageya. 'We have no horse.'

'Never mind, I will speak to the squire, he will lend you one.'

The doctor leaves, the light goes out, and again Varka hears: 'Bu, bu, bu.' In half an hour someone drives up to the cabin. . . . This is the cart for Yéfim to go to hospital in. . . . Yéfim gets ready and goes. . . .

And now comes a clear and fine morning. Pelageya is not at home; she has gone to the hospital to find out how Yéfim is. . . . There is a child crying, and Varka hears someone singing with her own voice:

'*Bayu, bayushki, bayú,* Nurse will sing a song to you. . . .'

Pelageya returns, she crosses herself and whispers:

'Last night he was better, towards morning he gave his soul to God. . . . Heavenly kingdom, eternal rest! . . . They say we brought him too late. . . . We should have done it sooner. . . .'

Varka goes into the wood, and cries, and suddenly someone slaps her on the nape of the neck with such force that her forehead bangs against a birch tree. She lifts her head, and sees before her her master, the shoe-maker.

'What are you doing, scabby?' he asks. 'The child is crying and you are asleep.'

He gives her a slap on the ear; and she shakes her head, rocks the cradle, and murmurs her lullaby. The green spot, the shadows from the trousers and the baby-clothes, tremble, wink at her, and soon again possess her brain. Again she sees a road covered with liquid mud. Men with satchels on their backs, and shadows lie down and sleep soundly. When she looks at them Varka passionately desires to sleep; she would lie down with joy; but mother Pelageya comes along and hurries her. They are going into town to seek situations.

'Give me a kopeck for the love of Christ,' says her mother to everyone she meets. 'Show the pity of God, merciful gentleman!'

'Give me here the child,' cries a well-known voice. 'Give me the child,' repeats the same voice, but this time angrily and sharply. 'You are asleep, beast!'

Varka jumps up, and looking around her remembers where she is; there is neither road, nor Pelageya, nor people, but only, standing in the middle of the room, her mistress who has come to feed the child. While the stout, broad-shouldered woman feeds and soothes the baby, Varka stands still, looks at her, and waits till she has finished.

And outside the window the air grows blue, the shadows fade and the green spot on the ceiling pales. It will soon be morning.

'Take it,' says her mistress buttoning her night-dress. 'It is crying. The evil eye is upon it!'

Varka takes the child, lays it in the cradle, and again begins rocking. The shadows and the green spot fade away, and there is nothing now to set her brain going. But, as before, she wants to sleep, wants passionately to sleep. Varka lays her head on the edge of the cradle and rocks it with her whole body so as to drive away sleep; but her eyelids droop again, and her head is heavy.

'Varka, light the stove!' rings the voice of her master from behind the door.

That is to say: it is at last time to get up and begin the day's work. Varka leaves the cradle, and runs to the shed for wood. She is delighted. When she runs or walks she does not feel the want of sleep as badly as when she is sitting down. She brings in wood, lights the stove, and feels how her petrified face is waking up, and how her thoughts are clearing.

'Varka, get ready the samovar!' cries her mistress.

Varka cuts splinters of wood, and has hardly lighted them and laid them in the samovar when another order comes:

'Varka, clean your master's goloshes!'

Varka sits on the floor, cleans the goloshes, and thinks how delightful it would be to thrust her head into the big, deep golosh, and slumber in it awhile. . . . And suddenly the golosh grows, swells, and fills the whole room. Varka drops the brush, but immediately shakes her head, distends her eyes, and tries to look at things as if they had not grown and did not move in her eyes.

'Varka, wash the steps outside . . . the customers will be scandalised!'

Varka cleans the steps, tidies the room, and then lights another stove and runs into the shop. There is much work to be done, and not a moment free.

But nothing is so tiresome as to stand at the kitchen-table and peel potatoes. Varka's head falls on the table, the potatoes glimmer in her eyes, the knife drops from her hand, and around her bustles her stout, angry mistress with sleeves tucked up, and talks so loudly that her voice rings in Varka's ears. It is torture, too, to wait at table, to wash up, and to sew. There are moments when she wishes, notwithstanding everything around her, to throw herself on the floor and sleep.

The day passes. And watching how the windows darken, Varka presses her petrified temples, and smiles, herself not knowing why. The darkness caresses her drooping eyelids, and promises a sound sleep soon. But towards evening the bootmaker's rooms are full of visitors.

'Varka, prepare the samovar!' cries her mistress.

It is a small samovar, and before the guests are tired of drinking tea, it has to be filled and heated five times. After tea Varka stands a whole hour on one spot, looks at the guests, and waits for orders.

'Varka, run and buy three bottles of beer!'

Varka jumps from her place, and tries to run as quickly as possible so as to drive away sleep.

'Varka, go for vodka! Varka, where is the cork-screw? Varka, clean the herrings!'

At last the guests are gone; the fires are extinguished; master and mistress go to bed.

'Varka, rock the cradle!' echoes the last order.

In the stove chirrups a cricket; the green spot on the ceiling, and the shadows from the trousers and baby-clothes again twinkle before Varka's half-opened eyes, they wink at her, and obscure her brain.

'*Bayu, bayushki, bayú,*' she murmurs, 'Nurse will sing a song to you. . . .'

But the child cries and wearies itself with crying. Varka sees again the muddy road, the men with satchels, Pelageya, and father Yéfim. She remembers, she recognises them all, but in her semi-slumber she cannot understand the force which binds her, hand and foot, and crushes her, and ruins her life. She looks around her, and seeks that force that she may rid herself of it. But she cannot find it. And at last, tortured, she strains all her strength and sight; she looks upward at the winking green spot, and as she hears the cry of the baby, she finds the enemy who is crushing her heart.

The enemy is the child.

Varka laughs. She is astonished. How was it that never before could she understand such a simple thing? The green spot, the shadows, and the cricket, it seems, all smile and are surprised at it.

An idea takes possession of Varka. She rises from the stool, and, smiling broadly with unwinking eyes, walks up and down the room. She is delighted and touched by the thought that she will soon be delivered from the child who has bound her, hand and foot. To kill the child, and then to sleep, sleep, sleep . . .

And smiling and blinking and threatening the green spot with her fingers, Varka steals to the cradle and bends over the child. . . . And having smothered the child she drops on the floor, and, laughing with joy at the thought that she can sleep, in a moment sleeps as soundly as the dead child.

AT THE MANOR

AT THE MANOR

Pavel Ilitch Rashevitch marched up and down the room, stepping softly on the Little Russian parquet, and casting a long shadow on the walls and ceiling; and his visitor, Monsieur Meyer, Examining Magistrate, sat on a Turkish divan, with one leg bent under him, smoked, and listened. It was eleven o'clock, and from the next room came the sound of preparations for supper.

'I don't dispute it for a moment!' said Rashevitch. 'From the point of view of fraternity, equality, and all that sort of thing the swineherd Mitka is as good a man as Goethe or Frederick the Great. But look at it from the point of view of science; have the courage to look actuality straight in the face, and you cannot possibly deny that the white bone* is not a prejudice, not a silly woman's invention. The white bone, my friend, has a natural-historical justification, and to deny it, in my mind, is as absurd as to deny the antlers of a stag. Look at it as a question of fact! You are a jurist, and never studied anything except the humanities, so you may well deceive yourself with illusions as to equality, fraternity, and that sort of thing. But, on my side, I am an incorrigible Darwinian, and for me such words as race, aristocracy, noble blood are no empty sounds.'

Rashevitch was aroused, and spoke with feeling. His eyes glittered, his pince-nez jumped off his nose, he twitched his shoulders nervously, and at the word 'Darwinian' glanced defiantly at the mirror, and with his two hands divided his grey beard. He wore a short, well-worn jacket, and narrow trousers; but the rapidity of his movements and the smartness of the short jacket did not suit him at all, and his big, long-haired, handsome head, which reminded one of a bishop or a venerable poet, seemed to be set on the body of a tall,

* Blue blood.

135

thin, and affected youth. When he opened his legs widely, his long shadow resembled a pair of scissors.

As a rule he loved the sound of his own voice; and it always seemed to him that he was saying something new and original. In the presence of Meyer he felt an unusual elevation of spirits and flow of thought. He liked the magistrate, who enlivened him by his youthful ways, his health, his fine manners, his solidity, and, even more, by the kindly relations which he had established with the family. Speaking generally, Rashevitch was not a favourite with his acquaintances. They avoided him, and he knew it. They declared that he had driven his wife into the grave with his perpetual talk, and called him, almost to his face, a beast and a toad. Meyer alone, being an unprejudiced new-comer, visited him often and willingly, and had even been heard to say that Rashevitch and his daughters were the only persons in the district with whom he felt at home. And Rashevitch reciprocated his esteem – all the more sincerely because Meyer was a young man, and an excellent match for his elder daughter, Zhenya.

And now, enjoying his thoughts and the sound of his own voice, and looking with satisfaction at the stout, well-groomed, respectable figure of his visitor, Rashevitch reflected how he would settle Zhenya for life as the wife of a good man, and, in addition, transfer all the work of managing the estate to his son-in-law's shoulders. It was not particularly agreeable work. The interest had not been paid into the bank for more than two terms, and the various arrears and penalties amounted to over twenty thousand roubles.

'There can hardly be a shadow of doubt,' continued Rashevitch, becoming more and more possessed by his subject, 'that if some Richard the Lion-hearted or Frederick Barbarossa, for instance, a man courageous and magnanimous, has a son, his good qualities will be inherited by the son, together with his bumps; and if this courage and magnanimity are fostered in the son by education and exercise, and he marries a princess also courageous and magnanimous, then these qualities will be transmitted to the grandson, and so on, until they become peculiarities of the species, and descend organically, so to speak, in flesh and blood. Thanks to severe sexual selection, thanks to the fact that noble families instinctively preserve themselves from base alliances, and that young people of position do not marry the devil knows whom, their high spiritual qualities have reproduced themselves from generation to generation, they have been perpetuated, and in the course of ages have become even more perfect and loftier. For all that is good in humanity we are indebted to Nature, to the regular, natural–historical, expedient course of things, strenuously in the course of centuries separating the white bone from the black. Yes, my friend! It is not the potboy's child, the cookmaid's brat who has given us literature, science, art, justice, the ideas of honour and of duty. . . . For all these, humanity is indebted exclusively to the white bone; and in this sense, from the point of view of natural history, worthless Sobakevitch,* merely because he is a white bone, is a million times higher and more useful than the best tradesman, let him endow fifty museums! You may say what you like, but if I refuse to give my hand to the potboy's or the cookmaid's son, by that refusal I preserve from stain the best that is on the earth, and subserve one of the highest destinies of Mother Nature, leading us to perfection. . . .'

Rashevitch stood still, and smoothed down his beard with both hands. His scissors–like shadow stood still also.

'Take our dear Mother Russia!' he continued, thrusting his hands into his pockets, and balancing himself alternately on toes and heels. 'Who are our best people? Take our first–class artists, authors, composers. . . . Who are they? All these, my dear sir, are representatives of the white bone. Pushkin, Gogol, Lermontoff, Turgenev, Tolstoy. . . . Were these cook–maid's children?'

'Gontcharoff was a tradesman,' said Meyer.

'What does that prove? The exception, my friend, proves the rule. And as to the genius of Gontcharoff there can be two opinions. But let us leave names and return to facts. Tell me how you can reply, sir, to the eloquent fact that when the potboy climbs to a higher place than he was born in – when he reaches eminence in literature, in science, in local government,

---

* Sobakevitch, a stupid, coarse country gentleman, is one of the heroes of Gogol's celebrated novel *Dead Souls*.

in law – what have you to say to the fact that Nature herself
intervenes on behalf of the most sacred human rights, and
declares war against him? As a matter of fact, hardly has the
potboy succeeded in stepping into other people's shoes when
he begins to languish, wither, go out of his mind, and
degenerate; and nowhere will you meet so many dwarfs,
psychological cripples, consumptives, and starvelings as
among these gentry. They die away like flies in autumn. And
it is a good thing. If it were not for this salutary degeneration,
not one stone of our civilisation would remain upon another –
the potboy would destroy it all. . . . Be so good as to tell me,
please, what this invasion has given us up to the present time?
What has the potboy brought with him?'

Rashevitch made a mysterious, frightened face, and
continued:

'Never before did our science and literature find themselves
at such a low ebb as now. The present generation, sir, has
neither ideas nor ideals, and all its activity is restricted to an
attempt to tear the last shirt off someone else's back. All your
present-day men who give themselves out as progressive and
incorruptible may be brought for a silver rouble; and modern
intelligent society is distinguished by only one thing, that is,
that if you mix in it you must keep your hand on your pocket,
else it will steal your purse.' Rashevitch blinked and smiled.
'Steal your purse!' he repeated, with a happy laugh. 'And
morals? What morals have we?' Rashevitch glanced at the
door. 'You can no longer be surprised if your wife robs you
and abandons you – that is a mere trifle. At the present day,
my friend, every twelve-year-old girl looks out for a lover;
and all these amateur theatricals and literary evenings are
invented only for the purpose of catching rich *parvenus* as
sweethearts. Mothers sell their daughters, husbands are asked
openly at what price they will sell their wives, and you may
even trade, my friend. . . .'

Up to this Meyer had said nothing, and sat motionless.
Now he rose from the sofa, and looked at the clock.

'Excuse me, Pavel Ilitch,' he said, 'but it's time for me to
go.'

But Rashevitch, who had not finished, took him by the
arm; set him down forcibly upon the sofa, and swore he

should not leave the house without supper. Meyer again sat motionless and listened; but soon began to look at Rashevitch with an expression of doubt and alarm, as if he were only just beginning to understand his character. When at last the maid entered, saying that the young ladies had sent her to say that supper was ready, he sighed faintly, and went out of the study first.

In the dining-room, already at table, sat Rashevitch's daughters, Zhenya and Iraida, respectively aged twenty-four and twenty-two. They were of equal stature, and both black-eyed and very pale. Zhenya had her hair down, but Iraida's was twisted into a high top-knot. Before eating anything each drank a glass of spirits, with an expression meant to imply that they were drinking accidentally, and for the first time in their lives. After this they looked confused, and tittered.

'Don't be silly, girls!' said Rashevitch.

Zhenya and Iraida spoke French to one another and Russian to their father and the visitor. . . . Interrupting one another, and mixing French and Russian, they began to remark that just at this time of the year, that is in August, they used to leave home for the Institute. How jolly that was! But now there was no place to go to for a change, and they lived at the manor-house winter and summer. How tiresome!

'Don't be silly, girls!' repeated Rashevitch.

'In short, that is exactly how things stand,' he said, looking affectionately at the magistrate. 'We, in the goodness and simplicity of our hearts, and from fear of being suspected of retrograde tendencies, fraternise – excuse the expression – with all kinds of human trash, and preach equality and fraternity with upstarts and *nouveaux riches!* Yet if we paused to reflect for a single minute we should see how criminal is our kindness. For all that our ancestors attained to in the course of centuries will be derided and destroyed in a single day by these modern Huns.'

After supper all went into the drawing-room. Zhenya and Iraida lighted the piano candles and got ready their music. . . . But their parent continued to hold forth, and there was no knowing when he would end. Bored and irritated, they looked at their egoist father, for whom, they concluded, the satisfaction of chattering and showing off his brains, was dearer than the future happiness of his daughters. Here was Meyer, the only young man who frequented the house – for the sake, they knew, of tender feminine society – yet the unwearying old man kept possession of him, and never let him escape for a moment.

'Just as western chivalry repelled the onslaught of the Mongols, so must we, before it is too late, combine and strike together at the enemy.' Rashevitch spoke apostolically, and lifted his right hand on high. 'Let me appear before the potboy no longer as plain Pavel Ilitch, but as a strong and menacing Richard the Lion-Heart! Fling your scruples behind you – enough! Let us swear a sacred compact that when the pot-boy approaches we will fling him words of contempt straight in the face! Hands off! Back to your pots! Straight in the face!' In ecstacy, Rashevitch thrust out a bent forefinger, and repeated: 'Straight in the face! In the face! In the face!'

Meyer averted his eyes. 'I cannot tolerate this any longer!' he said.

'And may I ask why?' asked Rashevitch, scenting the beginnings of a prolonged and interesting argument.

'Because I myself am the son of an artisan.'

And having so spoken, Meyer reddened, his neck seemed to swell, and tears sparkled in his eyes.

'My father was a plain working man,' he said in an abrupt, broken voice. 'But I can see nothing bad in that.'

Rashevitch was thunderstruck. In his confusion he looked as if he had been detected in a serious crime; he looked at Meyer with a dumbfounded face, and said not a word. Zhenya and Iraida blushed, and bent over their music. They were thoroughly ashamed of their tactless father. A minute passed in silence, and the situation was becoming unbearable when suddenly a sickly, strained voice – it seemed utterly *mal à propos* – stammered forth the words:

'Yes, I am a tradesman's son, and I am proud of it.'

And Meyer, awkwardly stumbling over the furniture, said good-bye, and walked quickly into the hall, although the trap had not been ordered.

'You will have a dark drive,' stammered Rashevitch, going after him. 'The moon rises late tonight.'

They stood on the steps in the darkness and waited for the horses. It was cold.

'Did you see the falling star?' asked Meyer, buttoning his overcoat.

'In August falling stars are very plentiful.'

When at last the trap drove round to the door, Rashevitch looked attentively at the heavens, and said, with a sigh:

'A phenomenon worthy of the pen of Flammarion. . . .'

Having parted from his guest, he walked up and down the garden, and tried to persuade himself that such a stupid misunderstanding had not really taken place. He was angry, and ashamed of himself. In the first place, he knew that it was extremely tactless and incautious to raise this accursed conversation about the white bone without knowing anything of the origin of his guest. He told himself, with perfect justice, that for him there was no excuse, for he had had a lesson before, having once in a railway carriage set about abusing Germans to fellow-passengers who, it turned out, were themselves Germans. . . . And in the second place he was convinced that Meyer would come no more. These *intellectuels* who have sprung from the people are sensitive, vain, obstinate, and revengeful.

'It is a bad business . . . bad . . . bad!' he muttered, spitting; he felt awkward and disgusted, as if he had just eaten soap. 'It is a bad business!'

Through the open window he could see into the drawing-room where Zhenya with her hair down, pale and frightened, spoke excitedly to her sister. . . . Iraida walked from corner to corner, apparently lost in thought; and then began to speak, also excitedly and with an indignant face. Then both spoke together. Rashevitch could not distinguish a word, but he knew too well the subject of their conversation. Zhenya was grumbling that her father with his eternal chattering drove every decent man from the house, and had today robbed them of their last acquaintance, it might have been husband; and now the poor young man could not find a place in the whole district wherein to rest his soul. And Iraida, if judged correctly from the despairing way in which she raised her arms, lamented bitterly their wearisome life at home and their ruined youth.

Going up to his bedroom, Rashevitch sat on the bed and undressed himself slowly. He felt that he was a persecuted man, and was tormented by the same feeling as though he had eaten soap. He was thoroughly ashamed of himself. When he had undressed he gazed sadly at his long, veined, old-man's legs, and remembered that in the country round he was nicknamed 'the toad,' and that never a conversation passed without making him ashamed of himself. By some extraordinary fatality every discussion ended badly. He began softly, kindly, with good intentions, and called himself genially an 'old student,' an 'idealist,' a 'Don Quixote'. But gradually, and unnoticed by himself, he passed on to abuse and calumny, and, what is more surprising, delivered himself of sincere criticisms of science, art, and morals, although it was twenty years since he had read a book, been farther than the government town, or had any channel for learning what was going on in the world around him. Even when he sat down to write a congratulatory letter he invariably ended by abusing something or somebody. And as he reflected upon this, it seemed all the more strange, since he knew himself in reality to be a sensitive, lachrymose old man. It seemed almost as if he were possessed by an unclean spirit which filled him against his will with hatred and grumbling.

'A bad business!' he sighed, getting into bed. 'A bad business!'

His daughters also could not sleep. Laughter and lamentation resounded through the house. Zhenya was in hysterics. Shortly afterwards Iraida also began to cry. More than once the barefooted housemaid ran up and down the corridor.

'What a scandal!' muttered Rashevitch, sighing, and turning uneasily from side to side. 'A bad business!'

He slept, but nightmares gave him no peace. He thought that he was standing in the middle of the room, naked, and tall, as a giraffe, thrusting out his forefinger, and saying:

'In the face! In the face! In the face!'

He awoke in terror, and the first thing he remembered was, that last evening a serious misunderstanding had occurred, and that Meyer would never visit him again. He remembered then that the interest had to be lodged in the bank, that he must find husbands for his daughters, and that he must eat and drink. He remembered sickness, old age, and unpleasantness; that winter would soon be upon him, and that there was no wood. . . .

At nine o'clock he dressed slowly, then drank some tea and ate two large slices of bread and butter. . . . His daughters did not come down to breakfast, they did not wish to see his face; and this offended him. For a time he lay upon the study sofa, and then sat at his writing-table and began to write a letter to his daughters. His hand trembled and his eyes itched. He wrote that he was now old, that nobody wanted him, and that nobody loved him; so he begged his children to forget him, and when he died, to bury him in a plain, deal coffin, without ceremony, or to send his body to Kharkoff for dissection in the Anatomical Theatre. He felt that every line breathed malice and affection . . . but he could not stop himself, and wrote on and on and on . . .

'The toad!' rang a voice from the next room; it was the voice of his elder daughter, an indignant, hissing voice. 'The toad!'

'The toad!' repeated the younger in echo. 'The toad!'

AN EVENT

AN EVENT

Morning. Through the frosty lacework which covered the window-panes a host of bright sunrays burst into the nursery. Vanya, a boy of six, with a nose like a button, and his sister Nina, aged four, curly-headed, chubby, and small for her age, awoke, and glared angrily at one another through the bars of their cots.

'Fie!' cried nurse. 'For shame, children! All the good people have finished breakfast, and you can't keep your eyes open . . .'

The sun-rays played merrily on the carpet, on the walls, on nurse's skirt, and begged the children to play with them. But the children took no notice. They had awakened on the wrong side of their beds. Nina pouted, made a wry face, and drawled:

'Te-ea! Nurse, te-ea!'

Vanya frowned, and looked about for an opportunity to pick a quarrel and roar. He had just blinked his eyes and opened his mouth, when out of the dining-room rang mother's voice:

'Don't forget to give the cat milk; she has got kittens.'

Vanya and Nina lengthened their faces and looked questioningly at one another. Then both screamed, jumped out of bed, and, making the air ring with deafening yells, ran barefooted in their nightdresses into the kitchen.

'The cat's got kittens! The cat's got kittens!' they screamed.

In the kitchen under a bench stood a small box, a box which Stepan used for coke when he lighted the stove. Out of this box gazed the cat. Her grey face expressed extreme exhaustion, her green eyes with their little black pupils looked languishing and sentimental. . . . From her face it was plain that to complete her happiness only one thing was lacking, and that was the presence of the father of her children, to whom she had given herself heart and soul. She attempted to mew, and opened her mouth wide, but only succeeded in making a hissing sound. . . . The kittens squealed.

The children squatted on the ground in front of the box, and, without moving, but holding their breath, looked at the cat. . . . They were astonished and thunderstruck, and did not hear the grumbling of the pursuing nurse. In the eyes of both shone sincere felicity.

In the up-bringing of children, domestic animals play an unnoticed but unquestionably beneficent part. Which of us cannot remember strong but magnanimous dogs, lazy lapdogs, birds who died in captivity, dull-witted but haughty turkey-cocks, kindly old-lady-cats who forgave us when we stood on their tails for a joke and caused them intense pain? It might even be argued that the patience, faithfulness, all-forgivingness and sincerity of our domestic animals act on the childish brain much more powerfully than the long lectures of dry and pale Karl Karlovitch, or the obscure explanations of the governess who tries to prove to children that water is composed of hydrogen and oxygen.

'What duckies!' cried Nina, overflowing with gay laughter. 'They're exactly like mice!'

'One, two, three!' counted Vanya. 'Three kittens. That is one for me, one for you, and one for somebody else.'

'Murrrrm . . . murrrrm,' purred the mother, flattered by so much attention. 'Murrrrm!'

When they had looked for a while at the kittens, the children took them from under the cat and began to smooth them down, and afterwards, not satisfied with this, laid them in the skirts of their nightdresses and ran from one room to another.

'Mamma, the cat's got kittens!' they cried.

Mother sat in the dining-room, talking to a stranger. When she saw her children unwashed, undressed, with their nightdresses on high, she got red, and looked at them severely.

'Drop your nightdresses, shameless!' she said. 'Run away at once, or you'll be punished.'

But the children paid no attention either to their mother's threats or to the presence of the stranger. They put the kittens down on the carpet and raised a deafening howl. Beside them walked the old cat, and mewed imploringly. When in a few minutes the children were dragged off to the nursery to dress, say their prayers, and have their breakfast, they were full of a passionate wish to escape from these prosaic duties and return to the kitchen.

Ordinary occupations and games were quite forgotten. From the moment of their appearance in the world the kittens obscured everything, and took their place as the living novelty and heart-swelling of the day. If you had offered Vanya or Nina a bushel of sweets for each kitten, or a thousand threepenny-bits, they would have rejected the offer without a moment's hesitation. Till dinner-time, in spite of the warm protests of nurse and the cook, they sat in the kitchen and played with the kittens. Their faces were serious, concentrated, and expressive of anxiety. They had to provide not only for the present condition, but also for the future of the kittens. So they decided that one kitten would remain at home with the old cat, so as to console its mother, that the other would be sent to the country-house, and that the third would live in the cellar and eat the rats.

'But why can't they see?' asked Nina. 'They have blind eyes, like beggars.'

The question troubled Vanya. He did his best to open one of the kitten's eyes, for a long time puffed and snuffled, but the operation was fruitless. And another circumstance worried the children extremely – the kittens obstinately refused the proffered meat and milk. Everything that was laid before their little snouts was eaten up by their grey mother.

'Let's build houses for the kittens,' proposed Vanya. 'We will make them live in different houses, and the cat will pay them visits. . . .' In three corners of the kitchen they set up old hat-boxes. But the separation of the family seemed premature; the old cat, preserving on her face her former plaintive and sentimental expression, paid visits to all the boxes and took her children home again.

'The cat is their mother,' said Vanya, 'but who is their father?'

'Yes, who is their father?' repeated Nina.

'They can't live without a father.'

For a long time Vanya and Nina discussed the problem, who should be father of the kittens. In the end their choice fell

on a big dark-red horse whose tail had been torn off. He had
been cast away in the store-room under the staircase, together
with the remnants of other toys that had outlived their
generation. They took the horse from the store-room and
stood it beside the box.

'Look out!' they warned him. 'Stand there and see that they
behave themselves.'

All this was said and done in a serious manner, and with an
expression of solicitude. Outside the box and the kittens,
Vanya and Nina would recognise no other world. Their
happiness had no bounds. But they were destined to endure
moments of unutterable torture.

Just before dinner Vanya sat in his father's study, and
looked thoughtfully at the table. Near the lamp, across a
packet of stamped paper, crawled a kitten. Vanya watched its
movements attentively, and occasionally poked it in the snout
with a pencil. . . . Suddenly, as if springing out of the floor,
appeared his father.

'What is this?' cried an angry voice.

'It is . . . it is a kitten, papa.'

'I'll teach you to bring your kittens here, wretched child!
Look what you've done! Ruined a whole package of paper!'

To Vanya's astonishment, his father did not share his
sympathy with kittens, and, instead of going into raptures and
rejoicing, pulled Vanya's ear, and cried:

'Stepan, take away this abomination!'

At dinner the scandal was repeated. . . . During the second
course the diners suddenly heard a faint squeal. They began to
search for the cause, and found a kitten under Nina's pinafore.

'Nina! Go out of the room!' said her father angrily. 'The
kittens must be thrown into the sink this minute! I won't
tolerate these abominations in the house!'

Vanya and Nina were terror-stricken. Death in the sink,
apart from its cruelty, threatened to deprive the cat and the
wooden horse of their children, to desolate the box, to destroy
all their plans for the future – that beautiful future when one
kitten would console its old mother, the second live in the
country, and the third catch rats in the cellar. . . . They began
to cry, and implored mercy for the kittens. Their father
consented to spare them, but only on the condition that the

children should not dare to go into the kitchen or touch the kittens again.

After dinner, Vanya and Nina wandered from one room to another and lauguished. The prohibition on going to the kitchen drove them to despair. They refused sweets; and were naughty, and rude to their mother. In the evening when Uncle Petrusha came they took him aside and complained of their father for threatening to throw the kittens into the sink.

'Uncle Petrusha,' they implored, 'tell mamma to put the kittens in the nursery. . . . Do!'

'Well . . . all right!' said their uncle, tearing himself away. 'Agreed!'

Uncle Petrusha seldom came alone. Along with him came Nero, a big black dog, of Danish origin, with hanging ears and a tail as hard as a stick. Nero was silent, morose, and altogether taken up with his own dignity. To the children he paid not the slightest attention; and, when he marched past them, knocked his tail against them as if they were chairs. Vanya and Nina detested him from the bottom of their hearts. But on this occasion practical considerations gained the upper hand over mere sentiment.

'Do you know what, Nina?' said Vanya, opening wide his eyes. 'Let us make Nero the father instead of the horse! The horse is dead, but Nero's alive.'

The whole evening they waited impatiently for their father to sit down to his game of *vint*, when they might take Nero to the kitchen without being observed. . . . At last father sat down to his cards, mother bustled around the samovar, and did not see the children. . . . The happy moment had come!

'Come!' whispered Vanya to his sister.

But at that very moment Stepan came into the room, and said with a grin:

'I beg your pardon, ma'am. Nero has eaten the kittens.'

Nina and Vanya turned pale, and looked with horror at Stepan.

'Yes, ma'am . . .' grinned the servant. 'He went straight to the box and gobbled them up.'

The children expected everyone in the house to rise in alarm and fly at the guilty Nero. But their parents sat calmly in their chairs, and only expressed surprise at the appetite of the big dog. Father and mother laughed. . . . Nero marched up to the table, flourished his tail, and licked himself complacently. . . . Only the cat seemed disturbed; she stretched out her tail, and walked about the room looking suspiciously at everyone and mewing plaintively.

'Now, children, time for bed! Ten o'clock!' cried mother.

And Vanya and Nina were put to bed, where they wept over the injured cat, whose life had been desolated by cruel, nasty, unpunished Nero.

WARD NO. 6

WARD NO. 6

I

At the side of the hospital yard stands a large wing, nearly surrounded by a forest of burdocks, nettles, and wild hemp. The roof is red, the chimney is on the point of tumbling, the steps are rotten and overgrown with grass, and of the plaster only traces remain. The front gazes at the hospital, the back looks into the fields, from which it is separated only by a grey, spiked fence. The spikes with their sharp points sticking upwards, the fence, the wing itself, have that melancholy, God-forsaken air which is seen only in hospitals and prisons.

If you are not afraid of being stung by nettles, come along the narrow path, and see what is going on inside. Open the hall-door and enter the hall. Here, against the walls and around the stove, are heaped whole mountains of rubbish. Mattresses, old tattered dressing-gowns, trousers, blue-striped shirts, worn-out footgear, all good-for-nothing, lie in tangled and crushed heaps, rot, and exhale a suffocating smell.

On the top of this rubbish heap, pipe eternally in mouth, lies the watchman Nikita, an old soldier. His face is coarse and drink-sodden, his hanging eye-brows give him the appearance of a sheep-dog, he is small and sinewy, but his carriage is impressive and his fists are strong. He belongs to that class of simple, expeditious, positive, and dull persons, who above all things in the world worship order, and find in this a justification of their existence. He beats his charges in the face, in the chest, in the back, in short, wherever his fists chance to strike; and he is convinced that without this beating there would be no order in the universe.

After you pass through Nikita's hall, you enter the large, roomy dormitory which takes up the rest of the wing. In this room the walls are painted a dirty blue, the ceiling is black with soot like the ceiling of a chimneyless hut; it is plain that in winter the stove smokes, and the air is suffocating. The windows are disfigured with iron bars, the floor is damp and splintered, there is a smell of sour cabbage, a smell of unsnuffed wicks, a smell of bugs and ammonia. And at the moment of entry all these smells produce upon you the impression that you have entered a cage of wild beasts.

Around the room stand beds, screwed to the floor. Sitting or lying on them, dressed in blue dressing-gowns, and wearing nightcaps after the manner of our forefathers, are men. It is the lunatic asylum, and these are the lunatics.

There are only five patients. One is of noble birth, the others are men of lower origin. The nearest to the door, a tall, thin man of the petty trading class, looks fixedly at one point: He has a red moustache and tear-stained eyes, and supports his head on one hand. In the books of the asylum his complaint is described as hypochondria; in reality, he is suffering from progressive paralysis. Day and night he mourns, shakes his head, sighs, and smiles bitterly. In conversation he seldom joins, and usually refuses to answer questions. He eats and drinks mechanically. Judged by his emaciation, his flushed cheeks, and his painful, hacking cough, he is wasting away from consumption.

Beside him is a little, active old man with a pointed beard, and the black, fuzzy hair of a negro. He spends all day in walking from window to window, or sitting on his bed, with legs doubled underneath him as if he were a Turk. He is as tireless as a bullfinch, and all day chirrups, titters, and sings in a low voice. His childish gaiety and lively character are shown also at night, when he rises to 'pray to God,' that is, to beat his breast with his clenched fists, and pick at the doors. This is Moséika, a Jew and an idiot. He went out of his mind twenty years ago when his cap factory was destroyed by fire.

Of all the captives in Ward No. 6, he alone has permission to leave the asylum, and he is even allowed to wander about the yard and the streets. This privilege, which he has enjoyed for many years, was probably accorded to him as the oldest inmate of the asylum, and as a quiet, harmless fool, the jester of the town, who may be seen in the streets surrounded by dogs and little boys. Wrapped in his old dressing-gown, with a ridiculous nightcap and slippers, sometimes barefooted, and generally without his trousers, he walks the streets, stopping at doorways and entering small shops to beg for kopecks. Sometimes he is given *kvas*, sometimes bread, sometimes a kopeck, so that he returns to the ward wealthy and sated. But all that he brings home is taken by Nikita for his own particular benefit. The old soldier does this roughly and angrily, turning out the Jew's pockets, calling God to witness that he will never allow him outside the asylum again, and swearing that to him disorder is the most detestable thing in the world.

Moséika loves to make himself useful to others. He fetches water for his companions, tucks them in when they go to bed, promises to bring each a kopeck when he next returns from the town, and to make them new caps. He feeds with a spoon his paralytic neighbour on the left; and all this he does, not out of sympathy for others or for consideration of humanity, but from a love of imitation, and in a sort of involuntary subjection to his neighbour on the right, Iván Gromof.

Iván Dmítritch Gromof is a man of thirty-three years of age. He is a noble by birth, and has been an usher in the law courts, and a government secretary; but now he suffers from the mania of persecution. He lies upon his bed twisted into a lump resembling a roll of bread, or marches from corner to corner for the sake of motion. He is always in a state of excitement and agitation; and seems strained by some dull, indefinable expectation. It needs but the slightest rustle in the hall, the slightest noise in the yard, to make him raise his head and listen intently. Is it for him they are coming? Are they searching for him? And his face immediately takes on an expression of restlessness and repulsion.

There is something attractive about his broad, high cheek-boned face, which reflects, as a mirror, the tortured wrestlings and eternal terror of his mind. His grimaces are strange and sickly; but the delicate lines engraven on his face by sincere suffering express reason and intelligence, and his eyes burn with a healthy and passionate glow. There is something attractive also in his character, in his politeness, his attentiveness, and in the singular delicacy of his bearing towards everyone except Nikita. If his neighbour drops a spoon or a button he jumps immediately out of bed and picks it up. When he wakes he invariably says, 'Good morning!' to his companions; and every evening on going to bed wishes them 'good night!'

But madness shows itself in other things besides his grimaces and continual mental tension. In the evening he wraps himself in his dressing-gown, and, trembling all over, and chattering his teeth, he walks from corner to corner, and in between the beds. He seems to be in a state of fever. From his sudden stoppages and strange looks at his fellow-prisoners it is plain that he has something very serious to say; but no doubt, remembering that they will neither listen nor understand, he says nothing, shakes his head impatiently, and continues his walk. But at last the desire to speak conquers all other considerations, and he gives way, and speaks passionately. His words are incoherent, gusty, and delirious; he cannot always be understood; but the sound of his voice expresses some exceptional goodness. In every word you hear the madman and the man. He speaks of human baseness, of violence trampling over truth, of the beautiful life on earth that is to come, and of the barred windows which remind him every moment of the folly and cruelty of the strong. And he hums medleys of old but forgotten songs.

II

Fifteen years before, in his own house, in the best street in the town, lived an official named Gromof – a solid and prosperous man. Gromof had two sons, Sergéi and Iván. Sergéi, when a student in the fourth class, was seized with consumption and died; and his death was the first of a series of misfortunes which overtook the Gromofs. A week after Sergéi's death his old father was tried for forgery and misappropriation of public moneys, and soon afterwards died of typhus in the prison infirmary. His house and all his belongings were sold by auction, and Iván Dmítritch and his mother remained without a penny.

When his father was alive, Iván Dmítritch studied at St. Petersburg University, received an allowance of sixty or seventy roubles a month, and had no idea of the meaning of poverty. Now he had to change his whole life. From early morning till late at night he gave cheap lessons to students and copied documents, yet starved, for all his earnings went to support his mother. The life was impossible, and Iván Dmítritch ruined his health and spirits, threw up his university studies, and returned home. Through interest he obtained an appointment as usher in the district school; but he was disliked by his colleagues, failed to get on with the pupils, and gave up the post. His mother died. For six months he lived without resources, eating black bread and drinking water, until at last he obtained an appointment as Usher of the Court. This duty he fulfilled until he was discharged owing to illness.

Never, even in his student days, had he had the appearance of a strong man. He was pale, thin, and sensitive to cold; he ate little and slept badly. A single glass of wine made him giddy and sent him into hysterics. His disposition impelled him to seek companionship, but thanks to his irritable and suspicious character he never became intimate with anyone, and had no friends. Of his fellow-citizens he always spoke with contempt, condemning as disgusting and repulsive their gross ignorance and torpid, animal life. He spoke in a tenor voice, loudly and passionately, and always seemed to be in a sincere state of indignation, excitement, or rapture. However he began a conversation, it ended always in one way – in a lament that the town was stifling and tiresome, that its people had no high interests, but led a dull, unmeaning life, varied only by violence, coarse debauchery and hypocrisy; that scoundrels were fed and clothed while honest men ate crusts; that the town was crying out for schools, honest newspapers, a theatre, public lectures, a union of intellectual forces; and that the time had come for the townspeople to awaken to, and be shocked at, the state of affairs. In his judgments of men he laid on his colours thickly, using only white and black, and recognising no gradations; for him humanity was divided into two sections, honest men and rogues – there was nothing between. Of woman and woman's love he spoke passionately and with rapture. But he had never been in love.

In the town, notwithstanding his nervous character and censorious temper, he was loved, and called caressingly

'Vanya.' His innate delicacy, his attentiveness, his neatness, his moral purity, his worn coat, his sickly appearance, the misfortunes of his family, inspired in all feelings of warmth and compassion. Besides, he was educated and well-read; in the opinion of the townsAn he knew everything; and occupied among them the place of a walking reference-book. He read much. He would sit for hours at the club, pluck nervously at his beard, and turn over the pages of books and magazines – by his face it might be seen that he was not reading but devouring. Yet reading was apparently merely one of his nervous habits, for with equal avidity he read everything that fell into his hands, even old newspapers and calendars. At home he always read, lying down.

III

One autumn morning. Iván Dmítritch, with the collar of his coat turned up, trudged through the mud to the house of a certain tradesman to receive money due on a writ of execution. As always in the morning, he was in a gloomy mood. Passing through a lane, he met two convicts in chains and with them four warders armed with rifles. Iván Dmítritch had often met convicts before, and they had awakened in him a feeling of sympathy and confusion. But this meeting produced upon him an unusual impression. It suddenly occurred to him that he too might be shackled and driven through the mud to prison. Having finished his work, he was returning home when he met a police-inspector, an acquaintance, who greeted him and walked with him a few yards down the street. This seemed to him for some reason suspicious. At home visions of convicts and of soldiers armed with rifles haunted him all day, and an inexplicable spiritual dread prevented him from reading or concentrating his mind. In the evening he sat without a fire, and lay awake all night thinking how he also might be arrested, manacled, and flung into prison. He knew that he had committed no crime, and was quite confident that he would never commit murder, arson, or robbery; but then, he remembered, how easy it was to commit a crime by accident or involuntarily, and how common were convictions on false evidence and owing to judicial errors! And in the present state of human affairs how probable, how little to be wondered at, were judicial errors! Men who witness the sufferings of others only from a professional standpoint; for instance, judges, policemen, doctors, became hardened to such a degree that even if they wished otherwise they could not resist the habit of treating accused persons formally; they got to resemble those peasants who kill sheep and calves in their back-yards without even noticing the blood. In view of the soulless relationship to human personality which everywhere obtains, all that a judge thinks of is the observance of certain formalities, and then all is over, and an innocent man perhaps deprived of his civil rights or sent to the galleys. Who indeed would expect justice or intercession in this dirty, sleepy little town, two hundred versts from the nearest railway? And indeed was it not ridiculous to expect justice when society regards every form of violence as rational, expedient, and necessary; and when an act of common mercy such as the acquittal of an accused man calls forth an explosion of unsatisfied vindictiveness!

Next morning Iván Dmítrich awoke in terror with drops of cold sweat on his forehead. He felt convinced that he might be arrested at any moment. That the evening's gloomy thoughts had haunted him so persistently, he concluded, must mean that there was some ground for his apprehensions. Could such thoughts come into his head without cause?

A policeman walked slowly past the window; that must mean something. Two men in plain clothes stopped outside the gate, and stood without saying a word. Why were they silent?

For a time, Iván Dmítritch spent his days and nights in torture. Every man who passed the window or entered the yard was a spy or detective. Every day at twelve o'clock the Chief Constable drove through the street on his way from his suburban house to the Department of Police, and every day it seemed to Iván Dmítritch that the Constable was driving with unaccustomed haste, and that there was a peculiar expression on his face; he was going, in short, to announce that a great criminal had appeared in the town. Iván Dmítritch shuddered at every sound, trembled at every knock at the yard-gate, and was in torment when any strange man visited his landlady. When he met a gendarme in the street, he smiled, whistled, and tried to assume an indifferent air. For whole nights, expecting arrest, he never closed his eyes, but snored carefully so that his landlady might think he was asleep; for if a man did not sleep at night it meant that he was tormented by the gnawings of conscience, and that might be taken as a clue. Reality and healthy reasoning convinced him that his fears were absurd and psychopathic, and that, regarded from a broad standpoint, there was nothing very terrible in arrest and imprisonment for a man whose conscience was clean. But the more consistently and logically he reasoned the stronger grew his spiritual torture; his efforts reminded him of the efforts of a pioneer to hack a path through virgin forest, the harder he worked with the hatchet the thicker and stronger became the undergrowth. So in the end, seeing that his efforts were useless, he ceased to struggle, and gave himself up to terror and despair.

He avoided others and became more and more solitary in his habits. His duties had always been detestable, now they became intolerable. He imagined that someone would hide money in his pockets and then denounce him for taking bribes, that he would make mistakes in official documents which were equivalent to forgery, or that he would lose the money entrusted to him. Never was his mind so supple and ingenious as when he was engaged in inventing various reasons for fearing for his freedom and honour. On the other hand, his interest in the outside world decreased correspondingly, he lost his passion for books, and his memory daily betrayed him.

Next spring when the snow had melted, the semi-decomposed corpses of an old woman and a boy, marked with indications of violence, were found in a ravine beside the graveyard. The townspeople talked of nothing but the discovery and the problem: who were the unknown murderers? In order to avert suspicion, Iván Dmítritch walked about the streets and smiled; and when he met his acquaintances, first grew pale and then blushed, and declared vehemently that there was no more detestable crime than the killing of the weak and defenceless. But this pretence soon exhausted him, and after consideration he decided that the best thing he could do was to hide in his landlady's cellar. In the cellar therefore, chilled to the bone, he remained all day, all next night, and yet another day, after which, waiting until it was dark, he crept secretly back to his room. Till daylight he stood motionless in the middle of the room, and listened. At sunrise a number of artisans rang at the gate. Iván Dmítritch knew very well that they had come to put up a new stove in the kitchen; but his terror suggested that they were constables in disguise. He crept quietly out of his room, and overcome by panic, without cap or coat, fled down the street. Behind him ran barking dogs, a woman called after him, in his ears the wind whistled, and it seemed to him that the scattered violences of the whole world had united and were chasing him through the town.

He was captured and brought home. His landlady sent for a doctor. Doctor Andréi Yéfimitch Rágin, of whom we shall hear again, prescribed cold compresses for his head, ordered him to take drops of bay rum, and went away saying that he would come no more, as it was not right to prevent people going out of their minds. So, as there were no means of treating him at home, Iván Dmítritch was sent to hospital, and put into the ward for sick men. He did not sleep at night, was unruly, and disturbed his neighbours, so that soon, by arrangement with Doctor Andréi Yéfimitch, he was transferred to Ward No. 6.

Before a year had passed, the townspeople had quite forgotten Iván Dmítritch; and his books, piled up in a sledge by his landlady and covered with a curtain, were torn to pieces by children.

IV

Iván Dmítritch's neighbour on the left, I have already said, was the Jew Moséika; his neighbour on the right was a fat, almost globular muzhik with a dull, meaningless face. This torpid, gluttonous, and uncleanly animal had long lost all capacity for thought and feeling. He exhaled a sharp, suffocating smell. When Nikita was obliged to attend on him he used to beat him terribly, beat him with all his strength and without regard for his own fists; and it was not this violence which was so frightful – the terror of that was mitigated by custom – but the fact that the stupefied animal made no answer to the blows either by sound or movement or even by expression in his eyes, but merely rocked from side to side like a heavy cask.

The fifth and last occupant of Ward No. 6 was a townsman who had served once as a sorter in the Post Office. He was a little, thin, fair-headed man, with a kindly, but somewhat cunning face. Judged by his clever, tranquil eyes, which looked out on the world frankly and merrily, he was the possessor of some valuable and pleasant secret. Under his pillow and mattress he had something hidden which he refused to show to anyone, not out of fear of losing it, but out of shame. Occasionally he walked to the window, and turning his back upon his fellow-prisoners, held something to his breast, and looked earnestly at it; but if anyone approached he became confused and hid it away. But it was not hard to guess his secret.

'Congratulate me!' he used to say to Iván Dmítritch. 'I have been decorated with the Stanislas of the second degree with a star. As a rule the second degree with a star is given only to foreigners, but for some reason they have made an exception in my case.' And then, shrugging his shoulders as if in doubt, he would add: 'That is something you never expected, you must admit.'

'I understand nothing about it,' answered Iván Dmítritch, gloomily.

'Do you know what I shall get sooner or later?' continued the ex-sorter, winking slyly. 'I shall certainly receive the Swedish Pole Star. An order of that kind is worth trying for. A white cross and a black ribbon. It is very handsome.'

In no other place in the world, probably, is life so monotonous as in the wing. In the morning the patients, with the exception of the paralytic and the fat muzhik, wash themselves in a great bucket which is placed in the hall, and dry themselves in the skirts of their dressing-gowns. After this they drink tea out of tin mugs brought by Nikita from the hospital. At midday they dine on *shtchi* made with sour cabbage, and porridge, and in the evening they sup on the porridge left over from dinner. Between meals they lie down, sleep, look out of the windows, and walk from corner to corner.

And so on every day. Even the ex-sorter talks always of the same decorations.

Fresh faces are seldom seen in Ward No. 6. Years ago the doctor gave orders that no fresh patients should be admitted, and in this world people rarely visit lunatic asylums for pleasure.

But once every two months comes Semión Lazaritch the barber. With Nikita's assistance, he cuts the patients hair; and on the consternation of the victims every time they see his drunken, grinning face, there is no need to dwell.

With this exception no one ever enters the ward. From day to day the patients are condemned to see only Nikita. But at last a strange rumour obtained circulation in the hospital. It was rumoured the doctor had begun to pay visits to Ward No. 6.

V

It was indeed a strange rumour!

Doctor Andréi Yéfimitch Rágin was a remarkable man in his way. In early youth, so they said, he was very pious, and intended to make a career in the Church. But when in the year 1863 he finished his studies in the gymnasium and prepared to enter the Ecclesiastical Academy, his father, a surgeon and a doctor of medicine, poured ridicule on these intentions, and declared categorically that if Andréi became a priest he would disown him for ever. Whether this story is true or not it is impossible to say, but it is certain that Andréi Yéfimitch more than once admitted that he had never felt any vocation for medicine or, indeed, for specialised sciences at all.

Certain it is, also, that he never became a priest, but completed a course of study in the medical faculty of his university. He showed no particular trace of godliness, and at the beginning of his medical career was as little like a priest as at the end.

In appearance he was as heavy and rudely built as a peasant. His bearded face, his straight hair, and his strong, awkward build recalled some innkeeper on a main road – incontinent and stubborn. He was tall and broad-shouldered, and had enormous feet, and hands with which, it seemed, he could easily crush the life out of a man's body. Yet his walk was noiseless, cautious, and insinuating; and when he met anyone in a narrow passage he was always the first to step aside, and to say – not as might be expected in a bass voice – in a soft, piping tenor: 'Excuse me!'

On his neck Andréi Yéfimitch had a small tumour which forbade his wearing starched collars; he always wore a soft linen or print shirt. Indeed, in no respect did he dress like a doctor; he wore the same suit for ten years, and when he did buy new clothing – at a Jew's store – it always looked as worn and crumpled as his old clothes. In one and the same frock-coat he received his patients, dined, and attended entertainments; and this not from penuriousness but from a genuine contempt for appearances.

When Andréi Yéfimitch first came to the town to take up his duties as physician to the hospital, that 'charitable institution' was in a state of inconceivable disorder. In the wards, in the corridors, and even in the open air of the yard it was impossible to breathe owing to the stench. The male attendants, the nurses and their children, slept in the dormitories together with the patients. It was complained that the hospital was becoming uninhabitable owing to the invasion of beetles, bugs, and mice. In the surgical department there were only two scalpels, nowhere was there a thermometer, and the baths were used for storing potatoes in. The superintendent, the housekeeper, and the feldscher robbed the sick, and of the former doctor, Andréi Yéfimitch's predecessor, it was said that he sold the hospital spirits secretly, and kept up a whole harem recruited from among the nurses and female patients. In the town these scandals were well-known and even exaggerated; but the townspeople were indifferent, and even excused the abuses on the ground that the patients were all either petty tradespeople or peasants who lived at home among conditions so much worse that they had no right to complain; such gentry, they added, must not expect to be fed on grouse! Others argued that as no small town had sufficient resources to support a good hospital without subsidies from the Zemstvo, they might thank God they had a bad one; and the Zemstvo refused to open a hospital in the town on the ground that there was already one.

When he inspected the hospital for the first time Andréi Yéfimitch saw at once that the whole institution was hopelessly bad, and in the highest degree dangerous to the health of the inmates. He concluded that the best thing to do was to discharge the patients and to close the hospital. But he knew that to effect this his wish alone was not enough; and he reasoned that if the physical and moral uncleanliness were driven from one place it would merely be transplanted to another; it was necessary, in fact, to wait until it cleaned itself out. To these considerations he added that if people opened a hospital and tolerated its abuses they must have need of it; and, no doubt, such abominations were necessary, and in the course of time would evolve something useful, as good soil results from manuring. And, indeed, on this earth there is nothing good that has not had evil germs in its beginnings.

Having taken up his duties, therefore, Andréi Yéfimitch looked upon the abuses with apparent indifference. He merely asked the servants and nurses not to sleep in the wards, and bought two cases of instruments; but he allowed the superintendent, the housekeeper, and the feldscher to remain in their positions.

Andréi Yéfimitch was passionately enamoured of intellect and honesty, but he had neither the character nor the confidence in his own powers necessary to establish around himself an intelligent and honest life. To command, to prohibit, to insist, he had never learned. It seemed almost that he had sworn an oath never to raise his voice or to use the imperative mood. . . . Even to use the words 'give' or bring' was difficult for him. When he felt hungry, he coughed irresolutely and said to his cook, 'Suppose I were to have a cup of tea,' or 'I was thinking about dining.' To tell the superintendent that he must cease his robberies, to dismiss him, or to abolish altogether his parasitical office he had not the strength. When he was deceived or flattered, or handed accounts for signature which he knew to have been falsified, he would redden all over and feel guilty, yet sign the accounts; and when the patients complained that they were hungry or had been ill-treated by the nurses, he merely got confused, and stammered guiltily:

'Very well, very well, I will investigate the matter. . . . No doubt there is some misunderstanding. . . .'

At first Andréi Yéfimitch worked very zealously. He attended to patients from morning until dinner-time, performed operations, and even occupied himself with obstetrics. He gained a reputation for exceptional skill in the treatment of women and children. But he soon began visibly to weary of the monotony and uselessness of his work. One day he would receive thirty patients, the next day the number had grown to thirty-five, the next day to forty, and so on from day to day, from year to year. Yet the death-rate in the town did not decrease, and the number of patients never grew less. To give any real assistance to forty patients in the few hours between morning and dinner-time was physically impossible; in other words, he became an involuntary deceiver. The twelve thousand persons received every year, he reasoned, were therefore twelve thousand dupes. To place the serious cases in the wards and treat them according to the rules of medical science was impossible, because there were no rules and no science; whereas if he left philosophy and followed the regulations pedantically as other doctors did, he would still be in difficulty, for in the first place were needed cleanliness and fresh air, and not filth; wholesome food, and not *shtchi* made of stinking sour cabbage; and honest assistants, not thieves.

And, indeed, why hinder people dying, if death is the normal and lawful end of us all? What does it matter whether some tradesman or petty official lives, or does not live, an extra five years? We pretend to see the object of medical science in its mitigation of suffering, but we cannot but ask ourselves the question: Why should suffering be mitigated? In the first place, we are told that suffering leads men to perfection; and in the second, it is plain that if men were really able to alleviate their sufferings with pills and potions, they would abandon that religion and philosophy in which until now they had found not only consolation, but even happiness. Pushkin suffered agonising torment before his death; Heine

lay for years in a state of paralysis. Why, then, interfere with
the sufferings of some mere Andréi Yéfimitch or Matrena
Savishin, whose lives are meaningless, and would be as
vacuous as the life of the amœba if it were not for suffering?

Defeated by such arguments, Andréi Yéfimitch dropped his
hands upon his knees, and ceased his daily attendances at the
hospital.

VI

His life passed thus. At eight in the morning he rose and took
his breakfast. After that he either sat in his study and read, or
visited the hospital. In the hospital in a narrow, dark corridor
waited the out-patients. With heavy boots clattering on the
brick floor, servants and nurses ran past them; emaciated
patients in dressing-gowns staggered by; and vessels of filth,
and corpses were carried out. And among them children cried
and draughts blew. Andréi Yéfemitch knew well that to the
fevered, the consumptive, and the impressionable such
surroundings were torment; but what could he do? In the
reception-room he was met by the feldscher, Sergéi
Sergéyitch, a little fat man, with a beardless, well-washed,
puffy face, and easy manners. Sergéi Sergéyitch always wore
clothes which resembled a senator's more than a surgeon's; in
the town he had a large practice, and believed that he knew
more than the doctor, who had no practice at all. In the corner
of the room hung a case of ikons with a heavy lamp in front;
on the walls were portraits of bishops, a view of Sviatogorsk
Monastery, and garlands of withered corn-flowers. Sergéi
Sergéyitch was religious, and the images had been placed in
the room at his expense; every Sunday by his command one of
the patients read the acathistus, and when the reading was
concluded, Sergéi Sergéyitch went around the wards with a
censer and sprinkled them piously.

There were many patients and little time. The examination
was therefore limited to a few short questions, and to the
distribution of such simple remedies as castor-oil and
ointments. Andréi Yéfimitch sat with his head resting on his
hands, lost in thought, and asked questions mechanically; and

Sergéi Sergéyitch sat beside him, and sometimes interjected a word.

'We become ill and suffer deprivation,' he would sometimes say, 'only because we pray too little to God.'

In these hours Andréi Yéfimitch performed no operations; he had got out of practice, and the sight of blood affected him unpleasantly. When he had to open a child's mouth, to examine its throat for instance, if the child cried and defended itself with its hands, the doctor's head went round and tears came into his eyes. He made haste to prescribe a remedy, and motioned to the mother to take it away as quickly as possible.

He quickly wearied of the timidity of the patients, of their shiftless ways, of the proximity of the pompous Sergéi Sergéyitch, of the portraits on the walls, and of his own questions – questions which he had asked without change for more than twenty years. And he would sometimes leave the hospital after having examined five or six patients, the remainder in his absence being treated by the feldscher.

With the pleasant reflection that thank God he had no private practice and no one to interfere with him, Andréi Yéfimitch on returning home would sit at his study-table and begin to read. He read much, and always with pleasure. Half his salary went on the purchase of books, and of the six rooms in his flat three were crowded with books and old newspapers. Above all things he loved history and philosophy; but of medical publications he subscribed only to *The Doctor*, which he always began to read at the end. Every day he read uninterruptedly for several hours, and it never wearied him. He read, not quickly and eagerly as Iván Dmítritch had read, but slowly, often stopping at passages which pleased him or which he did not understand. Beside his books stood a decanter of vodka, and a salted cucumber or soaked apple; and every half-hour he poured himself out a glass of vodka, and drank it without lifting his eyes from his book, and then – again without lifting his eyes – took the cucumber and bit a piece off.

At three o'clock he would walk cautiously to the kitchen door, cough, and say:

'Dáryushka, I was thinking of dining. . . .'

After a bad an ill-served dinner, Andréi Yéfimitch walked about his rooms, with his arms crossed on his chest, and thought. Sometimes the kitchen door creaked, and the red, sleepy face of Dáryushka appeared.

'Andréi Yéfimitch, is it time for your beer?' she would ask solicitously.

'No, not yet,' he would answer. 'I'll wait a little longer. . . .'

In the evening came the postmaster, Mikhail Averyanitch, the only man in the town whose society did not weary Andréi Yéfimitch. Mikhail Averyanitch had once been a rich country gentleman and had served in a cavalry regiment, but having ruined himself he took a position in the Post Office to save himself from beggary in his old age. He had a brisk, wholesome appearance, magnificent grey whiskers, well-bred manners, and a loud but pleasant voice. When visitors at the Post Office protested, refused to agree with him, or began to argue, Mikhail Averyanitch became purple, shook all over, and roared at the top of his voice: 'Silence!' so that the Post Office had the reputation of a place of terror. Mikhail Averyanitch was fond of Andréi Yéfimitch and respected his attainments and the nobility of his heart. But the other townspeople he treated haughtily as inferiors.

'Well, here I am!' he would begin. 'How are you, my dear? . . . But perhaps I bore you? Eh?'

'Oh the contrary. I am delighted,' answered the doctor. 'I am always glad to see you.'

The friends would sit on the study sofa and smoke for a time silently.

'Dáryushka, suppose I were to have a little beer . . .' said Andréi Yéfimitch.

The first bottle was drunk in silence. The doctor was lost in thought, while Mikhail Averyanitch had the gay and active expression of a man who has something very interesting to relate. The conversation was always begun by the doctor.

'What a pity!' he would say, slowly and quietly, looking away from his friend – he never looked anyone in the face. 'What a pity, my dear Mikhail Averyanitch, what a pity it is that there is not a soul in this town who cares to engage in an intellectual or interesting conversation! It is a great deprivation for us. Even the so-called intelligent classes never rise above commonplaces; the level of their development, I assure you, is no higher than that of the lower order.'

'Entirely true. I agree with you.'

'As you yourself know very well,' continued the doctor, pausing intermittently, 'as you know, everything in this world is insignificant and uninteresting except the higher phenomena of the human intellect. Intellect creates a sharp distinction between the animal and the man, it reminds the latter of his divinity, and to a certain extent compensates him for the immortality which he has not. As the result of this, intellect serves as the only fountain of enjoyment. When we say we see and hear around us no evidence of intellect, we mean thereby that we are deprived of true happiness. True, we have our books, but that is a very different thing from living converse and communication. If I may use a not very apt simile, books are the accompaniment, but conversation is the singing.'

'That is entirely true.'

A silence followed. From the kitchen came Dáryushka, and, with her head resting on her hands and an expression of stupid vexation on her face, stood at the door and listened.

'Akh!' sighed Mikhail Averyanitch, 'why seek intellect among the men of the present day?'

And he began to relate how in the old days life was wholesome, gay, and interesting, how the intellect of Russia was really enlightened, and how high a place was given to the ideas of honour and friendship. Money was lent without I.O.U.s, and it was regarded as shameful not to stretch out the hand of aid to a needy friend. What marches there were, what adventures, what fights, what companions-in-arms, what women! The Caucasus, what a marvellous country! And the wife of the commander of his battalion – what a strange woman! – who put on an officer's uniform and drove into the mountains at night without an escort. They said she had a romance with a prince in one of the villages.

'Heavenly mother! Lord preserve us!' sighed Dáryushka.

'And how we drank! How we used to eat! What desperate Liberals we were!'

Andréi Yéfimitch listened, but heard nothing; he was thinking of something else and drinking his beer.

'I often dream of clever people and have imaginary conversations with them,' he said, suddenly, interrupting

Mikhail Averyanitch. 'My father gave me a splendid education, but, under the influence of the ideas current in the sixties,
forced me to become a doctor. It seems to me that if I had
disobeyed him I might now be living in the very centre of the
intellectual movement – probably a member of some faculty.
Of course intellect itself is not eternal but transitory – but you
already know why I worship it so. Life is a vexatious snare.
When a reflecting man attains manhood and ripe
consciousness, he cannot but feel himself in a trap from which
there is no escape. . . . By an accident, without consulting his
own will, he is called from non-existence into life. . . . Why?
He wishes to know the aim and significance of his existence;
he is answered with silence or absurdities; he knocks but it is
not opened to him; and death itself comes against his will. And
so, as prisoners united by common misfortune are relieved
when they meet, men inclined to analysis and generalisation
do not notice the snare in which they live when they spend
their days in the exchange of free ideas. In this sense intellect is
an irreplaceable enjoyment.'

'Entirely true!'

And still with his face averted from his companion, Andréi
Yéfimitch, in a soft voice, with constant pauses, continues to
speak of clever men and of the joy of communion with them,
and Mikhail Averyanitch listens attentively and says: 'It is
entirely true.'

'Then you do not believe in the immortality of the soul?'
asks the postmaster.

'No, my dear Mikhail Averyanitch. I do not believe, and I
have no reason for believing.'

'I admit that I also doubt it. Still I have a feeling that I can
never die. "Come," I say to myself, "Come, old man, its time
for you to die." But in my heart a voice answers: "Don't
believe it, you will never die."'

At nine o'clock Mikhail Averyanitch takes leave. As he puts
on his overcoat in the hall, he says with a sigh:

'Yes, what a desert fate has planted us in! And what is worst
of all, we shall have to die here. *Akh!*'

VII

When he has parted from his friend, Andréi Yéfimitch sits at his table and again begins to read. The stillness of evening, the stillness of night is unbroken by a single sound; time, it seems, stands still and perishes, and the doctor perishes also, till it seems that nothing exists but a book and a green lampshade. Then the rude, peasant face of the doctor, as he thinks of the achievements of the human intellect, becomes gradually illumined by a smile of emotion and rapture. Oh, why is man not immortal? he asks. For what end exist brain-centres and convolutions, to what end vision, speech, consciousness, genius, if all are condemned to pass into the earth, to grow cold with it, and for countless millions of years, without aim or object, to be borne with it around the sun? In order that the human frame may decay and be whirled around the sun, is it necessary to drag man with his high, his divine mind, out of non-existence, as if in mockery, and to turn him again into earth?

Immortality of matter! What cowardice to console ourselves with this fictitious immortality! Unconscious processes working themselves out in Nature – processes lower even than folly, for in folly there is at least consciousness and volition, while in these processes there is neither! Yet they say to men, 'Be at rest, thy substance, rotting in the earth, will give life to other organisms' – in other words, thou wilt be more foolish than folly! Only the coward, who has more fear of death than sense of dignity, can console himself with the knowledge that his body in the course of time will live again in grass, in stones, in the toad. To seek immortality in the indestructibility of matter is, indeed, as strange as to prophesy a brilliant future for the case when the costly violin is broken and worthless.

When the clock strikes, Andréi Yéfimitch leans back in his chair, shuts his eyes, and thinks. Under the influence of the lofty thoughts which he has just been reading, he throws a glance over the present and the past. The past is repellent, better not think of it! And the present is but as the past. He knows that in this very moment, while his thoughts are sweeping round the sun with the cooling earth, in the hospital building in a line with his lodgings, lie men tortured by pain and tormented by uncleanliness; one cannot sleep owing to the insects, and howls in his pain; another is catching erysipelas, and groaning at the tightness of his bandages; others are playing cards with the nurses, and drinking vodka. In this very year no less than twelve thousand persons were duped; the whole work of the hospital, as twenty years before, is based on robbery, scandal, intrigue, nepotism, and gross charlatanry; altogether, the hospital is an immoral institution, and a source of danger to the health of its inmates. And Andréi Yéfimitch knows that inside the iron bars of Ward No. 6, Nikita beats the patients with his fists, and that, outside, Moséika wanders about the streets begging for kopecks.

Yet he knows very well that in the last twenty-five years a fabulous revolution has taken place in the doctor's art. When he studied at the university it had seemed to him that medicine would soon be overtaken by the lot of alchemy and metaphysics, but now the records of its feats which he reads at night touch him, astonish him, and even send him into raptures. What a revolution! what unexpected brilliance! Thanks to antiseptics, operations are every day performed which the great Pigorof regarded as impossible. Ordinary Zemstvo doctors perform such operations as the resection of the knee articulations, of a hundred operations on the stomach only one results in death, and the stone is now such a trifle that it has ceased to be written about. Complaints which were once only alleviated are now entirely cured. And hypnotism, the theory of heredity, the discoveries of Pasteur and Koch, statistics of hygiene, even Russian Zemstvo medicine! Psychiatry, with its classification of diseases, its methods of diagnosis, its method of cure – what a transformation of the methods of the past! No longer are lunatics drenched with cold water and confined in strait waistcoats; they are treated as human beings, and even – as Andréi Yéfimitch read in the newspapers – have their own special dramatic entertainments and dances. Andréi Yéfimitch is well aware that in the modern world such an abomination as Ward No. 6 is possible only in a town situated two hundred versts from a railway, where the Mayor and Councillors are half-educated tradesmen, who regard a doctor as a priest to whom everything must be entrusted without criticsm, even though he were to dose his patients with molten tin. In any other town the public and the Press would long ago have torn this little Bastille to pieces.

'But in the end?' asks Andréi Yéfimitch, opening his eyes. 'What is the difference? In spite of antiseptics and Koch and Pasteur, the essence of the matter has no way changed. Disease and death still exist. Lunatics are amused with dances and theatricals, but they are still kept prisoners. . . . In other words, all these things are vanity and folly, and between the best hospital in Vienna and the hospital here there is in reality no difference at all.'

But vexation and a feeling akin to envy forbid indifference. It all arises out of weariness. Andréi Yéfimitch's head falls upon his book, he rests his head comfortably on his hands and thinks:

'I am engaged in a bad work, and I receive a salary from the men whom I deceive. I am not an honest man. . . . But then by myself I am nothing; I am only part of a necessary social evil; all the officials in the district are bad, and draw their salaries without doing their work. . . . In other words, it is not I who am guilty of dishonesty, but Time. . . . If I were born two hundred years hence I should be a different man.'

When the clock strikes three, he puts out his lamp and goes up to his bedroom. But he has no wish to sleep.

VIII

Two years ago, in a fit of liberality, the Zemstvo determined to appropriate three hundred roubles a year to the increase of the *personnel* of the hospital, until such time as they should open one of their own. They sent, therefore, as assistant to Andréi Yéfimitch, the district physician Yevgénii Feódoritch Khobótoff. Khobótoff was a very young man, under thiry, tall and dark, with small eyes and high cheek-bones; evidently of Asiatic origin. He arrived in the town without a kopeck, with a small portmanteau as his only luggage, and was accompanied by a young, unattractive woman, whom he called his cook. This woman's child completed the party. Khobótoff wore a peaked cap and high boots, and – in winter

– a short fur coat. He was soon on intimate terms with the feldscher, Sergé Sergéyitch, and with the bursar, but the rest of the officials he avoided and denounced as aristocrats. He possessed only one book, 'Prescriptions of the Vienna Hospital in 1881,' and when he visited the hospital he always brought it with him. He did not care for cards, and in the evenings spent his time playing billiards at the club.

Khobótoff visited the hospital twice a week, inspected the wards, and received out-patients. The strange absence of antiseptics, cupping-glasses, and other necessaries seemed to trouble him, but he made no attempt to introduce a new order, fearing to offend Andréi Yéfimitch, whom he regarded as an old rogue, suspected of having large means, and secretly envied. He would willingly have occupied his position.

IX

One spring evening towards the end of March, when the snow had disappeared and starlings sang in the hospital garden, the doctor was standing at his gate saying good-bye to his friend the postmaster. At that moment the Jew Moséika, returning with his booty, entered the yard. He was capless, wore a pair of goloshes on his stockingless feet, and held in his hand a small bag of coins.

'Give me a kopeck?' he said to the doctor, shuddering from the cold and grinning.

Andréi Yéfimitch, who could refuse no one, gave him a ten-kopeck piece.

'How wrong this is!' he thought, as he looked at the Jew's bare legs and his ankles. 'Wet, I suppose?'

And impelled by a feeling of pity and squeamishness he entered the wing after Moséika, looking all the time now at the Jew's bald head, now at his ankles. When the doctor entered, Nikita jumped off his rubbish-heap and stretched himself.

'Good evening, Nikita!' said the doctor softly. 'Suppose you give this man a pair of boots . . . that is . . . he might catch cold.'

'Yes, your Honour. I will ask the superintendent.'

'Please. Ask him in my name. Say that I spoke about it.'

The door of the ward was open. Iván Dmítritch, who was lying on his bed, and listening with alarm to the unknown voice, suddenly recognised the doctor. He shook with anger, jumped off his bed, and with a flushed, malicious face, and staring eyeballs, ran into the middle of the room.

'It is the doctor!' he cried, with a loud laugh. 'At last! Lord, I congratulate you, the doctor honours us with a visit! Accursed monster!' he squealed, and in an ecstacy of rage never before seen in the hospital, stamped his feet. 'Kill this monster! No, killing is not enough for him! Drown him in the closet!'

Andréi Yéfimitch heard him. He looked into the ward and asked mildly:

'For what?'

'For what!' screamed Iván Dmítritch, approaching with a threatening face, and convulsively clutching his dressing-gown. 'For what! Thief!' He spoke in a tone of disgust, and twisted his lips as if about to spit.

'Charlatan! Hangman!'

'Be quiet!' said Andréi Yéfimitch, smiling guiltily. 'I assure you I have never stolen anything. . . . I see that you are angry with me. Be calm, I implore you, if you can, and tell me why you want to kill me.'

'For keeping me here.'

'I do that because you are ill.'

'Yes! Ill! But surely tens, hundreds, thousands of madmen live unmolested merely because you in your ignorance cannot distinguish them from the sane. You, the feldscher, the superintendent, all the rascals employed in the hospital are immeasurably lower in morals than the worst of us; why, then, are we here instead of you? Where is the logic?'

'It is not a question of morality or logic. It depends on circumstances. The man who is put here, here he stays, and the man who is not here lives in freedom, that is all. For the fact that I am a doctor and you a lunatic neither morals nor logic is responsible, but only empty circumstance.'

'This nonsense I do not understand!' answered Iván Dmítritch, sitting down on his bed.

Moséika, whom Nikita was afraid to search in the doctor's presence, spread out on his bed his booty – pieces of bread, papers, and bones; and trembling with the cold, talked Yiddish in a sing-song voice. Apparently he imagined that he was opening a shop.

'Release me!' said Iván Dmítritch. His voice trembled.

'I cannot.'

'Why not?'

'Because it is not in my power. Judge for yourself! What good would it do you if I released you? Suppose I do! The townspeople or the police will capture you and send you back.'

'Yes, that is true, it is true . . .' said Iván Dmítritch, rubbing his forehead. 'It is terrible! But what can I do? What?'

His voice, his intelligent, youthful face pleased Andréi Yéfimitch. He wished to caress him and quiet him. He sat beside him on the bed, thought for a moment, and said:

'You ask what is to be done. The best thing in your position would be to run away. But unfortunately that is useless. You would be captured. When society resolves to protect itself from criminals, lunatics, and inconvenient people, it is irresistible. One thing alone remains to you, to console yourself with the thought that your stay here is necessary.'

'It is necessary to no one.'

'Once prisons and asylums exist, someone must inhabit them. If it is not you it will be I, if not I then someone else. But wait! In the far future there will be neither prisons nor madhouses, nor barred windows, nor dressing-gowns. . . . Such a time will come sooner or later.'

Iván Dmítritch smiled contemptuously.

'You are laughing at me,' he said, winking. 'Such gentry as you and your assistant Nikita have no business with the future. But you may be assured, sir, that better times are in store for us. What if I do express myself vulgarly – laugh at me! – but the dawn of a new life will shine, and truth will triumph . . . and it will be on our side the holiday will be. I shall not see it, but our posterity shall. . . . I congratulate them with my whole soul, and rejoice – rejoice for them! Forward! God help you, friends!'

Iván Dmítritch's eyes glittered; he rose, stretched out his eyes to the window, and said in an agitated voice:

'For these barred windows I bless you. Hail to the truth! I rejoice!'

'I see no cause for rejoicing,' said Andréi Yéfimitch, whom Iván Dmítritch's movements, though they seemed theatrical, pleased. 'Prisons and asylums will no longer be, and justice, as you put it, will triumph. But the essence of things will never change, the laws of Nature will remain the same. Men will be diseased, grow old, and die, just as now. However glorious the dawn which enlightens your life, in the end of ends you will be nailed down in a coffin and flung into a pit.'

'But immortality?'

'Nonsense!'

'You do not believe, but I believe. Dostoyevsky or Voltaire or someone said that if there were no God men would have invented one. And I am deeply convinced that if there were no immortality it would sooner or later have been invented by the great human intellect.'

'You speak well,' said Andréi Yéfimitch, smiling with pleasure. 'It is well that you believe. With such faith as yours you would live happily though entombed in a wall. May I asked where you were educated?'

'I was at college, but never graduated.'

'You are a thoughtful and penetrating man. You would find tranquillity in any environment. The free and profound thought which aspires to the comprehension of life; and high contempt for the vanity of the world – these are two blessings higher than which no man can know. And these you will enjoy though you live behind a dozen barred windows. Diogenes lived in a tub, yet he was happier than all the kings of the earth.'

'Your Diogenes was a blockhead!' cried Iván Dmítritch gloomily. 'What do you tell me about Diogenes and the understanding of life?' He spoke angrily, and sprang up. 'I love life, love it passionately. I have the mania of persecution, a ceaseless, tormenting terror, but there are moments when I am seized by the thirst of life, and in those moments I fear to go out of my mind. I long to live . . . terribly!'

He walked up and down the ward in agitation, and continued in a lower voice:

'When I meditate I am visited by visions. Men come to me, I hear voices and music, and it seems to me that I am walking through woods, on the shores of the sea; and I long passionately for the vanities and worries of life. . . . Tell me! What is the news?'

'You ask about the town, or generally?'

'First tell me about the town, and then generally?'

'What is there? The town is tiresome to the point of torment. There is no one to talk to, no one to listen to. There are no new people. But lately we got a new doctor, Khobótoff, a young man.'

'He has been here. A fool?'

'Yes, an uneducated man. It is strange, do you know. If you judge by metropolitan life there is no intellectual stagnation in Russia, but genuine activity; in other words, there are real men. But for some reason or other they always send such fellows here. It is an unfortunate town.'

'An unfortunate town,' sighed Iván Dmítritch. 'And what news is there generally? What have you in the newspapers and reviews?'

In the ward it was already dark. The doctor rose, and told his patient what was being written in Russia and abroad, and what were the current tendencies of the world. Iván Dmítritch listened attentively, and asked questions. But suddenly, as if he had just remembered something terrible, he seized his head and threw himself on the bed, with his back turned to the doctor.'

'What is the matter?' asked Andréi Yéfimitch.

'You will not hear another word from me' said Iván Dmitrítch rudely. 'Go away!'

'Why?'

'I tell you, go away! Go to the devil!'

Andréi Yéfimitch shrugged his shoulders, sighed, and left the ward. As he passed through the hall, he said:

'Suppose you were to clear some of this away; Nikita. . . . The smell is frightful.'

'Yes, your Honour!'

'What a delightful young man!' thought Andréi Yéfimitch, as he walked home. 'He is the first man worth talking to whom I have met all the time I have lived in this town. He can reason and interests himself only with what is essential.'

As he read in his study, as he went to bed, all the time, he thought of Iván Dmítritch. When he awoke next morning, he remembered that he had made the acquaintance of a clever and interesting man. And he decided to pay him another visit at the first opportunity.

X

Iván Dmítritch lay in the same position as on the day before, holding his head in his hands, his legs being doubled up underneath him.

'Good morning, my friend,' said Andréi Yéfimitch. 'You are not asleep?'

'In the first place I am not your friend,' said Iván Dmítritch, keeping his face turned towards the pillow, 'and in the second, you are troubling yourself in vain; you will not get from me a single word.'

'That is strange,' said Andréi Yéfimitch. 'Yesterday we were speaking as friends, but suddenly you took offence and stopped short. . . . Perhaps I spoke awkwardly, or expressed opinions differing widely from your own.'

'You won't catch me!' said Iván Dmítritch, rising from the bed and looking at the doctor ironically and suspiciously. 'You may go and spy and cross-examine somewhere else; here there is nothing for you to do. I know very well why you came yesterday.'

'That is a strange idea,' laughed the doctor. 'But why do you assume that I am spying?'

'I assume it. . . . Whether spy or doctor it is all the same.'

'Yes, but . . . excuse me. . . .' The doctor sat on a stool beside the bed, and shook his head reproachfully. 'Even suppose you are right, suppose I am following your words only in order to betray you to the police, what would happen? They would arrest you and try you. But then, in the dock or in prison would you be worse off than here? In exile or penal servitude you would not suffer any more than now. . . . What, then, do you fear?'

Apparently these words affected Iván Dmítritch. He sat down quietly.

It was five o'clock, the hour when André Yéfimitch usually walked up and down his room and Dáryushka asked him whether it was time for his beer. The weather was calm and clear.

'After dinner I went out for a walk, and you see where I've come,' said the doctor. 'It is almost spring.'

'What month is it?' asked Iván Dmítritch. 'March?'

'Yes, we are at the end of March?'

'Is it very muddy?'

'Not very. The paths in the garden are clear.'

'How glorious it would be to drive somewhere outside the town!' said Iván Dmítritch, rubbing his red eyes as if he were sleepy, 'and then to return to a warm comfortable study . . . and to be cured of headache by a decent doctor. . . . For years past I have not lived like a human being. . . . Things are abominable here, – intolerable, disgusting!'

After last evening's excitement he was tired and weak, and he spoke unwillingly. His fingers twitched, and from his face it was plain that his head ached badly.

'Between a warm, comfortable study and this ward there is no difference,' said Andréi Yéfimitch. 'The rest and tranquillity of a man are not outside but within him.'

'What do you mean by that?'

'Ordinary men find good and evil outside, that is, in their carriages and comfortable rooms; but the thinking man finds them within himself.'

'Go and preach that philosophy in Greece, where it is warm and smells of oranges – it doesn't suit this climate. With whom was it I spoke of Diogenes? With you?'

'Yes, yesterday with me.'

'Diogenes had no need of a study and a warm house, he was comfortable without them. . . . Lie in a tub and eat oranges and olives! Set him down in Russia – not in December, but even in May. He would freeze even in May with the cold.'

'No. Cold, like every other feeling, may be disregarded. As Marcus Aurelius said, pain is the living conception of pain; make an effort of the will to change this conception, cease to complain, and the pain disappears. The wise man, the man of thought and penetration, is distinguished by his contempt for suffering; he is always content and he is surprised by nothing.'

'That means that I am an idiot because I suffer, because I am discontented, and marvel at the baseness of men.'

'Your discontent is in vain. Think more, and you will realise how trifling are all the things which now excite you. . . . Try to understand life – in this is true beatitude.'

'Understand!' frowned Iván Dmítritch. 'External, internal. . . . Excuse me, but I cannot understand you. I know only one thing,' he continued, rising and looking angrily at the doctor. 'I know only that God created me of warm blood and nerves; yes! and organic tissue, if it be capable of life, must respond to irritation. And I respond to it! Pain I answer with tears and cries, baseness with indignation, meanness with repulsion. In my mind, that is right, and it is that which is called life. The lower the organism the less susceptible is it, and the more feebly it responds to irritation; the higher it is the more sensitively it responds. How is it you do not know that? A doctor – yet you do not know such truisms! If you would despise suffering, be always contented, and marvel at nothing, you must lower yourself to the condition of that . . .' Iván Dmítritch pointed to the fat, greasy muzhik, 'or inure yourself to suffering until you lose all susceptibility – in other words, cease to live. Excuse me, but I am not a wise man and not a philosopher,' continued Iván Dmítritch irritably, 'and I do not understand these things. I am not in a condition to reason.'

'But you reason admirably.'

'The Stoics whom you travesty were remarkable men, but their teaching died two thousand years ago, and since then it has not advanced, nor will it advance, an inch, for it is not a practical or a living creed. It was successful only with a minority who spent their lives in study and trifled with gospels of all sorts; the majority never understood it. . . . A creed which teaches indifference to wealth, indifference to the conveniences of life, and contempt for suffering, is quite incomprehensible to the great majority who never knew either wealth or the conveniences of life, and to whom contempt for suffering would mean contempt for their own lives, which are made up of feelings of hunger, cold, loss, insult, and a Hamlet-like terror of death. All life lies in these feelings, and life may be hated or wearied of, but never despised. Yes, I repeat it, the teaching of the Stoics can never have a future; from the beginning of time, life has consisted in sensibility to pain and response to irritation.'

Iván Dmítritch suddenly lost the thread of his thoughts, ceased speaking, and rubbed his forehead irritably.

'I had something important to say, but have gone off the track,' he continued. 'What was I saying? Yes, this is it. One of these Stoics sold himself into slavery to redeem a friend. Now what does that mean but that even a Stoic responded to irritation, for to perform such a magnanimous deed as the ruin of one's self for the sake of a friend demands a disturbed and sympathetic heart. I have forgotten here in prison all that I learnt, otherwise I should have other illustrations. But think of Christ! Christ rebelled against actuality by weeping, by smiling, by grieving, by anger, even by weariness. Not with a smile did He go forth to meet suffering, nor did He despise death, but prayed in the garden of Gethsemane that this cup might pass from Him.'

Iván Dmítritch laughed and sat down.

'Suppose that contentment and tranquillity are not outside but within a man,' he continued. 'Suppose that we must despise suffering and marvel at nothing. But you do not say on what foundation you base this theory. You are a wise man? A philosopher?'

'I am not a philosopher, but everyone must preach this because it is rational.'

'But I wish to know why in this matter of understanding life, despiring suffering, and the rest of it, you consider yourself competent to judge? Have you ever suffered? What is your idea of suffering? Were you ever flogged when you were a child?'

'No, my parents were averse to corporal punishment.'

'But my father flogged cruelly. He was a stern hae-morrhoidal official with a long nose and a yellow neck. But what of you? In your whole life no one has ever laid a finger on you, and you are as healthy as a bull. You grew up under your father's wing, studied at his expense, and then dropped at once into a fat sinecure. More than twenty years you have lived in free lodgings, with free fire and free lights, with servants, with the right to work how, and as much as, you like, or to do nothing. By character you were an idle and a feeble man, and you strove to build up your life so as to avoid trouble. You left your work to feldschers and other scoundrels, and sat at home in warmth and quiet, heaped up money, read books, and enjoyed your own reflections about all kinds of exalted nonsense, and' – Iván Dmítritch looked at the doctor's nose – 'drank beer. In one word, you have not seen life, you know nothing about it, and of realities you have only a theoretical knowledge. Yes, you despise suffering and marvel at nothing for very good reasons; because your theory of the vanity of things, external and internal happiness, contempt for life, for suffering and for death, and so on – this is the philosophy best suited to a Russian lie-abed. You see, for instance, a muzhik beating his wife. Why interfere? let him beat her! It is all the same, both will be dead sooner or later, and then, does not the wife-beater injure himself and not his victim? To get drunk is stupid and wrong, but the man who drinks dies, and the woman who drinks dies also! A woman comes to you with a toothache. Well, what of that? Pain is the conception of pain, without sickness you cannot live, all must die, and therefore take yourself off, my good woman, and don't interfere with my thoughts and my vodka! A young man comes to you for advice: what should he do, how ought he to live? Before answering, most men would think, but your answer is always ready: Aspire to understand life and to real goodness! And what is this fantastic real goodness? No answer! We are imprisoned behind iron bars, we rot and we are tortured, but this, in reality, is reasonable and beautiful because between this ward and a comfortable warm study there is no real difference! A convenient philosophy; your conscience is clean, and you feel yourself to be a wise man. No, sir, this is not philosophy, not breadth of view, but idleness, charlatanism, somnolent folly. . . . Yes,' repeated Iván Dmítritch angrily. 'You despise suffering, but squeeze your finger in the door and you will howl for your life!'

'But suppose I do not howl,' said Andréi Yéfimitch, smiling indulgently.

'What! Well, if you had a stroke of paralysis, or if some impudent fellow, taking advantage of his position in the world, insulted you publicly, and you had no redress – then you would know what it meant to tell others to understand life and aspire to real good.'

'This is original,' said Andréi Yéfimitch, beaming with
satisfaction and rubbing his hands. 'I am delighted with your
love of generalisation; and the character which you have just
drawn is simply brilliant. I confess that conversation with you
gives me great pleasure. But now, as I have heard you out,
will you listen to me . . .'

XI

This conversation, which lasted for an hour longer,
apparently made a great impression on Andréi Yéfimitch. He
took to visiting the ward every day. He went there in the
morning, and again after dinner, and often darkness found
him in conversation with Iván Dmítritch. At first Iván
Dmítritch was shy with him, suspected him of some evil
intention, and openly expressed his suspicions. But at last he
got used to him; and his rude bearing softened into indulgent
irony.

A report soon spread through the hospital that Doctor
Andréi Yéfimitch paid daily visits to Ward No. 6. Neither the
feldscher, nor Nikita, nor the nurses could understand his
object; why he spent whole hours in the ward, what he was
talking about, or why he did not write prescriptions. His
conduct appeared strange to everyone. Mikhail Averyanitch
sometimes failed to find him at home, and Dáryushka was
very alarmed, for the doctor no longer drank his beer at the
usual hour, and sometimes even came home late for dinner.

One day – it was at the end of June – Doctor Khobótoff
went to Andréi Yéfimitch's house to see him on a business
matter. Not finding him at home, he looked for him in the
yard, where he was told that the old doctor was in the
asylum. Khobótoff entered the hall of the ward, and standing
there listened to the following conversation:

'We will never agree, and you will never succeed in
converting me to your faith,' said Iván Dmítritch irritably.
'You are altogether ignorant of realities, you have never
suffered, but only, like a leech, fed on the sufferings of others.
But I have suffered without cease from the day of my birth
until now. Therefore I tell you frankly I consider myself

much higher than you, and more competent in all respects. It is not for you to teach me.'

'I certainly have no wish to convert you to my faith,' said Andréi Yéfimitch softly, and evidently with regret that he was misunderstood. 'That is not the question, my friend. Suffering and joy are transitory – leave them, God be with them! The essence of the matter is that you and I recognise in one another men of thought, and this makes us solid however different our views. If you knew, my friend, how I am weary of the general idiocy around me, the lack of talent, the dullness – if you knew the joy with which I speak to you! You are a clever man, and it is a pleasure to be with you.'

Khobótoff opened the door and looked into the room. Iván Dmítritch with a nightcap on his head and Doctor Andréi Yéfimitch sat side by side on the bed. The lunatic shuddered, made strange faces, and convulsively clutched his dressing-gown; and the doctor sat motionless, inclining his head, and his face was red and helpless and sad. Khobótoff shrugged his shoulders, laughed, and looked at Nikita. Nikita also shrugged his shoulders.

Next day Khobótoff again came to the wing, this time together with the feldscher. They stood in the hall and listened:

'Our grandfather, it seems, is quite gone,' said Khobótoff going out of the wing.

'Lord, have mercy upon us – sinners!' sighed the pompous Sergéi Sergéyitch, going round the pools in order to keep his shiny boots clear of the mud. 'I confess, my dear Yevgéniï Feódoritch, I have long expected this.'

XIII

After this incident, Andréi Yéfimitch began to notice that he was surrounded by a strange atmosphere of mystery. . . . The servants, the nurses, and the patients whom he met looked questioningly at one another, and whispered among themselves. When he met little Masha, the superintendent's daughter, in the hospital garden, and smilingly went over to her, as usual, to stroke her hair, for some inexplicable reason she ran away. When the postmaster, Mikhail Averyanitch, sat listening to him he no longer said: 'Entirely true!' but got red in the face and stammered, 'Yes, yes . . . yes . . .' and sometimes, looking at his friend thoughtfully and sorrowfully, advised him to give up vodka and beer. But when doing this, as became a man of delicacy, he did not speak openly, but dropped gentle hints, telling stories, now of a certain battalion commander, an excellent man, now of the regimental chaplain, a first-rate little fellow, who drank a good deal and was taken ill, yet having given up drink got quite well. Twice or thrice Andréi Yéfimitch was visited by his colleague Khobótoff, who also asked him to give up spirits, and, without giving him any reasons, advised him to try bromide of potassium.

In August Andréi Yéfimitch received a letter from the Mayor asking him to come and see him on very important business. On arriving at the Town Hall at the appointed time he found awaiting him the head of the recruiting department, the superintendent of the district school, a member of the Town Council, Khobótoff, and a stout, fair-haired man, who was introduced as a doctor. This doctor, who bore an unpronounceable Polish name, lived on a stud-farm some thirty versts away, and was passing through the town on his way home.

'Here is a communication about your department,' said the Town Councillor, turning to Andréi Yéfimitch. 'You see, Yevgénii Feódoritch says that there is no room for the dispensing room in the main building, and that it must be transferred to one of the wings. That, of course, is easy, it can be transferred any day, but the chief thing is that the wing is in want of repair.'

'Yes, we can hardly get on without that,' answered Andréi Yéfimitch after a moment's thought. 'But if the corner wing is to be fitted up as a dispensary you will have to spend at least five hundred roubles on it. It is unproductive expenditure.'

For a few minutes all were silent.

'I had the honour to announce to you, ten years ago,' continued Andréi Yéfimitch in a soft voice, 'that this hospital, under present conditions, is a luxury altogether beyond the means of the town. It was built in the forties, when the means for its support were greater. The town wastes too much money on unnecessary buildings and sinecure offices. I think that with the money we spend we could keep up two model hospitals; that is, of course, with a different order of things.'

'Well, then, let us reform the present order,' said the Town Councillor.

'I have already had the honour to advise you to transfer the medical department to the Zemstvo.'

'Yes, and hand over to the Zemstvo funds which it will pocket,' laughed the fair-haired doctor.

'That is just what happens,' said the Town Councillor, laughing also.

Andréi Yéfimitch looked feebly at the fair-haired doctor, and said:

'We must be just in our judgments.'

Again all were silent. Tea was brought in. The chief of the recruiting department, apparently in a state of confusion, touched Andréi Yéfimitch's hand across the table, and said:

'You have quite forgotten us, doctor. But then you were always a monk; you don't play cards, and you don't care for women. We bore you, I'm afraid.'

And all agreed that it was tiresome for any decent man to live in such a town. Neither theatres, nor concerts, and at the last club-dance about twenty women present and only two men. Young men no longer danced, but crowded round the supper-table or played cards together. And Andréi Yéfimitch, in a slow and soft voice, without looking at those around him, began to lament that the citizens wasted their vital energy, their intellects, and their feelings over cards and scandal, and neither cared nor knew how to pass the time in interesting conversation, in reading, or in taking advantage of the pleasures which intellect alone yields. Intellect is the only interesting and distinguished thing in the world; all the rest is petty and base. Khobótoff listened attentively to his colleague, and suddenly asked:

'Andréi Yéfimitch, what is the day of the month?'

Having received an answer, he and the fair-haired doctor, both in the tone of examiners convinced of their own incapacity, asked Andréi Yéfimitch a number of other questions; what was the day of the week, how many days were there in the year, and was it true that in Ward No. 6 there was a remarkable prophet?

In answer to this last question Andréi Yéfimitch got red in the face, and said:

'Yes, he is insane. . . . But he is a most interesting young man.'

No other questions were asked.

As Andréi Yéfimitch put on his coat, the chief of the recruiting department put his hand on his shoulder and said, with a sigh:

'For us – old men – it is time to take a rest.'

As he left the Town Hall, Andréi Yéfimitch understood that he had been before a commission appointed to test his mental sanity. He remembered the questions put to him, reddened, and for the first time in his life felt pity for the medical art.

'My God!' he thought. 'These men have only just been studying psychiatry and passing examinations! Where does their monstrous ignorance come from? They have no ideas about psychiatry.'

For the first time in his life he felt insulted and angry.

Towards evening Mikhail Averyanitch came to see him. Without a word of greeting, the postmaster went up to him, took him by both hands, and said in an agitated voice:

'My dear friend, my dear friend, let me see that you believe in my sincere affection for you. Regard me as your friend!' And preventing Andréi Yéfimitch saying a word, he continued in extreme agitation: 'You know that I love you for the culture and nobility of your mind. Listen to me, like a good man! The rules of their profession compel the doctors to hide the truth from you, but I, in soldier style, will tell it to you flatly. You are unwell! Excuse me, old friend, but that is the plain truth, and it has been noticed by everyone around you. Only this moment Doctor Yevgénii Feódoritch said that for the benefit of your health you needed rest and recreation. It is entirely true! And things fit in admirably. In a few days I will take my leave, and go off for change of air. Prove to me that you are my friend, and come with me. Come!'

'I feel very well,' said Andréi Yéfimitch, after a moment's thought; 'and I cannot go. Allow me to prove my friendship in some other way.'

To go away without any good reason, without his books, without Dáryushka, without beer – suddenly to destroy the order of life observed for twenty years – when he first thought of it, the project seemed wild and fantastic. But he remembered the talk in the Town Hall, and the torments which he had suffered on the way home; and the idea of leaving for a short time a town where stupid men considered him mad, delighted him.

'But where do you intend to go?' he asked.

'To Moscow, to Petersburg, to Warsaw. . . . In Warsaw I spent some of the happiest days of my life. An astonishing city! Come!'

XIII

A week after this conversation, Andréi Yéfimitch received a formal proposal to take a rest, that is, to retire from his post, and he received the proposal with indifference. Still a week later, he and Mikhail Averyanitch were sitting in the post tarantass and driving to the railway station. The weather was cool and clear, the sky blue and transparent. The two hundred versts were traversed in two days and two nights. When they stopped at the post-houses and were given dirty glasses for tea, or were delayed over the horses, Mikhail Averyanitch grew purple, shook all over, and roared 'Silence! Don't argue!' . . . And as they sat in the tarantass he talked incessantly of his travels in the Caucasus and in Poland. What adventures he had, what meetings! He spoke in a loud voice, and all the time made such astonished eyes that it might have been thought he was lying. As he told his stories he breathed in the doctor's face and laughed in his ear. All this incommoded the doctor and hindered his thinking and concentrating his mind.

For reasons of economy they travelled third-class, in a non-smoking carriage. Half of the passengers were clean. Mikhail Averyanitch struck up acquaintance with all, and as he shifted from seat to seat, announced in a loud voice that it was a mistake to travel on these tormenting railways. Nothing but rascals around! What a different thing to ride on horseback; in a single day you cover a hundred versts, and at the end feel wholesome and fresh. Yes, and we had been cursed with famines as the result of the draining of the Pinsky marshes! Everywhere nothing but disorder! Mikhail Averyanitch lost his temper, spoke loudly, and allowed no one else to say a word. His incessant chatter, broken only by loud laughter and expressive gesticulations, bored André Yéfimitch.

'Which of us is the more mad?' he asked himself. 'I who do my best not to disturb my fellow-travellers, or this egoist who thinks he is cleverer and more interesting than anyone else, and gives no one a moment's rest?'

In Moscow, Mikhail Averyanitch donned his military tunic without shoulder-straps, and trousers with red piping. Out of doors he wore an army forage-cap and cloak, and was saluted by the soldiers. To Andréi Yéfimitch he began to seem a man who had lost all the good points of the upper classes and retained only the bad. He loved people to dance attendance on him even when it was quite unnecessary. Matches lay before him on the table and he saw them, yet he roared to the waiter to hand them to him; he marched about in his underclothing before the chambermaid; he addressed the waitresses – even the elderly ones – indiscriminately as 'thou,' and when he was irritated called them blockheads and fools. This, thought Andréi Yéfimitch, is no doubt gentlemanly, but it is detestable.

First of all, Mikhail Averyanitch brought his friend to the Iverskaya.* He prayed piously, bowed to the ground, shed tears, and when he had finished, sighed deeply and said:

'Even an unbeliever feels himself at peace after he has prayed. Kiss the image, dear!'

Andréi Yéfimitch got red in the face and kissed the image; and Mikhail Averyanitch puffed out his lips, shook his head, prayed in a whisper; and again into his eyes came tears. After this they visited the Kremlin and inspected the Tsar-Cannon and the Tsar-Bell, touched them with their fingers, admired the view across the Moscow River, and spent some time in the

---

* A celebrated ikon kept in a small chapel near the Moscow Town Hall. It is supposed to possess miraculous healing virtues.

Temple of the Saviour and afterwards in the Rumiantseff Museum.

They dined at Testoff's.* Mikhail Averyanitch stroked his whiskers, gazed long at the *menu*, and said to the waiter in the tone of a gourmet who feels at home in restaurants:

'We'll see what you'll feed us with today, angel!'

XIV

The doctor walked and drank and ate and inspected, but his feelings remained unchanged; he was vexed with Mikhail Averyanitch. He longed to get a rest from his companion, to escape from him, but the post-master considered it his duty not to let him out of his sight, and to see that he tasted every possible form of recreation. For two days Andréi Yéfimitch endured it, but on the third declared that he was unwell, and would remain all day at home. Mikhail Averyanitch said that in that case he also would remain at home. And indeed, he added, a rest was necessary, otherwise they would have no strength left. Andréi Yéfimitch lay on the sofa with his face to the wall, and with clenched teeth listened to his friend, who assured him that France would sooner or later inevitably destroy Germany, that in Moscow there are a great many swindlers, and that you cannot judge of the merits of a horse by its appearance. The doctor's heart throbbed, his ears hummed, but from motives of delicacy he could not ask his friend to leave him alone or be silent. But happily Mikhail Averyanitch grew tired of sitting in the room, and after dinner went for a walk.

Left alone, Andréi Yéfimitch surrendered himself to the feeling of rest. How delightful it was to lie motionless on the sofa and know that he was alone in the room! Without solitude true happiness was impossible. The fallen angel was faithless to God probably only because he longed for solitude, which angels knew not. Andréi Yéfimitch wished to reflect upon what he had seen and heard in the last few days. But he could not drive Mikhail Averyanitch out of his mind.

* A Moscow restaurant noted for genuine Russian cookery.

'But then he obtained leave and came with me purely out of friendship and generosity,' he thought with vexation. 'Yet there is nothing more destable than his maternal care. He is good and generous and a gay companion – but tiresome! Intolerably tiresome! He is one of those men who say only clever things, yet you cannot help feeling that they are stupid at bottom.'

Next day Andréi Yéfimitch said he was still ill, and remained in his room. He lay with his face to the back of the sofa, was bored when he was listening to conversation, and happy only when he was left alone. He was angry with himself for leaving home, he was angry with Mikhail Averyanitch, who every day became more garrulous and free-making; to concentrate his thoughts on a serious, elevated plane he failed utterly.

'I am now being tested by the realities of which Iván Dmítritch spoke,' he thought, angered at his own pettiness. 'But this is nothing. . . . I will go home, and things will be as before.'

In St. Petersburg the incidents of Moscow were repeated; whole days he never left his room, but lay on the sofa, and rose only when he wanted to drink beer.

All the time, Mikhail Averyanitch was in a great hurry to get to Warsaw.

'My dear friend, why must I go there?' asked Andréi Yéfimitch imploringly. 'Go yourself, and let me go home. I beg you!'

'Not for a million!' protested Mikhail Averyanitch. 'It is an astonishing city! In Warsaw I spent the happiest days of my life.'

Andréi Yéfimitch had not the character to persist, and with a twinge of pain accompanied his friend to Warsaw. When he got there he stayed all day in the hotel, lay on the sofa, and was angry with himself, and with the waiters who stubbornly refused to understand Russian. Mikhail Averyanitch, healthy, gay, and active as ever, drove from morning to night about the city and sought out his old acquaintances. Several nights he stayed out altogether. After one of these nights, spent it is uncertain where, he returned early in the morning, dishevelled and excited. For a long time he walked up and down the room, and at last stopped and exclaimed:

'Honour before everything!'

Again he walked up and down the room, seized his head in his hands, and declaimed tragically:

'Yes! Honour before everything! Cursed be the hour when it entered my head to come near this Babylon! . . . My dear friend,' he turned to Andréi Yéfimitch, 'I have lost heavily at cards. Lend me five hundred roubles!'

Andréi Yéfimitch counted the money, and gave it silently to his friend. Mikhail Averyanitch, purple from shame and indignation, cursed incoherently and needlessly, put on his cap, and went out. After two hours' absence he returned, threw himself into an armchair, sighed loudly, and said:

'Honour is saved! Let us go away, my friend! Not another minute will I rest in this accursed city! They are all scoundrels! . . . Austrian spies!'

When the travellers returned it was the beginning of November, and the streets were covered with snow. Doctor Khobótoff occupied Andréi Yéfimitch's position at the hospital, but lived at his own rooms, waiting until Andréi Yéfimitch returned and gave up the official quarters. The ugly woman whom he called his cook already lived in one of the wings.

Fresh scandals in connection with the hospital were being circulated in the town. It was said that the ugly woman had quarrelled with the superintendent, who had gone down before her on his knees and begged forgiveness. On the day of his return Andréi Yéfimitch had to look for new lodgings.

'My friend,' began the postmaster timidly, 'forgive the indelicate question, what money have you got?'

Andréi Yéfimitch silently counted his money, and said: 'Eighty-six roubles.'

'You don't understand me,' said Mikhail Averyanitch in confusion. 'I ask what means have you – generally?'

'I have told you already – eighty-six roubles . . . Beyond that I have nothing.'

Mikhail Averyanitch was well aware that the doctor was an honest and straightforward man. But he believed that he had at least twenty thousand roubles in capital. Now learning that his friend was a beggar and had nothing to live on, he began to cry, and embraced him.

XV

Andréi Yéfimitch migrated to the three-windowed house of Madame Byelof, a woman belonging to the petty trading class. In this house were only three rooms and a kitchen. Of these rooms two, with windows opening on the street, were occupied by the doctor, while in the third and in the kitchen lived Dáryushka, the landlady, and three children. Occasionally the number was added to by a drunken workman, Madame Byelof's lover, who made scenes at night and terrified Dáryushka and the children. When he came, sat in the kitchen, and demanded vodka, the others were crowded out, and the doctor in compassion took the crying children to his own room, and put them to sleep on the floor. This always gave him great satisfaction.

As before, he rose at eight o'clock, took his breakfast, and sat down and read his old books and reviews. For new books he had no money. But whether it was because the books were old or because the surroundings were changed, reading no longer interested him, and even tired him. So to pass the time he compiled a detailed catalogue of his books, and pasted labels on the backs; and this mechanical work seemed to him much more interesting than reading. The more monotonous and trifling the occupation the more it calmed his mind, he thought of nothing, and time passed quickly. Even to sit in the kitchen and peel potatoes with Dáryushka or to pick the dirt out of buckwheat meal interested him. On Saturdays and Sundays he went to church. Standing at the wall, he blinked his eyes, listened to the singing, and thought of his father, his mother, the university, religion; he felt calm and melancholy, and when leaving the church, regretted that the service had not lasted longer.

Twice he visited the hospital for the purpose of seeing Iván Dmítritch. But on both occasions Gromof was unusually angry and excited; he asked to be left in peace, declared that he had long ago wearied of empty chatter, and that he would regard solitary confinement as a deliverance from these accursed, base people. Was it possible they would refuse him that? When Andréi Yéfimitch took leave of him and wished him good night, he snapped and said:

'Take yourself to the devil!'

And Andréi Yéfimitch felt undecided as to whether he should go a third time or not. But he wished to go.

In the old times Andréi Yéfimitch had been in the habit of spending the time after dinner in walking about his rooms and thinking. But now from dinner to tea-time he lay on the sofa with his face to the wall and surrendered himself to trivial thoughts, which he found himself unable to conquer. He considered himself injured by the fact that after twenty years' service he had been given neither a pension nor a grant. True he had not done his duties honestly, but then were not pensions given to all old servants indiscriminately, without regard to their honesty or otherwise? Modern ideas did not regard rank, orders, and pensions as the reward of moral perfection or capacity, and why must he alone be the exception? He was absolutely penniless. He was ashamed to pass the shop where he dealt or to meet the proprietor. For beer alone he was in debt thirty-two roubles. He was in debt also to his landlady. Dáryushka secretly sold old clothing and books, and lied to the landlady, declaring that her master was about to come in to a lot of money.

Andréi Yéfimitch was angry with himself for having wasted on his journey the thousand roubles which he had saved. What could he not do with a thousand roubles now? He was annoyed, also, because others would not leave him alone. Khobótoff considered it his duty to pay periodical visits to his sick colleague; and everything about him was repulsive to Andréi Yéfimitch – his sated face, his condescending bad manners, the word 'colleague,' and the high boots. But the greatest annoyance of all was that he considered it his duty to cure André Yéfimitch, and even imagined he was curing him. On every occasion he brought a phial of bromide of potassium and a rhubarb pill.

Mikhail Averyanitch also considered it his duty to visit his sick friend and amuse him. He entered the room with affected freeness, laughed unnaturally, and assured Andréi Yéfimitch that today he looked splendid, and that, glory be to God! he was getting all right. From this alone it might be concluded that he regarded the case as hopeless. He had not yet paid off the Warsaw debt, and being ashamed of himself and constrained, he laughed all the louder, and told ridiculous anecdotes. His stories now seemed endless, and were a source of torment both to Andréi Yéfimitch and to himself.

When the postmaster was present, Andréi Yéfimitch usually lay on the sofa, his face turned to the wall, with clenched teeth, listening. It seemed to him that a crust was forming about his heart, and after every visit he felt the crust becoming thicker, and threatening to extend to his throat. To exorcise these trivial afflictions he ēflected that he, and Khobótoff, and Mikhail Averyanitch would, sooner or later, perish, leaving behind themselves not a trace. When a million years had passed by, a spirit flying through space would see only a frozen globe and naked stones. All – culture and morals – everything would pass away: even the burdock would not grow. Why, then, should he trouble himself with feelings of shame on account of a shopkeeper, of insignificant Khobótoff, of the terrible friendship of Mikhail Averyanitch. It was all folly and vanity.

But such reasoning did not console him. He had hardly succeeded in painting a vivid picture of the frozen globe after a million years of decay, when from behind a naked rock appeared Khobótoff in his topboots, and beside him stood Mikhail Averyanitch, with an affected laugh, and a shamefaced whisper on his lips: 'And the Warsaw debt, old man, I will repay in a few days . . . without fail!'

XVI

Mikhail Averyanitch arrived after dinner one evening when Andréi Yéfimitch was lying on the sofa. At the same time came Khobótoff with his bromide of potassium. Andréi Yéfimitch rose slowly, sat down again, and supported himself by resting his hands upon the sofa edge.

'Today, my dear,' began Mikhail Averyanitch, 'today your complexion is much healthier than yesterday. You are a hero! I swear to God, a hero!'

'It's time, indeed it's time for you to recover, colleague,' said Khobótoff, yawning. 'You must be tired of the delay yourself.'

'Never mind, we'll soon be all right,' said Mikhail Averyanitch gaily. 'Why, we'll live for another hundred years! Eh?'

'Perhaps not a hundred, but a safe twenty,' said Khobótoff consolingly. 'Don't worry, colleague, don't worry!'

'We'll let them see!' laughed Mikhail Averyanitch, slapping his friend on the knee. 'We'll show how the trick is done! Next summer, with God's will, we'll fly away to the Caucasus, and gallop all over the country – trot, trot, trot! And when we come back from the Caucasus we'll dance at your wedding!' Mikhail Averyanitch winked slyly. 'We'll marry you, my friend, we'll find the bride!'

Andréi Yéfimitch felt that the crust had risen to his throat. His heart beat painfully.

'This is absurd,' he said, rising suddenly and going over to the window. 'Is it possible you don't understand that you are talking nonsense?'

He wished to speak to his visitors softly and politely, but could not restrain himself, and, against his own will, clenched his fists, and raised them threateningly above his head.

'Leave me!' he cried, in a voice which was not his own. His face was purple and he trembled all over. 'Begone! Both of you! Go!'

Mikhail Averyanitch and Khobótoff rose, and looked at him, at first in astonishment, then in terror.

'Begone both of you!' continued Andréi Yéfimitch. 'Stupid idiots! Fools! I want neither your friendship nor your medicines, idiots! This is base, it is abominable!'

Khobótoff and the postmaster exchanged confused glances, staggered to the door, and went into the hall. Andréi Yéfimitch seized the phial of bromide of potassium, and flung it after them, breaking it upon the threshold.

'Take yourselves to the devil!' he cried, running after them into the hall. 'To the devil!'

After his visitors had gone he lay on the sofa, trembling as if in fever, and repeated –

'Stupid idiots! Dull fools!'

When he calmed down, the first thought that entered his head was that poor Mikhail Averyanitch must now be terribly ashamed and wretched, and that the scene that had passed was something very terrible. Nothing of the kind had ever happened before. What had become of his intellect and tact? Where were now his understanding of the world and his philosophical indifference?

All night the doctor was kept awake by feelings of shame and vexation. At nine o'clock next morning, he went to the post office and apologised to the postmaster.

'Do not refer to what happened!' said the postmaster, with a sigh. Touched by Andréi Yéfimitch's conduct, he pressed his hands warmly. 'No man should trouble over such trifles. . . . Lubiakin!' he roared so loudly that the clerks and visitors trembled. 'Bring a chair! . . . And you just wait!' he cried to a peasant woman, who held a registered letter through the grating. 'Don't you see that I am engaged? . . . We will forget all that,' he continued tenderly, turning to Andréi Yéfimitch. 'Sit down, my old friend!'

He stroked his eyebrows silently for a minute, and continued:

'It never entered my head to take offence. Illness is a very strange thing, I understand that. Yesterday your fit frightened both the doctor and myself, and we talked of you for a long time. My dear friend, why will you not pay more attention to your complaint? Do you think you can go on living in this way? Forgive the plain speaking of a friend.' He dropped his voice to a whisper. 'But you live among hopeless surroundings – closeness, uncleanliness, no one to look after you, nothing to take for your ailment. . . . My dear friend, both I and the doctor implore you with all our hearts – listen to our advice – go into the hospital. There you will get wholesome food, care and treatment. Yevgénïi Feódoritch – although, between ourselves, *de mauvais ton* – is a capable man, and you can fully rely upon him. He gave me his word that he would take care of you.'

Andréi Yéfimitch was touched by the sincere concern of his friend, and the tears that trickled down the postmaster's cheeks.

'My dear friend, don't believe them!' he whispered, laying his hand upon his heart. 'It is all a delusion. My complaint lies merely in this, that in twenty years I found in this town only one intelligent man, and he was a lunatic. I suffer from no

disease whatever; my misfortune is that I have fallen into a
magic circle from which there is no escape. It is all the same
to me – I am ready for anything.'

'Then you will go into the hospital?'

'It is all the same – even into the pit.'

'Give me your word, friend, that you will obey Yevgénii
Feódoritch in everything.'

'I give you my word. But I repeat that I have fallen into a
magic circle. Everything now, even the sincere concern of
my friends, tends only to the same thing – to my
destruction. I am perishing, and I have the courage to
acknowledge it.'

'Nonsense, you will get all right!'

'What is the use of talking like that?' said Andréi
Yéfimitch irritably. 'There are very few men who at the
close of their lives do not experience what I am experiencing
now. When people tell you that you have disease of the
kidneys or a dilated heart, and set about to cure you; when
they tell you that you are a madman or a criminal – in one
word, when they begin to turn their attention on to you –
you may recognise that you are in a magic circle from which
there is no escape. You may try to escape, but that makes
things worse. Give in, for no human efforts will save you.
So it seems to me.'

All this time, people were gathering at the grating. Andréi
Yéfimitch disliked interrupting the postmaster's work, and
took his sleeve. Mikhail Averyanitch once more made him
give his word of honour, and escorted him to the door.

The same day towards evening Khobótoff, in his short fur
coat and high boots, arrived unexpectedly, and, as if nothing
had happened the day before, said:

'I have come to you on a matter of business, colleague. I
want you to come with me to a consultation. Eh?'

Thinking that Khobótoff wanted to amuse him with a
walk, or give him some opportunity of earning money,
Andréi Yéfimitch dressed, and went with him into the street.
He was glad of the chance to redeem his rudeness of the day
before, thankful for the apparent reconciliation, and grateful
to Khobótoff for not hinting at the incident. From this
uncultured man who would have expected such delicacy?

'And where is your patient?' asked Andréi Yéfimitch.

'At the hospital. For a long time past I have wanted you to see him. . . . A most interesting case.'

They entered the hospital yard, and passing through the main building, went to the wing where the lunatics were confined. When they entered the hall, Nikita as usual jumped up and stretched himself.

'One of them has such strange complications in the lungs,' whispered Khobótoff as he entered the ward with Andréi Yéfimitch. 'But wait here. I shall be back immediately. I must get my stethoscope.'

And he left the room.

XVII

It was already twilight. Iván Dmítrich lay on his bed with his face buried in the pillow; the paralytic sat motionless, and wept softly and twitched his lips; the fat muzhik and the ex-sorter slept. It was very quiet.

Andréi Yéfimitch sat on Iván Dmítritch's bed and listened. Half an hour passed by, but Khobótoff did not come. Instead of Khobótoff came Nikita carrying in his arm a dressing-gown, some linen, and a pair of slippers.

'Please to put on these, your Honour,' he said calmly. 'There is your bed, this way, please,' he added, pointing at a vacant bed, evidently only just set up. 'And don't take on; with God's will you will soon be well!'

Andréi Yéfimitch understood. Without a word he walked over to the bed indicated by Nikita and sat upon it. Then, seeing that Nikita was waiting, he stripped himself and felt ashamed. He put on the hospital clothing; the flannels were too small, the shirt was too long, and the dressing-gown smelt of smoked fish.

'You will soon be all right, God grant it!' repeated Nikita.

He took up Andréi Yéfimitch's clothes, went out, and locked the door.

'It is all the same,' thought André Yéfimitch, shamefacedly gathering the dressing-gown around him, and feeling like a convict in his new garments. 'It is all the same. In dress clothes, in uniform . . . or in this dressing-gown.'

But his watch? And the memorandum book in his side pocket? And the cigarettes? Where had Nikita taken his clothes? To the day of his death he would never again wear trousers, a waistcoat, or boots. It was strange and incredible at first. Andréi Yéfimitch was firmly convinced that there was no difference whatever between Madame Byeloff's house and Ward No. 6, and that all in this world is folly and vanity; but he could not prevent his hands trembling, and his feet were cold. He was hurt, too, by the thought that Iván Dmítritch would rise and see him in the dressing-gown. He rose, walked up and down the room, and again sat down.

He remained sitting for half an hour, weary to the point of grief. Would it be possible to live here a day, a week, even years, as these others had done? He must sit down, and walk about and again sit down; and then he might look out of the window, and again walk from end to end of the room. And afterwards? Just to sit all day still as an idol, and think! No, it was impossible.

Andréi Yéfimitch lay down on his bed, but almost immediately rose, rubbed with his cuff the cold sweat from his forehead, and felt that his whole face smelt of dried fish. He walked up and down the ward.

'This is some misunderstanding . . .' he said, opening his arms. 'It only needs an explanation, it is a misunderstanding. . . .'

At this moment Iván Dmítritch awoke. He sat up in bed, rested his head on his hands, and spat. Then he looked dly at the doctor, apparently at first understanding nothing. But soon his sleepy face grew contemptuous and malicious.

'So they have brought you here, my friend,' he began in a voice hoarse from sleep. He blinked one eye. 'I am very glad! You drank other men's blood, and now they will drink yours! Admirable.'

'It is some misunderstanding . . .' began Andréi Yéfimitch, frightened by the lunatic's words. He shrugged his shoulders and repeated. 'It is a misunderstanding . . . of some kind.'

Iván Dmítritch again spat, and lay down on his bed.

'Accursed life!' he growled. 'But what is most bitter, most abominable of all, is that this life ends not with rewards for suffering, not with apotheoses as in operas, but in death; men come and drag the corpse by its arms and legs into the cellar. Brrrrr! . . . Well, never mind! . . . For all that we have suffered in this, in the other world we will be repaid with a holiday! From the other world I shall return hither as a shadow, and terrify these monsters! . . . I will turn their heads grey!'

Moséika entered the ward, and seeing the doctor, stretched out his hand, and said:

'Give me a kopeck!'

XVIII

Andréi Yéfimitch went across to the window, and looked out into the fields. It was getting dark, and on the horizon rose a cold, livid moon. Near the hospital railings, a hundred fathoms away, not more, rose a lofty, white building, surrounded by a stone wall. It was the prison.

'That is actuality,' thought Andréi Yéfimitch, and he felt terrified.

Everything was terrible: the moon, the prison, the spikes in the fence, and the blaze in the distant bonemill. Andréi Yéfimitch turned away from the window, and saw before him a man with glittering stars and orders upon his breast. The man smiled and winked cunningly. And this, too, seemed terrible.

He tried to assure himself that in the moon and in the prison there was nothing peculiar at all, that even sane men wear orders, and that the best of things in their turn rot and turn into dust. But despair suddenly seized him, he took hold of the grating with both hands, and jerked it with all his strength. But the bars stood firm.

That it might be less terrible, he went to Iván Dmítritch's bed, and sat upon it.

'I have lost my spirits, friend,' he said, stammering; trembling, and rubbing the cold sweat from his face. 'My spirits have fallen.'

'But why don't you philosophise?' asked Iván Dmítritch ironically.

'My God, my God! . . . Yes, yes! . . . Once you said that in Russia there is no philosophy; but all philosophise, even triflers. But the philosophising of triflers does no harm to anyone,' said Andréi Yéfimitch as if he wanted to cry. 'But why, my dear friend, why this malicious laughter? Why should not triflers philosophise if they are not satisfied? For a clever, cultivated, proud, freedom-loving man, built in the image of God, there is no course left but to come as doctor to a dirty, stupid town, and lead a life of jars, leeches, and gallipots. Charlatanry, narrowness, baseness! Oh, my God!'

'You chatter nonsense! If you didn't want to be a doctor, why weren't you a minister of state?'

'I could not. We are weak, my friend. I was indifferent to things, I reasoned actively and wholesomely, but it needed but the first touch of actuality to make me lose heart, and surrender. . . . We are weak, we are worthless! . . . And you also, my friend. You are able, you are noble, with your mother's milk you drank in draughts of happiness, yet hardly had you entered upon life when you wearied of it. . . . We are weak, weak!'

In addition to terror and the feeling of insult, Andréi Yéfimitch had been tortured by some importunate craving ever since the approach of evening. Finally he came to the conclusion that he wanted to smoke and drink beer.

'I am going out, my friend,' he said. 'I will tell them to bring lights. . . . I cannot in this way. . . . I am not in a state. . . .'

He went to the door and opened it, but immediately Nikita jumped up and barred the way.

'Where are you going to? You can't, you can't!' he cried. 'It's time for bed!'

'But only for a minute. . . . I want to go into the yard. . . . I want to have a walk in the yard,' said Andréi Yéfimitch.

'You can't. I have orders against it. . . . You know yourself.'

Nikita banged the door and set his back against it.

'But if I go out what harm will it do?' asked Andréi Yéfimitch. 'I don't understand! Nikita, I must go out!' he cried in a trembling voice. 'I must go!'

'Don't create disorder; it is not right!' said Nikita in an edifying tone.

'The devil knows what is the meaning of this!' suddenly screamed Iván Dmítritch, jumping from his bed. 'What right has he to refuse to let us go? How dare they keep us here? The law allows no man to be deprived of freedom without a trial! This is violence . . . tyranny!'

'Of course it is tyranny,' said Andréi Yéfimitch, encouraging Gromof. 'I must go! I have to go out! He has no right! Let me out, I tell you!'

'Do you hear, stupid dog!' screamed Iván Dmítritch, thumping the door with his fists. 'Open, or I will smash the door! Blood-sucker!'

'Open!' cried Andréi Yéfimitch, trembling all over. 'I demand it!'

'Talk away!' answered Nikita through the door. 'Talk away!'

'Go, then, for Yevgénïï Feódoritch! Say that I ask him to come . . . For a minute!'

'Tomorrow he will come all right.'

'They will never let us go!' cried Iván Dmítritch. 'We will all die here! Oh, God, is it possible that in the other world there is no hell, that these villains will be forgiven? Where is there justice? Open, scoundrel, I am choking!' Gromof cried out in a hoarse voice, and flung himself against the door. 'I will dash my brains out! Assassins!'

Nikita flung open the door, and with both hands and his knees roughly pushed Andréi Yéfimitch back into the room, and struck him with his clenched fist full in the face. It seemed to Andréi Yéfimitch that a great salt wave had suddenly dashed upon his head and flung him upon his bed; in his mouth was a taste of salt, and the blood seemed to burst from his gums. As if trying to swim away from the wave, he flourished his arms and seized the bedstead. But at this moment Nikita struck him again and again in the back.

Iván Dmítritch screamed loudly. He also had evidently been beaten.

Then all was quiet. Liquid moonlight poured through between the iron bars, and on the floor lay a network shadow. All were terrified. Andréi Yéfimitch lay on the bed and held his breath in terror, awaiting another blow.

It seemed as if someone had taken a sickle, thrust it into his chest and turned it around. In his agony he bit his pillow and ground his teeth, and suddenly into his head amid the chaos flashed the intolerable thought that such misery had been borne year after year by these helpless men who now lay in the moonlight like black shadows about him. In twenty years he had never known of it, and never wanted to know. He did not know, he had no idea of their wretchedness, therefore he was not guilty; but conscience, as rude and unaccommodating as Nikita's fists, sent an icy thrill through him from head to foot. He jumped from his bed and tried to scream with all his might, to fly from the ward and kill Nikita, and Khobótoff, and the superintendent, and the feldscher, and himself. But not a sound came from his throat, his feet rebelled against him, he panted, he tore his gown and shirt, and fell insensible on the bed.

XIX

Next morning his head ached, his ears hummed, and he was weak. The memory of his weakness on the day before made him feel ashamed. Yesterday he had shown a petty spirit, he had feared even the moon, and honestly expressed feelings and thoughts which he had never suspected could exist in himself. For instance, the thought about the discontent of philosophic triflers. But now he was quite indifferent.

He neither ate nor drank, but lay motionless and silent.

'It is all the same to me,' he thought when he was questioned. 'I shall not answer . . . It is all the same. . . .'

After dinner Mikhail Averyanitch brought him a quarter of a pound of tea and a pound of marmalade. Dáryushka also came, and for a whole hour stood beside the bed with a dull expression of uncomprehending affliction. Doctor Khobótoff also paid him a visit. He brought a phial of bromide of potassium, and ordered Nikita to fumigate the ward.

Towards evening Andréi Yéfimitch died from an apoplectic stroke. At first he felt chill, and sickness; something loathsome like rotting sour cabbage or bad eggs seemed to permeate his whole body even to his fingers, to extend from his stomach to his head, and to flow in his eyes and ears. A green film appeared before his eyes. Andréi Yéfimitch realised that his hour had come; and remembered that Iván Dmítritch, Mikhail Averyanitch, and millions of others believed in immortality. But immortality he did not desire, and thought of it only for a moment. A herd of antelopes, extraordinarily beautiful and graceful, of which he had been reading the day before, rushed past him; then a woman stretched out to him a hand holding a registered letter. . . . Mikhail Averyanitch said something. Then all vanished and Andréi Yéfimitch died.

The servants came in, took him by the shoulders and legs, and carried him to the chapel. There he lay on a table with open eyes, and at night the moon shone down upon him. In the morning came Sergéi Sergéyitch, piously prayed before a crucifix, and closed the eyes of his former chief.

Next day Andréi Yéfimitch was buried. Only Mikhail Averyanitch and Dáryushka were present at the funeral.